CAST OF CHARACTERS

Major Charles Kemp. An original member of the Foothold Club and a professional army man, whose cadets are holding training maneuvers during the club's annual dinner meet.

Professor Julius Wiernick. An odious, intolerant man but a brilliant mountaineer.

Eve Wiernick. His sultry second wife, many years his junior.

Jack James Griffith. A Welsh climbing guide with the airs of an Englishman.

Peter Lumley. A young member whose father, Jack Lumley, perished in a climbing accident on the Matterhorn decades earlier.

Mark Stonor. The outgoing president of the Foothold Club.

Donald Ferguson. A Scotsman and the incoming present of the club.

Flora Massey. Ferguson's pretty niece, the object of Peter Lumley's affections.

Dr. Tom Paton. A genial physician, one of the club's original members.

Dr. Richard Paton. His equally genial son, also a mountaineer.

George Sheldrake. The Grand Old Man of the Foothold Club.

Frank Hibberd. A schoolmaster and veteran of three Himalayan expeditions.

Mrs. Julia Hengist. An original member who is also Peter Lumley's aunt.

Goerge Thripp. An original member of the club and a stickler for organization.

Galu Regmi. A young Nepalese, half Sherpa, now one of Major Kemp's cadets.

Abercrombie "Filthy" Lewker. The noted Shakespearean actor-manager and mountaineer, also a gifted amateur detective.

Detective-Inspector George Grimmett. An old friend and ally of Lewker's, whom he has invited to be his guest at the Foothold Club's annual dinner meet.

Plus assorted Foothold Club membe   and the cadets.

The Abercrombie Lewker novels

The Detective Novels

Death on Milestone Buttress (1951)*
Murder on the Matterhorn (1951)
The Youth Hostel Murders (1952)*
The Corpse in the Crevasse (1952)
Death Under Snowdon (1952)*
A Corpse at Camp Two (1954)
Murder of an Owl (1956)
The Ice Axe Murders (1958)
Swing Away, Climber (1959)
Holiday with Murder (1960)
Death Finds a Foothold (1961)*
Lewker in Norway (1963)
Death of a Weirdy (1965)
Lewker in Tirol (1967)
Fat Man's Agony (1969)

The Spy Novels

Traitor's Mountain (1945)
Kidnap Castle (1947)
Hammer Island (1947)

*Reprinted by The Rue Morgue Press

Death Finds
a Foothold

Glyn Carr

Rue Morgue Press

Lyons / Boulder

The cover picture shows a hiker taking in the awe-inspiring view at Crib-Goch on the 'Snowdon Horseshoe' ridge walk, facing Mount Snowdon, a favorite spot for "Filthy" Lewker.

About Glyn Carr

Glyn Carr was born Showell Styles in Four Oaks, Warwickshire, England, in 1908 and died at his longtime home in Wales in 2005. He did his first mountain trek at the age of three and spent the rest of his life scrambling on rocks, snow, ice and mountains. During World War II Styles used his shore leave from the Royal Navy to pioneer new ascents in North Africa and Malta. After he was discharged, Styles led two exploring and climbing expeditions to the Lyngen Peninsula, 250 miles from the Arctic Circle, where he climbed seven virgin peaks. In 1954, he led an expedition to the Himalayas to attempt a 22,000-foot peak in the Manaslu range in Nepal. He published numerous books on climbing as well as young adult fiction. If you look upon a mountain climb as taking place in a large, open-air locked room, then Showell Styles was right to choose Glyn Carr as his pseudonym for fifteen detective novels featuring Abercrombie Lewker, all of which concern murders committed among the crags and slopes of peaks scattered around the world. There's no doubt that John Dickson Carr, the king of the locked room mystery, would have agreed that Styles managed to find a way to lock the door of a room that had no walls and only the sky for a ceiling. In fact, it was while Styles was climbing a pitch on the classic Milestone Buttress on Tryfan in Wales that it struck him "how easy it would be to arrange an undetectable murder in that place, and by way of experiment I worked out the system and wove a thinnish plot around it." That book was, of course, *Death on Milestone Buttress*, which first appeared in 1951 and was published for the first time in the United States by the Rue Morgue Press in 2000. Upon its original publication Styles' English publisher, Geoffrey Bles, immediately asked for more climbing mysteries. Over the next eighteen years, Styles produced another fourteen Lewker books (fifteen, counting one last, currently lost unpublished manuscript) before he halted the series, having run out "of ways of slaughtering people on steep rock-faces."

Death Finds

a Foothold

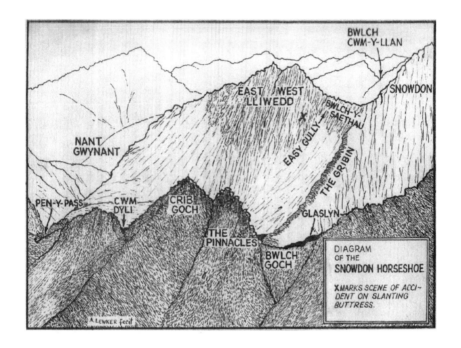

Diagram labels: BWLCH CWM-Y-LLAN, SNOWDON, EAST WEST LLIWEDD, BWLCH-Y-SAETHAU, NANT GWYNANT, EASY GULLY, THE GRIBIN, PEN-Y-PASS, CWM DYLI, CRIB GOCH, GLASLYN, THE PINNACLES, BWLCH GOCH

DIAGRAM
OF THE
SNOWDON HORSESHOE

X MARKS SCENE OF ACCI-
DENT ON SLANTING
BUTTRESS.

A. LEWKER fecit

Prologue

Thirty feet overhead, as Dr. Zukmayer fumbled and clawed his way up-ward, the snow-plastered rocks of the Hörnli Ridge vanished into gray and freezing mist. In that mist the figure of his guide, Frido Taugwalder, moved ghostlike, squatly foreshortened, pulling impatiently on the rope that linked him to his charge. Now and again Taugwalder growled in-junctions—come faster, trust to the rope, the two Englishmen in front were almost out of sight—and Dr. Zukmayer did his best to obey. He was very cold and very unhappy. There was a small icicle depending from his bulbous nose and his molded rubber boot soles slithered horri-bly on rocks that were coated with *verglas*. If he had not been a physi-cian, if this had not been a rescue party, the little doctor would never have set out up the northeast ridge of the Matterhorn for the second time in two days, in conditions which had driven all aspiring mountaineers down to the fleshpots of Zermatt.

He struggled round the side of a pinnacle, gloved hands clutching at slippery rock, and found himself close to the guide on a narrow tongue of snow. He recognized the place. Here, at 5 a.m. on the previous morn-ing, he had looked up and seen the final tower of the Matterhorn blazing like a great torch overhead, the first part of all the mountain world to receive the fire of the climbing sun. The tongue of snow had been a rock slab then, and he had been exalted and happy—yes, even though the fearful precipices on either hand had scared him—to be making the as-cent he had so long coveted. Little man Zukmayer had known fellowship with the enormous Matterhorn, had felt the great peak's welcome. Now it was very different. The storm of last night had changed everything. One might more easily imagine oneself welcomed by a hippogriff or a tornado than by this frigid monster of rock, shrouded in grey mists, up whose spine he was crawling at a height of nearly 13,000 feet.

The voices of the Englishmen came down out of the obscurity. They sounded jerky and anxious. "*Kommen sie!*" grunted Taugwalder. The doctor kicked the packed snow from his boots and climbed on.

Yesterday Dr. Zukmayer and his guide had seized one of the few good days in the bad season of 1934 to climb the Matterhorn by the Hörnli. The brief promise of the morning had held until eleven and then had ended in one of those sudden and violent storms for which the Matterhorn is famous. By that time they had been nearly down to the Belvedere, but the thunder and the hail and the blinding whirl of snow that followed had caused them to take more than an hour over the last five hundred feet of descent and the doctor had been very glad indeed to see the solid shape of the hut-hotel loom through the flying murk below. The weather grew worse. It was too bad to descend to Zermatt, whither all prudent mountaineers had fled that morning. Dr. Zukmayer and Frido Taugwalder were thus the only climbers at the Belvedere when the two Englishmen reached it early in the afternoon. The Englishmen had almost reached the limit of endurance. They had traversed the Matterhorn guideless, up the Italian ridge and down the Hörnli, and had been caught by the storm. There had been a party of four, climbing in pairs, and the other two were still on the mountain, they said. When two hours had passed and their friends had failed to come in, they had wanted to set off up the ridge to look for them, but Frido Taugwalder had spoken so strongly against it that they had given up the idea. It was plain suicide, said the guide emphatically, to go up the ridge in such weather. The two missing men might have found shelter in the Solvay refuge 1600 feet below the summit. If they hadn't—he shrugged his big shoulders—there was still a small chance that they would survive. A very small chance. But it was better to wait until the weather moderated, so that one of the porters from the Belvedere could go down to the inn at the Schwarzsee and fetch men who would carry up the stretcher and first aid equipment.

So they had waited. At three next morning the wind and snow had stopped, leaving the mountain clad in snow and ice and mist. A porter had started down to the Schwarzsee at the earliest possible moment and an hour later the four climbers had started up the ridge. No one asked little Dr. Zukmayer if he was willing to go up with the first search party, and he did not raise any objection. He was a physician and he was a mountaineer. In both roles tradition demanded his utmost help. But more than once in the first two hours of that grim second ascent he found himself wishing he had taken up tennis or even *boule* instead of mountaineering. He wished also that the Englishmen in front would go more slowly; he was in his fiftieth year, and (he told himself resentfully) naturally less agile than men who must be his juniors by a good twenty years. Panting, he hauled himself over a difficult corner and reached a slanting platform with grey emptiness on three sides and the ridge towering into the mist above. Taugwalder had halted there and so had the Englishmen.

"Solvay," the guide said briefly.

The tiny hutch of the refuge, tucked into a nook secure from falling stones, was snow-coated and silent. One of the Englishmen tugged the door open. The place was empty. He pushed up his snow-goggles and looked at his companion who nodded and began to climb on without a word. Taugwalder followed them. Before Dr. Zukmayer had started after him there was a shout from fifty feet above, and when he had puffed and scrabbled his way up to the spot he found the three hurriedly belaying themselves to the rock spikes of a steep and broken section of the ridge. At their feet, in a narrow chasm below a projecting rock, a man was huddled. There was a rope round his waist and it was wound in many coils round the projection; evidently he had safeguarded himself before seeking the shelter of the crack. His body in its red hooded jacket was thinly powdered with snow.

"'Nother couple of minutes and he'd have reached the refuge," muttered one of the Englishmen. "Must have left Jack higher up. Wonder why they unroped."

"He's wearing Jack's windproof," said the other with somber finality.

"In the snowstorm he not know where," Taugwalder said in his labored English. "He choose best shelter, *hein*? Not much snow on him."

Dr. Zukmayer paid no attention to their conversation. His terrors and discomforts had left him and he was on his knees by the motionless body, careless of whether or not Taugwalder was safeguarding him with the rope on the precarious rocks. He thought he had seen the thin vapor of breath hovering for an instant about the pinched nostrils which projected above a swathing scarf.

He got his hand inside the man's clothing—with some difficulty, for the climber had on two windproof jackets and two thick sweaters—and felt warmth and the faint movement of the heart.

"The coffee, quickly," he said incisively. "He yet lives."

There were startled exclamations. The thermos flask of warm coffee laced with rum was handed to him. He pulled back the frozen lower folds of the two hoods and gently forced some of the liquid between the blue lips. At the second attempt there was a convulsive movement of the throat—the man swallowed.

"Raise him, please," said Dr. Zukmayer.

Moving gingerly on the icy slabs, the taller of the two Englishmen managed to support the upper part of the man's body while the doctor coaxed more coffee into him.

"What's the verdict, Doctor?" he muttered. "He's alive—but will he live?"

"I think so, yes—if he can be got down without delay. He has maintained body-warmth. You see he has much clothing. There may be frostbite—*ach*, he now moves!"

The man stirred slightly. His eyes opened, looked questingly from side to side. The Englishman, leaning over him beside Zukmayer, spoke loudly and firmly.

"You're all right—understand? You're all right and we're going to get you down. Now tell us—*where's Jack?*"

The blue lips moved stiffly. It took a moment or two for the word to form itself and be uttered.

"Dead."

"Where did you leave him?"

A pause again. Words came a little more easily but very faintly.

"Up—not—far—I think—"

The man's eyes closed. The Englishman stood up.

"We'd better go on and look for him," he said to his companion. "As far as the first fixed rope, anyway."

As he was speaking a loud hail floated up from the grayness below. Taugwalder answered it with a bellow of *patois*.

"The men from Schwarzsee," he told the others. "They bring stretcher."

"Good," the Englishman nodded. "You'll wait for them, then. We shan't go beyond the Shoulder."

The two of them climbed on up the ridge, to be lost to sight almost at once in the mist. Dr. Zukmayer busied himself in preparing the rescued man for a stretcher descent. He reflected, as he worked, that if this man's comrade had not died when he did there might now have been two corpses on the mountain. The survivor had clearly taken from the body all this extra clothing, the red windproof jacket and probably a sweater and the heavy woolen mitts he was wearing beneath the windproof gauntlets; possibly also the loose outer trousers of Grenfell cloth which he wore in addition to thick tweed breeches. These things alone had kept him alive through the night.

The party from the Schwarzsee reached their perch on the ridge five minutes later; there were seven men, six of them guides and the seventh a Swiss doctor, an experienced mountaineer. Dr. Zukmayer, finding his comments on the patient brusquely received, surprised himself by suggesting to Taugwalder that they should go up after the Englishmen. The guide agreed and they went on up the ridge. It was more difficult, almost vertical *gendarmes* and a very narrow crest, but the doctor climbed more confidently now. The knowledge that he had helped to save one life gave him a feeling almost of exhilaration. There was a sense of lifting weather in the air, and the mist was undoubtedly thinner. On the gray overhead, like a negative image appearing on a photographic plate in the developing-dish, the white-streaked black precipice of the Shoulder loomed dark and enormous. Swarming up a corner where all the holds were filled with frozen snow, Dr. Zukmayer came to a more level crest just below the Shoulder and found Taugwalder and the two Englishmen standing together on a ledge overlooking the eastern precipice.

"You have not found him?" he panted as he approached.

The answer came after a pause.

"He's down there. Must have fallen."

Dr. Zukmayer stepped cautiously to the edge and looked down. The vast wall of rock fell dizzily away into the mist. At one place, a little to the right and about forty feet down, a slanting shelf interrupted the smooth sweep of the wall. Rocks and stones, the debris of the Matterhorn's continuous disintegration, evidently fell across the shelf, for it was covered with shale, but this morning the stonefalls were checked by the hand of frost. The shattered wall immediately above the shelf was nearly vertical—unclimbable. On the narrow slope of shale the body of a man was lying. It was plainly a corpse, for its clothing—flannel trousers and a shirt of green-and-yellow check pattern—was stained with great blotches that had spread in brighter crimson across the snow that powdered the shale. The doctor sucked in his breath with a hissing sound. His round face was very pale.

Behind him Taugwalder growled a question at the Englishmen.

"This is your comrade?"

"Yes. Poor devil. Went over the edge in the snowstorm, probably."

Dr. Zukmayer swung round. "But if—" he began.

"He fell, Doctor." The tall Englishman's voice was like the rasp of a file on metal. "He's dead. The other man's alive. You say he'll recover. Which of the two should now concern us, Doctor?"

The little doctor shivered. He looked away from the three hooded and goggled figures beside him, to the Shoulder whose dark bulk hovered above them like the wing of Lucifer.

"Perhaps you are right," he said in a low voice. "We should hasten to assist with the stretcher." He hesitated. "And of the man down there we shall report—"

"That he fell and was killed. As he was, Doctor."

"As he was," repeated Dr. Zukmayer slowly.

He turned away and nodded to his guide. Taugwalder held the rope as he began the descent. At the Solvay refuge they found that another four men had come up from the Schwarzsee and the laden stretcher was already on its way down the ridge. The weather was beginning to clear. Half an hour later, when the two Englishmen caught them up, the clouds were opening to reveal the smiling valley of Zermatt five thousand feet below.

Chapter 1

Three Letters

1. From Sir Abercrombie Lewker to
Detective-Inspector George Grimmett

13 Sheridan Place W.1
January 16, 1961

My dear Grimm,

How doth your worship? Passing well, I trust. For myself, I am in reasonable health—which is more, alas! than can be said for my wife. Lady Lewker is abed, recovering from the assaults of that distemper known for some obscure reason as 'influenza.' (The word, I fancy, is Italian, and bears no relevance whatever to the nature of the disease.) However, I come at once to the nub and core of this letter by way of three facts, of which Georgie's indisposition is the first. The second fact is your temporary residence in North Wales as the guest of a chief constable; of this I am informed by our mutual friend (the phrase is horrid but convenient) the Assistant Commissioner at Scotland Yard. The third fact is that my wife and I were to have joined the annual dinner meet of the Foothold Club, which is to be held at the Pen-y-Pass Hotel next week-end, from the 20th to the 23rd of this month; our places are booked, as also is a room at the P-y-P with two beds, but Georgie cannot now accompany me.

Under, or in (I spare you the arguments for and against these prepositions) the circumstances contained by the aforementioned facts, I was reminded of a wish expressed by you during our cooperation on the Case of the Murdered Owl: that you might some day have the opportunity of observing a gathering of mountaineers—a clutch of climbers, to coin a collective noun—in their natural haunts. Emboldened by this remembrance, I venture to invite you, my dear Grimm, to be my guest on this occasion. I know you will not be offended, as a lesser man might be, at a last-minute invitation to fill a place originally intended for someone else.

As you probably know, the Pen-y-Pass is less than twenty miles from the scene of your junketings with the chief constable, which are, I understand, to terminate before the weekend. Sir Frederick Claybury has assured me that Scotland Yard will tolerate your further absence until Tuesday the 24th. I have therefore every hope that you will pleasure me by accepting. I myself shall drive from London on Friday, arriving at the P.Y.P. about seven in the evening.

I think, Grimm, it would be a good plan to give you some preliminary information about this dinner meet.

The meet was first held in 1935, two years after the founding of the Foothold Club, and has taken place at the Pen-y-Pass every year since then with the exception of the war years, 1939 to 1944. It is distinct and different from the annual dinner (which is held in London and may be attended by any of the club's four hundred members) in that only the president, past presidents, and original members of the Foothold Club are privileged to attend; each, however, is entitled to bring one guest, who may or may not be a mountaineer. You will not be the only non-climber present, therefore. Usually there are less than thirty people at the meet and the majority of those are naturally middle-aged or even older; thus the gathering or clutch will not be wholly representative of the modern climber, though it will not, I hope, be any the less interesting on that account to a student of human eccentricity like yourself.

The dinner, which takes place on Saturday, is informal as far as dress is concerned. The day preceding it is spent by those present in climbing or hill-walking, as is the Sunday also. There is a tendency for original members to demonstrate to each other that they still retain their original agility; the original member whose guest you will be, however, does not intend to take part in the demonstration. On Monday most of the party leave.

I look forward confidently, my dear Grimm, to your company. The food at the Pen-y-Pass is excellent and their bitter beer is well kept. Until—and during—our encounter, then:

> May good digestion wait on appetite
> And health on both.

Georgie asks me to convey to you her kindest regards. I send my unfailing respect and amity.

Yours sincerely,
Abercrombie Lewker

Post Scriptum. If, as I understand, you have been assisting Major Wightman-Jones to shoot rabbits on his estate, you will have with you a pair of stout boots. Bring them with you to the Pen-y-Pass.

A.L.

From Colonel Finlay, O.C. Training, Shoreburst

(Duplicated Circular)

EXERCISE ALL SAINTS—INSTRNS TO GUIDES RMAS/OC/71/
DX dated 6/1/61

Opening Narrative

1. A triumphant surge of WELSH nationalism has resulted in the partition of ENGLAND and WALES. The violent events leading up to this have worsened the previous good relations between the two countries and a state of cold war now exists.

2. Clandestine operations by ENGLISH agents have taken place in WALES and vice versa.

Guides' Position

3. Guides representing defecting WELSHMEN have been approached by the famous ENGLISH agent Major Kemp and have consented to lead parties of ENGLISH soldiers from the comparatively safe dropping areas near the PEN-Y-PASS Hotel over the SNOWDON massif, to within reach of military objectives farther west.

4. Agents are naturally extremely scared, for the wild WELSH farmers will assuredly cut their throats if they catch them, and should therefore lead their parties as quickly as possible over the SNOWDON range and be rid of them as soon as they can (providing that it is safe from a mountaineering point of view to do so).

Timing

5. Agents are asked to be at their RVs by 0545 hrs on 21 Jan 61.
RVs
6. (a) Your RV is .... LLYN TEYRN. (548642 OS 107) ....

(b) Your gps are .... WELLINGTON 8 .... and .... PICTON 8 ....

(c) They have been ordered to meet you at .... 0545 ....

Recognition

7. The ENGLISH soldiers have been instructed to approach with the words "A DEWI SANT". You should reply "CROESO I CYMRU". Their mastery of the WELSH language is, however, negligible, so please make allowances.

Welsh Shepherds and Farmers

8. Posses of shepherds and farmers, armed with rifles and of violent temperament, are known to patrol the mountains and if seen should be avoided.

Completion

9. Exercise H.Q. will be at the Pen-y-Pass. After releasing your gps please check in at H.Q.

> "Saint GEORGE for ENGLAND"
> "And may we give the dragon's tail a damn good twist!"

(Signals exchanged between Admiral KEYES and Captain CARPEN-TER RN before the blocking of ZEEBRUGGE, 23rd April 1918)

To .... Peter Lumley Esq. ....
    ...... c/o Pen-y-Pass Hotel ......
    .... Caernarvonshire ....

3. From? (Typewritten; unsigned; undated)

You thought youd got away with it but its catching up with you you dirty skunk your not fit to live and wont if you persist in taking the job so watch out.

Chapter II

Results of Three Letters

The headlights of Sir Abercrombie Lewker's veteran Wolseley conjured familiar sights out of the darkness ahead as the big car topped the moorland rise west of Capel Curig. A rushy hollow on the right where a stream came tumbling down from the Glyders, a corner rugged with boulders, then—a quarter of a mile away in front of the moving jets of light—the yellow gleam of windows cheerful in a void of blackness. Sir Abercrombie stopped the car and climbed down somewhat stiffly into the road. The reflected glow of the car lamps lit his squat figure and its incongruous clothing; the woolen 'balaclava' beloved of senior mountaineers and the luxurious overcoat, fur-collared, with which it was his pleasure to perpetuate the sartorial tradition of the great actor-managers. A ten-hour journey in January in the ancient tourer necessitated these garments, for the Wolseley's hood and sidescreens were only moderately protective and Sir Abercrombie regarded car heaters as sybaritic.

He took off the balaclava and allowed the night wind to ruffle the tufts of hair that fringed his bald head. He also sniffed the cold air, largely and with enormous satisfaction. It was redolent of all that he loved most in North Wales; of moorland and bog myrtle, of height and space, of wet gray rock—of mountains. A very faint aroma of wood smoke came to his nostrils on the westerly wind and told of bright fires in the solitary inn whose windows beckoned through the dark, and like a distant trumpet-note rising above this orchestration of scents he discerned a tang, an acridity—perhaps not so much a scent as a feeling in the atmosphere. He reached into the car and switched off the headlamps.

The night was clear and pricked with stars, but the firmament was screened to westward by the enormous black shapes of mountains. Right above the yellow gleams of the inn rose a dark peak in mysterious silhouette, and as his eyes grew more accustomed to the darkness Sir Abercrombie saw that the pointed summit of this peak was aglimmer with streaks of silver. His nose had not deceived him, then—there was snow on Crib Goch and Snowdon summit would be helmeted in white.

He lowered his gaze from three thousand feet to nine hundred, to the little *llyn* whose black waters, hardly disturbed by the faint breeze, glinted with the yellow lights of the inn beyond it. The Pen-y-Gwryd Hotel, rival and predecessor of the Pen-y-Pass Hotel a mile farther on, kept an export bitter of notable quality, he remembered; remembered, too, the seasoned traveler of *The Winter's Tale* and his "For a quart of ale is a dish for a king." Arrival at the Pen-y-Pass, greetings of fellow members already arrived for the dinner meet, garaging of car, finding of bedroom—these would seriously delay the refreshing draught. Besides, though ten people had been butchered and a few hundred others mutilated and maimed on British roads that day (if the usual average had been maintained) by way of homage to the god of speed, Sir Abercrombie's car had taken no part in the carnage. By virtue of never exceeding thirty-five miles an hour and of regarding all other road users as prima facie lunatics, he had twice in the 240 miles from London avoided being crashed into by another car. That merited a modest celebration, with a pint pot if not with Autolycus's quart. He got into the car again, switched on the headlights, and drove to the Pen-y-Gwryd.

Sir Abercrombie Lewker, inheritor of the mantle worn before him by Tree and Martin Harvey, had their gift of commanding an audience by his mere appearance on the scene. He made no sound beyond the click of the latch as he entered the bar of the Pen-y-Gwryd, but the four people in the bar instantly ceased talking and turned to face him as he came in. Three of them were men, the fourth a woman. The actor-manager recognized a fellow member of the Foothold Club, one Major Charles Kemp; the others were unknown to him.

"Well, well, well!" said Kemp, very hail-fellow. "Another deserter from the P.Y.P., and none other than Sir Abercrombie Lewker in person. Come and join us, sir. What'll you have?"

He was shortish and dark, graying at the temples, with a neat mustache above sensual lips. Lewker remembered him as a Himalayan climber of some note in the days when Britain had an army in India.

"I thank you, Major," he boomed affably. "Export bitter—a pint, if I may suggest it—would comfort a traveler who left the metropolis an hour before the worshipp'd sun peered forth the golden window of the east."

The major barked at the man behind the bar.

"You've not been to Pen-y-Pass yet, then?" he added to Lewker.

"Thought I hadn't seen you there. Here—let me introduce you. You haven't met Mrs. Wiernick, I think. This is Sir Abercrombie Lewker, Eve."

"I've seen you from the stalls," smiled the girl, giving him her hand, "and Julius—my husband—has told me about some of your Alpine climbs."

"Ancient history, I fear, Mrs. Wiernick," said Sir Abercrombie deprecatingly, and allowed his appreciative glance to dwell on her.

Eve Wiernick was worth looking at. Hair as truly black and glossy as the raven's wing, eyes that could be called green set very slightly aslant in a face of vivid and provocative beauty, slimness and curves well revealed in a dark-blue ski suit with a red silk scarf at the throat. She could not be more than thirty; Julius Wiernick, he recalled, must be well over fifty.

"Peter Lumley—also a Footholder," Kemp was saying. "Jack Jones-Griffith, bachelor of this parish."

The two men mumbled conventionally. Peter Lumley was a very large young man with unkempt red hair and a reserved, not to say sullen, manner; he wore a faded red anorak that clashed fearsomely with the color of his hair. Jones-Griffith, an older man, was as tall as Lumley but leaner. Like the major, he wore a tweed suit and a collar and tie, but whereas Kemp's tweeds were old and good Jones-Griffith's were new and badly cut. His weather-beaten face and choleric blue eye flicked up a card in the files of Sir Abercrombie's memory.

"Munich climb, two summers ago," he pronounced. "The afternoon was intolerably hot. You, Mr. Jones-Griffith, were leading the climb and Professor Wiernick was your second."

"That's raight," Jones-Griffith said, staring; his Welsh accent (he had been born Welsh-speaking, guessed Sir Abercrombie) was overlaid with imitation-superior-English distortions.

"I recall it clearly," pursued the actor-manager, "because I was on Pinnacle Rib, on the other side of the gully, at the time. I was in full sunshine but you were in shadow, and I envied you consumedly."

"Your beer, sir," said Kemp, pushing a pint tankard towards him.

"Thank you. On the afternoon of which I speak I would have offered a kingdom, had I possessed one—not, like Richard of Gloucester, for a horse, but for—this."

He raised the tankard in courteous salute and drank. Eve Wiernick nodded at him and sipped her martini.

"I can remember my husband saying much the same when he came into the P.Y.G. after that day's climbing," she said. "I rang for a pint of beer the moment I saw him."

"You'd only been married a year then, m'dear, hadn't you?" said Kemp, with a quick glance. "You picked up the art of man-management devilish quick."

Eve's green eyes gave him a slow sidelong look. "It takes longer to learn some things," she said.

Peter Lumley spoke abruptly. "What about these rifles?"

"Oh, ah," said Kemp. He scowled over his shoulder at a party of three climbers who were just coming in. "Let's take our drinks into the alcove there. May as well be comfortable."

There was an efficient convector heater in the little alcove opposite the bar and they found themselves seats there round a small circular table. It was Peter Lumley who placed a chair for Sir Abercrombie and invited him, with an awkward gesture, to sit in it.

"Rifles," said the major; he glanced at Lewker. "Sir Abercrombie won't know what we're talkin' about. Fact is, sir, it's maneuvers, as they used to call it. Exercise. Officer Cadets, for the chastenin' of. Laid on for tomorrow and Sunday, thus linkin' up nicely with the dinner meet and gettin' my exes paid by the W.O."

"I suppose you fixed that yourself, Charles," murmured Mrs. Wiernick lazily. "Typical, if you don't mind my saying so."

"For old acquaintance' sake, m'dear, you can say anything you damn well please." Kemp addressed the actor-manager, "There's two bus-loads comin' up from Shorehurst overnight. Keen lads. Full paratroop equipment—oh, sorry, Eve."

He struck a match and leaned forward to hold it to Mrs. Wiernick's cigarette.

"Isn't it just possible, Charles," she said in her sleepy voice, "that one or two people don't know what position you hold at Shorehurst?"

Kemp grinned at her a trifle sheepishly. "Oh, ah. Fact is, Sir Abercrombie, I'm Second-in-Command Training. Exercise Dogsbody, that's me. Well, anyway, these lads—the officer cadets, bless 'em—de-bus in the small hours of tomorrow at points along the roads near the Pen-y-Pass pub. They're supposed to have been dropped by parachute. The unlikely assumption is that Wales is at war with England. At least, Jones-Griffith thinks it's unlikely. I gather he's an anti-Welsh-Nationalist."

Jones-Griffith sat up, his blue eyes glinting. "That's raight," he said emphatically. "It isn't sense to antagonize England as some Welshmen are trying to do. In my humble opinion Major Kemp's exercise is a mistake, as tending to—"

"I dare say I'll agree with you before the weekend's over," Kemp cut in. "However—their objective's a secret arms factory on the other side of Snowdon near Rhyd-ddu. It's a disused slate quarry actually. I know it looks like pretty inaccurate droppin' by our aircraft, but we've got to give the lads a real tough trek. We can't risk 'em getting crag-bound on Snowdon in midwinter, though, so I've laid on guides—supposed to be defectin' Welshmen—who'll take the groups over the worst of it. The groups'll be lyin' doggo here and there just off the road, poor ginks, and the guides'll happen along in the dark and exchange passwords as per the best adventure yarns. Not borin' you, am I?"

"Not at all," boomed the actor-manager affably. "Pray continue."

He was enjoying his beer. He had glanced surreptitiously at his watch and it was just after six-thirty, so that he could linger over his pint and then drive the last mile up to Pen-y-Pass to arrive well before seven, the time he had mentioned in his letter to George Grimmett.

"Lumley and Jones-Griffith here are actin' as guides," the major went on; obviously he was an enthusiast. "They make contact at oh-five-four-five and take their groups as far as the saddle southeast of Snowdon summit, Bulk-Something—Bulkysytho."

"Bwlch-y-Saethau," amended Jones-Griffith irritably.

"As you say. They leave their groups there and the lads push on by themselves over a lower pass on the west. To liven things up a bit we've got one or two fellers to act as Welsh guerrillas and dodge about on that pass takin' potshots with rifles—blank ammo for them, naturally. The lads get an issue of live ammo."

He paused to drink from his glass of whisky.

"Your officer cadets will have real bullets in their rifles?" Lewker queried in some surprise.

"Not to slay the Welsh guerrillas with. Touch of realism. I was round at the old quarry this mornin', riggin' up dummies in likely positions. Idea is, they advance in cover and open fire on the dummies. When they've taken the position they can see from the bullet-holes what sort of shootin' they've made. They bivouac that night in the quarry—it's assumed they blow up the arms factory, their objective—and start back at first light on Sunday by the same route. On Bulky Whatsit there'll be more potshots from the guerrillas to finish off the operation realistically. As before, our men take evasive action. I'm short of enemy types, so Lumley and Jack are goin' up to Bulky on Sunday mornin' again, this time as enemy

Welsh—and by the by, you fellers had better be up there by oh-eight-double-oh in case the lads make a start in the dark. All right?"

"All raight, Major," said Jones-Griffith.

"Rifles?" demanded Peter Lumley.

"Oh, ah, your rifles. Draw 'em from me p.m. Saturday. There'll be spares and ammo comin' up with the buses and we're usin' the tin shanty across the road from the Pen-y-Pass as a store." The major leaned back and drained his glass. "Thank the Lord the weather's pretty fair," he added. "Any funny business like accidents or search-parties—headlines in the papers and all that—and my name'd be mud with the C.O."

"Not to mention someone being hurt," murmured Eve Wiernick. She blew a long cloud of smoke and looked at him through it. "You always were an egocentric, Charles, if that's the word I want."

"Got to think of the Army's reputation, m'dear," said Kemp; he seemed rather to enjoy the girl's gibes. "Besides, haven't I roped in two good mountaineers to be on the spot if anything goes wrong? Lumley here traversed the Matterhorn last summer—that's right, isn't it, Peter?—and Jones-Griffith's a professional rock-climbin' guide and knows Snowdon like the palm of his hand."

Lumley stared into the bottom of his empty glass. "Plenty of hard snow high up," he muttered.

"Not below two thousand five hundred feet," put in the Welshman.

"That's about as high as the lads go," Kemp said. "At least, I hope so. We've got one type in Wellington—that's one of the groups—who's a bit unpredictable. He's a Nepalese, half a Sherpa, named Galu Regmi. Big grin all the time but you never know what's behind it. Regmi's lived most of his life on the Himalayan snowline in some village up near Everest and I'm told he pretty near went mad with joy when he heard there was likely to be snow up here." He stood up, and Lewker, who had finished his beer, rose with him. "Let's have some more drinks. Same again, everybody? Eve? Sir Abercrombie?"

"By your leave, Major," boomed the actor-manager, "I will decline. My dinner-guest is arriving at the Pen-y-Pass Hotel this evening and I should be there to welcome him."

He bowed to Eve Wiernick, who crinkled her disturbing eyes at him, and went out of the alcove with Kemp, who was making for the bar.

"You'll find most of the gang there," remarked the major. "Old Thripp's been checkin' 'em in and I gather there's only two or three stragglers to come. Well—see you at nineteen-thirty hours. That's dinnertime at the P.Y.P."

Sir Abercrombie went out to his car. Overhead the stars shone steadily, the night air was as cold and clear as the water of a hilltop spring, the black mountain-shapes shouldered boldly up to the very floor of heaven and its patinas of bright gold. The beer and the company in the Pen-y-Gwryd had been a pleasant and reviving change after the long hours of driving along the A5. Yet, as the Wolseley chugged bravely up the long hill that leads to the top of Llanberis Pass, its driver was conscious of a quite irrational feeling of unease, and was vaguely irritated because he could not lay a finger on its cause. He remembered now hearing that Professor Wiernick, a widower, had married again three years ago. Eve was an unexpected sort of partner for acid-tongued Julius Wiernick, the most opinionated and intolerant man Lewker had ever met; and she and Charles Kemp were apparently in process of renewing an old friendship. But that was not the cause of his disquiet. Jones-Griffith? One of the four professional climbing guides of North Wales and presumably Anglophile. Peter Lumley? A silent young man—older than he looked, possibly thirtyish. There had been a kind of brooding atmosphere about Lumley, as if his thoughts were permanently occupied with matters of a depressing nature, but there was nothing very remarkable about that. Charles Kemp was the professional army man; full of his job and with the traditional military eye for feminine attractions. Very hearty and open, Major Kemp. And he had paid for that excellent bitter beer.

The actor-manager shook off these misty reflections as the car plodded round a corner of hewn rock. His headlights showed only the stone wall on the left of the roadway and the beginning of the rocky hillside on the right, but he knew that below the wall the ground dropped steeply away for eight hundred feet into the deep-sunk Vale of Gwyant and that the crags of Moel Berfedd hung in the darkness overhead. Lights appeared in front, on top of the hill, and then a square white shape flanked by the darker buildings of byres. He drew in under the whitewashed wall of the Pen-y-Pass Hotel, stopped his engine, and got out.

The old inn stands eleven hundred feet above the sea, on the crest of the Pass of Llanberis and on the very knees of Snowdon. On one side the deep cleft of the pass drops with its curling road towards Caernarvon and the Straits, on the other the mountainsides sweep down in fold and ridge to the lakes and woods of eastern valleys. Behind the inn the craggy steeps of Glyder Fawr end above the kitchen windows, and in front, across the road and beyond the leveled patch of the car park with its ugly corrugated-iron shed, the divergent paths by which Snowdon summit may be reached mount sinuously round buttress and corner into the hidden heart of Cwm Dyli. Darkness hid these familiar sights from Sir Abercrombie as he stood for a moment savoring (as middle-aged mountaineers will) the fragrance of youthful ardor and mountain holidays long ago. Only the sharp peak of Crib Goch was still definite above the shadowy bulk of surrounding hills, incredibly high against the stars, lifting its silver-blue glint of snow towards the wheeling planets.

It was not a Shakespearean quotation but four lines from Winthrop Young's *Pen-y-Pass Song* that came to the actor-manager's mind:

> And the wind from Cwm Idwal, Cwm Llydaw, Cwm Glas,
> Comes whispering over the scree:
> Come back, mountain friends, to your youth on the pass;
> Come home, mountain climber, to me.

The night wind was steadily astir among the rocks, bringing up from the valley the distant voices of many little streams to mingle with the subdued hum of human voices that came from behind the curtained windows of the inn. The purposeful note of a car climbing the road on the Llanberis side entered suddenly as it came round an invisible corner below the pass.

"Hallo there?" called an inquiring voice.

Lewker turned and saw a spectacled face protruding tortoiselike from the lamplit porch of the hotel. He recognized George Thripp, the original member upon whom devolved the organization of the Foothold Club's dinner meet. He boomed a greeting.

"That's Lewker, isn't it? Good man, good man." Thripp peered earnestly at the paper in his hand. "That makes twenty-two of us arrived so far. Only the Patons and your guest—Mr. Grimmett, isn't it?—still to come." He came out of the porch, a lean worried-looking man in the late fifties, to shake the actor-manager's hand. "Nice to see you again. The president will be pleased, too—he told me he didn't think you'd come. How is Lady Lewker, may I ask?"

"Better, I thank you, though not well enough to face the journey from London. My tardy substitution of Grimmett did not cause too much trouble, I trust?"

"Not the least trouble," returned Thripp; he shivered slightly. "If the wind drops it may freeze. Grimmett—the name is vaguely familiar. Haven't I heard, or read, of an Inspector Grimmett, a Scotland Yard detective officer?"

"You have. He is identical with my guest."

"Oh," said Thripp. "Yes. Well—there's just room for your car, I believe. Let me see—" He pulled another paper from his pocket and scrutinized it anxiously in the light from one of the Wolseley's sidelamps. "Yes, in the end of the farthest shed, along there."

The car coming up the pass had slowed as it approached the crest. Now its headlamp-beams winked out and it stopped in front of the inn. A square broad-shouldered man got out and came towards them.

"Grimm!" exclaimed Sir Abercrombie, and held out his hand.

Detective-Inspector Grimmett grasped it warmly. The dim light showed his square-cut, sandy-mustached face creased in a broad smile.

"This is grand, sir, so it is," he said in his pleasant countrified voice.

Sir Abercrombie performed introductions. Thripp said worriedly that he was afraid there was no room for another car under cover and Grimmett replied that he had antifreeze in his radiator and would park by the side of the sheds.

"Good—good." Thripp took out yet another slip of paper and peered anxiously at it. "Your room is number seven. There's a washbasin. You don't mind sharing? If Williams is punctual, as I've repeatedly urged him to be, we shall eat in forty minutes' time—and I must press on. Got to type the names for dinner places."

He trotted back into the hotel.

"Takes his job seriously," commented the inspector.

"He does it well, Grimm. Thripp has organized this dinner meet for the past six years, and each time it worries him more. However—" Sir Abercrombie clapped his old friend on the shoulder—"bring that gutless modern machine of yours into the yard and let us take ourselves within doors. The air bites shrewdly here."

While Grimmett brought his new Austin saloon up the uneven slope to the byres, the actor-manager took his rucksack and suitcase from the Wolseley's rear seat. Except in the summer there was no hotel porter at the P.Y.P., so he decided to make a second journey to disembark his boots, ice-axe, and rope and put the car in the shed. The inspector joined him with a suitcase in one hand and a pair of heavy nailed boots in the other and they went in through the porch.

The roomy hall-cum-bar inside was just as Lewker remembered it from the days of his first Welsh climbs. The dim staircase on the right as you came in, the rectangular Victorian furniture, the bar-hatch with its stained-glass window opposite the front door, the colored prints of misadventures with horseless carriages and the framed mountain collotypes of the same period—everything was unchanged. The enormous and apparently ageless canine called Monty, so draped in shaggy hair that it was impossible to distinguish its bows from its stern, was still lord of the place and was receiving with supercilious tolerance the advances of a pretty girl in a tartan skirt. Three men who were drinking aperitifs near the bar-hatch called greetings to the actor-manager as he and Grimmett started up the stairs. Another man, descending the stairs, halted them.

"My dear Lewker!" he said in a loud and nasal voice. "This is very condescending of you. I've as yet had no opportunity of congratulating you on your knighthood, or of discovering why they gave it you."

"And I, my dear Wiernick," boomed Sir Abercrombie urbanely, "have as yet had no opportunity of congratulating you on your most fortunate marriage. I met your wife in the Pen-y-Gwryd half an hour ago."

Professor Julius Wiernick's thin gray eyebrows drew together. He was tall and thin, with a pointed beard that gave him the look of an elderly Mephistopheles.

"No doubt," continued the actor-manager, "a more convenient opportunity for discussing our undeserved good fortune will occur later. At the moment I am, as you see, burdened with fardels."

"Elizabethan as ever, I perceive," said the professor acidly, and went on his way down the stairs.

Lewker and Grimmett gained the dimly-lit passage above.

"Julius Wiernick," said Lewker as they went along peering at room numbers, "professes anthropology at Morchester University and used to be the club's finest rock-climber."

"Seems to have a rare bite to his tongue," Grimmett remarked.

"It is a gift that has cost him dear. I doubt whether he has one friend in the club, or anywhere else. Here is number seven. Pray go in, Grimm."

The bedroom was small but neat, with a washbasin and taps in one corner and two beds, one of which was close to the tightly-shut window. Sir Abercrombie dumped his baggage on the floor and after a short struggle succeeded in opening the window. It was in the front of the hotel, and when he put his head out he could see the lights of the Wolseley a little to the left below him. The window of his room in Sheridan Place looked upon rows of other windows, but tomorrow morning he would look out and see Crib Goch challenging and beckoning high overhead as it had done when he was a boy.

"Take your choice of beds, Grimm," he said over his shoulder.

"This one near the door'll do me, sir," replied the inspector, with a grin. "Then you'll be handy to climb out and go mountaineering in the night, if you want to."

"For the moment, at least, I shall follow the White Queen's advice and use the regular way."

Sir Abercrombie went out and descended the stairs again. Thripp, brandishing a large square of cardboard on which a plan was drawn in black and red ink, waylaid him as he reached the hall.

"We're at small tables tonight," he said a trifle breathlessly. "I've arranged the seating. You and your guest will be with the two Patons—they've not come yet, but they said they'd be here for dinner. This is the table, here by the middle window."

The actor-manager noted the table's position gravely and thanked him.

"There is a small matter for which I beg your attention," he added. "My guest is here in a private capacity. It is not necessary, I think, to inform the company that he is a Detective Inspector."

"Oh, dear!" Thripp was instantly worried. "Awfully sorry, Lewker, but I've already told the president—no one else, though. Look here, shall I see Stonor and ask him to keep it quiet?"

Sir Abercrombie said hastily that there was no need to do that and soothed him with a compliment on his work of organizing the dinner meet. Thripp, looking only a trifle less worried, trotted off towards the group by the bar and he went out to the Wolseley.

On the other side of the road two men in windproof jackets were sitting on the stone wall with their faces towards the dark bulk of the mountains, smoking cigarettes and talking in low voices. As he got his climbing equipment out of the car he could hear some of their talk … *round a little rib on the left … But that'd take you on to Mallory's Slab. … No, no—well away from Shallow Gully, a damned awkward traverse with one good handhold. …*" It was very pleasant to hear the old climbing 'shop' again, in the old atmosphere. He dumped boots and ice-axe and rope in the porch and prepared to get into the car.

"Lewker! I say!"

The man who came out of the inn in a hurry was one of those who had been standing by the bar-hatch. Sir Abercrombie had some slight acquaintance with him. Donald Ferguson, like himself, was an Original Member of the Foothold Club and had been a notable mountaineer in his heyday.

"It's long since we met last, I know," Ferguson said quickly, "but I've a wee favor to ask." He noticed the pair on the other side of the road and lowered his voice; he was a stockily-built man with a bristle of white hair. "Yon busybody Thripp has saddled me with this."

He held a slip of paper under the actor-manager's nose. Sir Abercrombie inquired mildly what it was.

"It's a list of the guests," said Ferguson. "Thripp's picked on me to make a short speech of welcome after dinner tonight. I told him I'd not do it—I'm no good at that sort of thing. He said I could find someone else to do it if I liked. The man may be a bonny organizer," he ended in an irritable undertone, "but he's a bluidy nuisance."

"I will undertake the task if you wish," said Sir Abercrombie.

"That's damned good of you." Ferguson, with a sigh of relief, handed over the paper and Lewker stowed it in his pocket. "It's more in your line than in mine and I ventured to seize on you while I had the chance. You're away down to the P.Y.G., I'm thinking."

"By no means. Merely about to garage my car."

"Oh. Charles Kemp and some others have gone down there and I thought maybe you were joining them. Well, we'll be meeting later. My niece Flora wants to meet you—she's a mighty fan of Sir Abercrombie Lewker's."

Ferguson bolted back into the hotel as if fearful that Sir Abercrombie might change his mind. As he wheeled the Wolseley into her appointed place in the byre farthest from the inn the actor-manager reflected that it was typical of George Thripp to introduce a formal speech into the informal Friday-night gathering; Thripp, a retired bank manager, revelled in committees and speeches, proposings and secondings. Rather odd, though, that Donald Ferguson should decline to make that short speech of welcome. According to Dr. Tom Paton, who was on the Foothold Club committee and had recently dined with the Lewkers, Ferguson was to succeed the present president of the club, Mark Stonor, when the latter's two years of office terminated in March. The president of a senior mountaineering club like the Foothold would have a good deal of speechmaking to do, whether it was 'in his line' or not.

Having covered the Wolseley's bonnet with a car-rug, Sir Abercrombie strolled back to the inn, sniffing the air as he walked. It was very cold, but an instinct born of many winter visits to North Wales hinted to him that the wind might back to the southwest, bringing warmer air and the possibility of mist on the hills tomorrow. As he came round to the front of the inn he noticed that the three lit windows above the porch (one was the window of the room he was sharing with Grimmett) were all open; the senior members of the Foothold Club evidently preserved that fondness for fresh air, irrespective of its temperature, which had brought execration upon them in a hundred Alpine huts.

Grimmett's ruddy features beamed at him from the folds of a briskly-plied towel as he came into the bedroom.

"Lashings of hot water, sir," he announced. "That's a comfort, being as we're nigh on twelve hundred feet up."

"A British mountaineer, Grimm, requires two things in his ideal home-from-home—hot water and cold air. However, let us not be too aggressively British in January." Sir Abercrombie closed the window and turned on the electric fire that stood in the hearth. "There is to be a sufficient dispensation of hot air this evening, so we may as well acclimatize ourselves. I am to deliver a speech of welcome to yourself and our other guests."

He told the inspector of Ferguson's request, divesting himself of overcoat and jacket as he did so. Grimmett looked interested.

"I heard you talking outside and thought I recognized the other voice," he said. "I've heard Donald Ferguson on the radio and the telly. He's the youth center man, I reckon."

"That is he. Ferguson of Fergolocks, once of the little locksmith business in the Gorbals, now acquiring the backing of church and state for his nationwide chain of youth centers. It is a good line to take nowadays, Grimm. Ferguson may climb into the Cabinet one day."

"I thought I recognised him when we came in." Grimmett regarded his sandy-gray mustache in the mirror over the washbasin. "There was another chap in the hall who looked like Arthur Penberthy—the Conservative M.P. who held Harborough West in the by-election."

"It was Penberthy. You will find among us, Grimm, the choice and master spirits of this age. The president himself is the greatest living authority on the Aramaic language. Lord Rendall, who is a Past president and never misses a dinner meet, was Her Majesty's ambassador in Rome and is practically inarticulate. But"—Sir Abercrombie turned from his unpacking to wag a cautionary finger—"it is to be remembered, Grimm, that here these things are of secondary moment. Above a thousand feet we are all mountaineers, and Rendall's most notable achievement—the Weisshorn guideless by the ordinary route—places him well below Frank Hibberd, a secondary-modern schoolmaster who was one of the two men to reach the summit of Kangri in the Nepal Himalaya."

"I'll remember," promised Grimmett. "Reckon I'd better keep quiet about my mountaineering triumphs," he added with a grin. "I've been up Snowdon once—by the train, when I was a kid."

"My dear Grimm! That was a deed of dreadful note, whose blackness, excusable perhaps in early youth, should be expunged at all costs before you shuffle off this mortal coil. Some form of penance is indicated. I suggest a second ascent of Snowdon tomorrow, with me, by some less degrading route."

Grimmett looked dubious. "I'm no mountaineer, sir," he protested. "Besides, there's snow up above, seemingly."

"You will enjoy yourself," Lewker reassured him. "Have you not spent the last few days tramping the chief constable's moors? You should be in excellent trim for a mountain walk."

"All right, sir," said the inspector resignedly. "I'll have a go. I'm in your hands, so to speak."

Sir Abercrombie beamed approvingly at him and took his place at the washbasin.

"There is one other matter, Grimm," he boomed as he removed the stains of travel. "I am by no means averse to receiving the proper tokens of respect from those by whom they are due. A youthful member of this club, for example, may call me 'sir' and thereby pleasure me. But from you—whom I count, if I may say so, as a friend and equal—the expression is superfluous. Can you, do you think, eliminate it from our conversation?"

The inspector stopped attacking his sandy hair with a pair of military hairbrushes and scratched his head instead. He looked both pleased and doubtful.

"It'd be a mite difficult," he said slowly. "What with me calling Sir Frederick Claybury 'sir' and you being a personal friend of his, and the three murder cases we've worked on together with you as a sort of unofficial chief tec, so to speak—"

"I resent that, Grimm," interrupted Sir Abercrombie severely. "Chief tec, unofficial or otherwise, I have never been. The amateur, gifted maybe, perhaps not unhelpful, has ever been my role in our happy collaborations. As for Sir Frederick, he is the assistant commissioner and your professional superior. I am not."

"Well," said Grimmett, "if it isn't to be 'sir', sir, what do I call you?"

The actor-manager twinkled at him and resumed his jacket.

"Those who know me best," he said thoughtfully, "persist in addressing me as Filthy. There are only three of them and I am not greatly desirous of adding to their number."

"I should think not, indeed," Grimmett said with complete gravity.

"Then we have Abercrombie, or Sir Abercrombie, the latter alternative adding one more to an already ponderous four syllables. The nomenclatural sins of the parents, Grimm, are too often visited upon the children. On the whole, and bearing in mind that I continually, and without your permission, call you Grimm, I think an abbreviated form would be suitable."

"Aber, sir, or Crombie?" queried the inspector innocently.

"No jesting, Grimm, I beg of you. Words, and particularly names, are serious matters. Aber is the Welsh word for a confluence of waters and Crombie suggests I know not what. Some young friends of mine have chosen to call me Sir Ab, and I shall not object if you adopt that usage."

Grimmett, wagging his head uncertainly, pulled on his gray tweed coat.

"All right, sir—Sir Ab, I mean," he agreed reluctantly. "I'll do my best. That which we call a rose, by any other word would smell as sweet."

"Thank you. I see," added Sir Abercrombie approvingly, "that you correctly follow the folio and quarto of 1609 in using 'word' rather than 'name'."

"But," continued Grimmett, "I won't guarantee to keep it up if we run against one of those nasty little affairs that seem to crop up whenever you get into the mountains, same as if you were a magnet and murderers were made of iron filings."

Sir Abercrombie adjusted his tie and glanced at his watch.

"We have ten minutes before dinner is due to be served," he said. "I would like an aperitif, if you will join me. As for murder, or any other crime for that matter, such an inconsonancy is highly improbable in the gathering of grave and reverend signiors which—"

His hand was on the door-handle when there came a knock at the bedroom door to interrupt him. He opened the door. The man who stood there looking apologetic was clad in an old-fashioned knickerbocker suit that hung loosely on his thin frame. Rather long iron-gray hair seemed appropriate to a face that might have been that of a poet or an artist but for the stern and humorless mouth, and the slight stoop of the shoulders suggested a scholar. He extended a bony hand.

"Nice to see you, Lewker," he said in an unexpectedly deep voice. "I heard your unmistakable tones—my room is next door—and wondered if I might speak to you for a moment confidentially."

"I'll go on down and wait for you, sir—Sir Ab," said Grimmett, preparing to pass.

The man in the knickerbocker suit held up a hand in protest. "No—I'd rather you stayed, if you will. You see, Thripp told me you were in the detective police force, Mr.—er—"

"George Grimmett," put in Lewker. "Grimm, this is Mark Stonor, presi-

dent of the Foothold Club. You had better come in, Stonor," he added as
the two men shook hands.

It was Stonor who closed the door behind them and shot the bolt. He
seemed slightly ashamed of the precaution.

"It's rather a serious matter," he explained apologetically. "I know little
about these things, but I suppose secrecy is to be observed. I also understand that if a—hum—criminal is to be—ah—traced, the detectives or
police should be informed as soon as possible. Hence, my dear Lewker,
this intrusion, for which I hope you'll forgive me."

"Of course, Mr. President. And what, pray, is your trouble?"

"This," said Stonor.

He took from his pocket a crumpled slip of paper. At first sight Sir
Abercrombie thought it might be yet another of Thripp's memorandums.
When the president had straightened it out and handed it to him he saw
that the paper bore three lines of typewriting:

*"You thought youd got away with it but its catching up with you you
dirty skunk your not fit to live and wont if you persist in taking the job so
watch out."*

Chapter III

Introductions and Speculations

Lewker's pouchy face wrinkled in a frown of distaste as he read the typed words. There was no other writing or mark on the slip of paper. The frown was his only immediate comment.

"Do you wish Grimmett to see this?" he asked Stonor.

"Of course, if Inspector Grimmett doesn't mind."

The actor-manager handed over the paper. "It was, I presume, received by you?"

Stonor nodded. "It was."

"Indeed. How, pray, did it arrive?"

"I don't quite know. I found it in my car."

Grimmett coughed gently and Sir Abercrombie turned to him.

"Well, Grimm? What do you make of the thing?"

"Typed on an old Remington portable," replied the inspector concisely. "I'd say by someone not used to typing, or else using two fingers."

"May I ask how you—ah—deduce that, Inspector?" asked the president curiously.

"From the uneven spacing, sir, and the fact that some letters are a good deal blacker than others, showing uneven striking of the keys."

"Very illuminating," said Stonor politely; he seemed, thought Lewker, to be more interested in the minutiae of detection than in the content of the message.

"Was it in an envelope?" Grimmett asked.

"No. Just as you see it."

"And how did it come into your hands, sir?"

"I told you—I found it in my car."

"Just so," nodded Grimmett patiently. "But what was the time when you found it? Did you find it before you left home today?"

"Goodness, no!" Stonor looked surprised at the question. "It was little more than an hour ago. We all had tea at five—my arrival was nicely timed for that hour—and it wasn't until six, or a minute or two later, that I came out to fetch my suitcase, which I'd left in the car. I found the letter then, lying crumpled up on the driving-seat. Part of the typewriting was showing, so of course I read it."

"Had you locked the car?" asked the inspector.

Stonor hesitated a moment. "Yes—and the windows were shut. But it's a convertible, and the note could have been pushed in between the window-top and the material of the hood."

Sir Abercrombie, still frowning, put a question.

"Have you any idea, Stonor, from whom this unpleasant missive comes?"

Stonor lifted his long thin hands and let them fall. "Not the slightest. Not the very slightest."

"The message amounts to a threat. Your life, in fact, is threatened."

"It appears so."

"And you can think of no one who would conceivably send you such a message?"

"Not a soul that I know of."

The actor-manager rubbed his chin. He contemplated the grave ascetic countenance of the president with some impatience.

"Then what, may I ask, do you wish Grimmett or myself to do about it," he inquired.

Stonor looked mildly surprised. "Well—I don't quite know," he said. "You see, Lewker, I didn't think you'd be coming—how is Lady Lewker, by the by? Better, I trust?—and when I heard you were here, and knowing of your successful essays in the detection of crime, I considered you would not be offended if I brought this anonymous letter to your notice. Ought I to place it in the hands of the local police officers, do you think?"

"That's the proper procedure, sir, so it is," Grimmett answered him. "That's what everyone who receives an anonymous letter like this one ought to do, and if they did it they'd be a lot better off. But in this case"— he glanced at Sir Abercrombie—"you might like us to try and get a bit more out of it first."

Lewker transferred his frowning gaze from the president to the inspector and then returned it to Stonor, who had gone over to stand in front of the electric fire and was warming his hands at it.

"May I ask, Mr. President," he boomed gravely, "whether you have any fear that this threat against your life, as it appears to be, will result in action?"

"No—no, I cannot say that I have. As I told you, I don't know of anyone who would wish to kill me, or even to do me an injury."

"Hum. Then you are totally unaware of any action which—to quote the letter—you have got away with and which is catching up with you?"

"Totally unaware, my dear Lewker."

"Have you any intention of taking a job?"

"None." Stonor turned. "Unless—I am engaged at the moment in the deciphering of certain papyri brought from the Middle East. It is just possible that they may throw more light on some passages in the Second Gospel. But—who would wish to stop me from doing so?"

The actor-manager shook his head and scrutinized the creased slip of paper, which he had taken from the inspector.

"The lack of punctuation and the single spelling-mistake," he reflected aloud, "appear to indicate a sender whose education has been neglected. The use of the word 'persist', on the other hand, could be held to suggest that the semi-illiterate style is assumed."

"That's rather clever," Stonor said admiringly. "But even if there were a rival scholar jealous of my researches, which there is not so far as I know, he would hardly resort to anonymous letters and threats, would he?"

There was a little pause. The president blinked hopefully at the two sleuths. Grimmett blew through his mustache, impatiently and audibly.

"The only thing we get, seemingly," he said, "is that the chap who landed this letter on you must have been in the barn where you garaged your car between five and six p.m. this evening. Either he's staying in the hotel, guest or member of staff, or he passed it at that time. Pretty wide open, it looks."

"It is possible," Lewker said slowly, "that the note was not intended for Mr. Stonor at all. The sender could have put it in the wrong car."

"I say, Lewker!" Stonor's thin face lit up. "That's very likely it. But"— his joy faded—"I don't know, you know. There's no other Ford Consul in the barns, and besides, my suitcase was on the back seat with my name on it in black letters."

As he finished speaking the swelling resonance of a gong sounded from the hall downstairs. Sir Abercrombie folded the anonymous letter carefully, still frowning. His little eyes fixed themselves on the president's large gray ones.

"I take it that this is the only letter of its kind you have received?" he said.

Stonor paused for the fraction of a second before replying, but his gaze did not waver from Lewker's.

"Yes," he said mildly. "Yes, of course. That's what is so strange."

"Well, we had better go down," Sir Abercrombie said more briskly. "Frankly, Stonor, I do not see what we can do about the matter. I would advise you to ignore it, for the present at least. With your permission, Grimmett will keep this letter. If"—he gave a slight emphasis to his words—"you can at any time add to what you have told us, I hope you will do so."

The president moved towards the door, pausing to nod and smile at them.

"Of course. And my thanks to you both. The mere telling of my problem has greatly relieved my mind."

He unbolted the door and went out. Grimmett, placing the slip of paper in his pocketbook, looked askance at Sir Abercrombie.

"And he *could* add to it, I reckon," he muttered. "That wasn't the first he'd had, I'll wager."

"Possibly not," agreed the actor-manager thoughtfully. "However—as Lucetta remarks, dinner is ready and your father stays. Lead on, son Grimm."

They went down the stairs. In the hall there was now a considerable throng of Footholders, all moving slowly towards the open doors of the dining room. George Thripp, his spectacled face a trifle less worried than usual, nodded at Lewker.

"Everyone's arrived," he said with great satisfaction. "Twenty-five of us. Don't forget—table by middle window, with the Patons."

A small and very bony woman in tweeds looked over her shoulder and grinned at the actor-manager. Two bright black eyes glittered in a face wizened and lined like an old leather glove.

"If someone sits at the wrong table," she remarked, "George Thripp will have kittens. How are you, Sir Abercrombie?"

She had a voice that reminded Grimmett of the klaxon horns popular in his youth. Sir Abercrombie introduced his friend to Mrs. Julia Hengist, an Original Member of the Foothold Club.

"The oldest living Original Member, if you please," amended Mrs. Hengist with pride. "I top George Sheldrake's seventy-two years by just fourteen months."

The inspector said politely that she didn't look it and Mrs. Hengist cocked a grizzled eyebrow at him.

"Oh yes I do," she retorted. "I can still lead a V. Diff., though." She peered round Lewker's bulk as someone came in through the outer door. "Come on, Peter—you're late. Where the devil have you been?"

Peter Lumley's voice said apologetically that he was just going to nip up and brush his hair.

"My nephew," Mrs. Hengist said resignedly to Lewker. "I brought him along as my guest. As good as his father was on rock, but no manners to speak of."

"I had the pleasure of meeting him in the Pen-y-Gwryd this evening," Lewker told her. "He is taking part, as I understand, in some army maneuvers organized by Major Kemp."

"Tomfoolery!" snapped Peter's aunt. "And Charles Kemp should have known better than to bring his cadets up here on the dinner meet weekend. The hills are overcrowded enough as it is."

She preceded them into the dining-room and made for her table.

"What's a V. Diff.?" inquired Grimmett as they followed.

"A rock-climb graded Very Difficult in the climbers' guidebook. Broadly speaking, there are five main standards, from Moderate to Very Severe. Very Difficult is the third standard."

"And she climbs that sort of thing at seventy-three?"

"Not only climbs, but leads," said Lewker. "The leader, who goes first up the climb, has naturally a harder task than those who come up afterwards with the protection of the leader's rope from above. But Julia Hengist was one of the earliest woman climbers——" He broke off to beam at a big gray-haired man who had risen from his seat to greet them. "Grimm, this is Dr. Tom Paton, whom I last saw hanging upside down in the Mummery Crack on the Grépon. And his son Dr. Richard Paton, a climber of more upright habits than his father."

"I resent that, Lewker," growled Dr. Tom, shaking hands. "Dick does a damn sight more hanging upside down than I ever did. This damn tension-climbing demands it, I understand."

"One tries to keep head uppermost, at least," grinned his son. "You'd better sit next to me, Mr. Grimm," he added. "Dad and Sir Abercrombie will want to reminisce about Alpine climbing in the Year One."

"Thank you, Doctor. Er—Grimmett is the name."

Richard glanced sharply at him as he sat down. "Sorry. Inspector Grimmett, I think? I followed the Tourballes poisoning case and your picture was in the papers. I thought the medical evidence was devilish thin—or isn't one allowed to say that sort of thing to you?"

Grimmett, answering casually amid the buzz of cheerful talk and the increasing clatter of dishes, thought he had never seen a father and son more alike facially. Dr. Richard was not so broad as his father, though he was quite as tall, but both men had the same blunt, pleasant features and jutting brows, the same brilliant light-brown eyes, the same crisply curling mane of hair—Richard's already graying above the ears in preparation for matching Dr. Tom's silvery thatch.

"Dr. Richard, Grimm, is our honorary secretary," said Sir Abercrombie. "He it is who knows all that there is to be known about the members of this club. Apply to him, therefore, for identification of our fellow-diners."

"This club has now four hundred and twelve members, Sir Abercrombie," Richard pointed out. "One can't keep tabs on that many, believe me."

"Lewker thinks everyone's got a damn tape-recorder memory like himself," grunted Dr. Tom. "Far as I'm concerned, I don't even know some of the members here tonight. Who's that pretty youngster at the president's table? Haven't seen her before."

The six tables in the room were arranged symmetrically in two rows of three, each with four people at it except the center table opposite the one at which they were sitting. Here Mark Stonor's slightly goatlike countenance faced the room, with two women and two men at the same table. One of the men was Donald Ferguson, the other a tall, elderly man with a drooping mustache whom Sir Abercrombie identified, for Grimmett's benefit, as Lord Rendall, a past president of the club.

"The slightly equine lady beside him is Lady Rendall," he added. "The girl is unknown to me, though I saw her earlier this evening in the hall."

"She's not a member," Richard said. "Flora Massey's her name. She's Donald Ferguson's niece and housekeeper, here as his guest. She's done some climbing—in fact, I took her up her first climb, North Buttress on Tryfan, last July."

Dr. Tom, possibly aware of some unusual inflection in his son's voice, gave him a brief but penetrating look from beneath his shaggy brows.

"Nice-looking gel," he commented.

"Not bad at all," agreed Richard, carefully careless.

The waitress with the soup reached their table and conversation lapsed. The Patons *père et fils* clearly placed conversation second to action when they were hungry, and both Sir Abercrombie and the inspector liked their food. The main course, arriving with exemplary promptitude, featured the customary meat of Wales.

"Mutton," said Dr. Tom approvingly. "I never agreed with Sheldrake, who used to grumble in the old days about farmhouse mutton. He had a verse about it:

The dose you'll more or less repeat
On each successive day,
Till when you meet a mountain sheep
You'll turn the other way."

"That's more hopeful than A.G. Godley's lines about Swiss food, anyway," countered Dr. Richard. "If I remember them aright:

You will dine on mule and marmot, and on mutton made from goats,
You will taste the various horrors of Helvetian table d'hôtes."

"Geoffrey Sheldrake," the actor-manager told Grimmett, "is the white-haired man at Mrs. Hengist's table. He is the Grand Old Man of the Foothold Club, and climbed with Winthrop Young and, I believe, with Archer Thomson."

"Not to mention Thomas Paton," nodded Richard, winking at his father.

Dr. Tom grunted. "Sheldrake may be the G.O.M. of the club," he said, "but Mark Stonor's the general supervisor and always has been. That's our president, Mr. Grimmett. Stonor it was who really started the Foothold Club twenty-eight years ago and it's been his pride and joy ever since. I believe he'd destroy every one of his damn papyri if by doing so he could raise the Foothold Club to the status of the Alpine Club."

The hum of talk was rising now that the edge of appetite had been blunted. Cassata Marguerite with a *compote* of cherries, which followed the main dish, was a small obstacle to the conversation of old mountaineering friends reunited. Lewker and Thomas Paton became immersed in a discussion of the relative merits of Vibram soles and clinker nails for all-round mountaineering. Dr. Richard turned to Grimmett.

"You've met George Thripp, I expect? He's at that table over there, with his wife and the Rossiters. Terrific organizer—we have to sit where he says, even tonight. Bit of a fusspot but people like him."

"Mr. Thripp's done a good job, seemingly," the inspector remarked. "Everyone's happy, judging by sight and sound."

As he spoke, a loud and rather nasal voice from the next table rose momentarily above the general chatter.

"My dear Penberthy! I will believe in the efficacy of the system when Parliament no longer consists of a parcel of careerists who have one and all sold their souls for a seat in it."

Richard raised his eyebrows and grinned at the inspector.

"That's Julius Wiernick," he murmured. "The club's Naughty Boy—or one should perhaps say Naughty Old Boy, for he's fifty-seven if he's a day. He insults everyone on sight. I expect Thripp put the Wiernicks and the Penberthys together because Penberthy can be trusted not to get up and walk away in a huff. He's an M.P. and makes a point of tolerating everybody—even a man who tells him he's a soul-selling careerist."

"Which of the ladies is Mrs. Wiernick?" inquired Grimmett.

"The young one, black hair. Rather attractive, isn't she?" Richard glanced quickly round the room. "Let's see—who else is there? Oh, Reid Cable and his wife—he's Under-Secretary for Fuel—with Charles Kemp and Frank Hibberd. Hibberd's done some notable things in the Nepal Himalaya, and Kemp's an army wallah. That gives you the lot of us, I think."

Dr. Tom chipped in. "Wiernick was in Nepal with Hibberd's expedition in '54. They had a damn awful row—Wiernick was rude to a local god in one of the Himalayan villages or something—and they haven't been on speaking terms since."

"It's passed over lightly in the book Hibberd wrote about the expedition," said his son, "but it seems the professor went out of his way to profane the village temple at some place called Khamche. They nearly had a massacre on their hands because of it. Anyway, the careful Thripp has put them as far away from each other as he can."

"Mountaineers," boomed Sir Abercrombie, "are not normally preservers of ill-will, save in one or two notable cases like the famous feud between Coolidge and Whymper."

He helped himself to biscuits and Danish blue from the plate proffered by the waitress. The elder Paton nodded.

"Coolidge must have had more than a touch of Wiernick's waspishness," he said. "I shouldn't wonder if we have a feud or two on our hands in this club when Wiernick publishes his memoirs. He's writing 'em, so he told me—asked me the name of the guide who beat me in a drinking-match we had in Breuil twenty years ago, because the story was going in his book. I told him to publish and be damned."

"Wiernick's made it up with Donald Ferguson, anyway," Richard said. "They were drinking sherry together in the hall. Hallo, what on earth is Thripp doing? Seems to be making faces at someone over here."

"I fancy," said Sir Abercrombie, "that he is making them at me."

He rose slowly to his feet. There was no need to bang on the table for silence. As always, his actor's gift of presence required attention and got it. He delivered his speech of welcome in five sentences, only one of which contained a Shakespearean quotation, and sat down amid polite applause. George Thripp's high voice announced that coffee was served in the lounge, and the twenty-five Footholders drifted loungewards by twos and threes. In front of Lewker and the inspector walked Professor Wiernick and his wife, joined as they passed out of the room by Charles Kemp. The professor's nasal tones were heard again.

"I hear, my dear Kemp, that your juvenile soldiery are arriving in Snowdonia to undergo training. I presume that you yourself will instruct them in the chief military arts of rape and pillage?"

The words could have been jocular, but in Julius Wiernick's mouth they sounded deliberately insulting. Major Kemp's reply was inaudible. Sir Abercrombie observed, however, that the back of his neck took on an unpleasing shade of red.

In the lounge the professor was at once hailed by Donald Ferguson, who was extracting a large book from a bookshelf in the corner, and the two settled down on a sofa to pore over the volume in apparent amity. To the clinking of coffee-cups the members of the Foothold Club formed into cheerful groups. Sir Abercrombie and Dr. Tom and Grimmett made themselves comfortable within reasonable distance of the blazing fire, while Richard, excusing himself, took his coffee-cup to the other side of the room where Flora Massey was talking with Frank Hibberd and the Penberthys. Peter Lumley, who was also in attendance, scowled rather obviously as Richard shook hands with Flora.

"A climbing-rope's worse than a holiday cruise for starting romances," growled the observant Dr. Tom, applying a match to his pipe. "I suppose Dick'll sign on that wench for a climb tomorrow, always providing young Lumley hasn't bagged her first."

"Mr. Lumley is a nonstarter, I imagine," Sir Abercrombie told him. "I am informed that Major Kemp has acquired his assistance for tomorrow's army exercise."

"Then Dick will certainly cry off our proposed circuit of the Snowdon Horseshoe. What is this damn exercise of Kemp's, anyway?"

Lewker repeated what Kemp had told him in the Pen-y-Gwryd that evening. The doctor wagged his head.

"Better if they kept that sort of thing for summer," he said. "These boys may be tough, but Snowdon in winter isn't a place to lark about on. Didn't a Marine commando die from exposure last winter, merely walking over the Glyders?"

"Kemp appears to have taken sensible precautions. Moreover, one of his cadets is a Nepalese accustomed to Himalayan conditions."

"All very well, Lewker, so long as they keep together. I wouldn't risk anything alone in this weather—not even the Horseshoe, though I've done the damn thing a score of times at least."

"I have heard that conditions are not really bad on the tops." Sir Abercrombie put down his coffee-cup. "If, Doctor, Miss Massey captures your son and he is unable to come with you on the Snowdon Horseshoe, would you object if Grimmett and I accompanied you on the traverse tomorrow?"

"Now wait a bit, sir—Sir Ab," Grimmett said, startled. "I might consider walking up by a path—"

"Fine!" Dr. Tom cut him short. "Splendid, Lewker. Has Mr. Grimmett got an ice-axe? No? Tell you what—he can borrow Dick's. He won't want it if he goes rock-climbing with his wench."

Grimmett blew through his mustache protestingly.

"But I've never done any mountaineering, Doctor. I reckon I'd—"

"All the better, Mr. Grimmett. You couldn't have a finer introduction. The Horseshoe of Snowdon's the grandest ridge-walk in England and Wales—nothing as good south of Skye."

"And it is not at all difficult, Grimm," boomed the actor-manager soothingly. "Boy Scouts do the Horseshoe in summer. I have met an infant of six months on it, though to be sure it was carried on its father's back."

"I've taken a cocker spaniel on the trip," added the doctor. "You'll be missing a damn good thing if you cry off."

The inspector perceived that he would have to agree. He was slightly comforted by the term 'ridge-walk,' which seemed to imply that the traverse of the Snowdon Horseshoe was merely a matter of putting one foot in front of another, and he was a good walker; but his comfort was diminished when he remembered that an ice-axe was considered essential.

"I reckon I'll come along, then, if you'll put up with me," he said resignedly.

"Good man," approved Dr. Tom. "I've got a hundred-and-twenty-foot nylon medium, Lewker. We'll take that."

"Nylon?" murmured the inspector suspiciously. "Medium?"

"Rope," explained Dr. Paton. "Just in case, you know. The Crib Goch knife-edge can be awkward if it's iced up."

Grimmett's heart sank again. "Rope ... knife-edge ... iced up." The words conjured up a fearsome picture of three human specks clinging like flies to a blade of green ice desperately far above solid ground and safety. He caught Sir Abercrombie's twinkling glance and summoned a wry grin in response.

"Well, Dick—roped her in for a climb?" demanded Dr. Tom.

Richard, who had come back and was putting down his empty coffee-cup with a faintly disgruntled air, shook his head.

"If it's Flora Massey you mean," he said, "she's booked to do Slanting Buttress with her uncle tomorrow. Apparently Professor Wiernick's going with them. They're making a rope of three, so one can't very well tag on."

"Bad luck," sympathized his father with heavy jocularity. "Still, you could always hang about at the bottom of Lliwedd in case one of them falls off and she has to be rescued."

"What—fall off Slanting Buttress?" Richard retorted good-humoredly. "It's a Moderate. Wiernick could go up it blindfold, and Mr. Ferguson is nearly as good."

Here Mrs. Hengist and Eve Wiernick came over to them. The oldest living Original Member gestured imperatively with a clawlike hand.

"Don't get up," she said, "though it's nice to see you making the preliminary wriggles. Men over fifty still know the meaning of the word manners. Mr. Grimmett, you've not met Mrs. Wiernick, I think?"

Grimmett, mumbling politely, got up and Eve gave him her hand and a smile. She had exchanged her ski-suit for a close-fitting frock of a green material that emphasized the color of her eyes.

"I want a leader," announced Mrs. Hengist. "I've undertaken to get George Sheldrake and his daughter up Horned Crag tomorrow. The Penberthys want to come but neither of 'em is keen to lead. What about you, Sir Abercrombie?"

"Alas, dear lady, I am already committed." Sir Abercrombie needed that ice-axe for the inspector. "Possibly Dr. Richard—?"

"The very man. You'll lead the Penberthy rope, won't you, Doctor?"

Richard looked a trifle dashed. "Well—"

"Splendid!" said Mrs. Hengist briskly. "Mabel Penberthy will be delighted to have a muscular surgeon hauling her up the sticky bits. Come along and we'll fix up about rope and time of starting and so forth."

She led Richard away towards a large fresh-colored woman who was sharing a sofa with the imposing gentleman whom Grimmett had recognized as the member for Harborough West.

"Poor Dick!" chuckled Dr. Tom. "The Penberthy tips the scale at eleven stone seven, at a guess."

"Too unkind, Doctor," Eve Wiernick said in her sleepy voice. "Mabel is certainly not more than ten stone. It's that awful frock that makes her look heavier."

"Miaow, miaow," remarked Major Kemp, arriving heartily. "I heard that. Good dinner, Sir Abercrombie, what?"

"Excellent, Major."

"Better than Shorehurst mess, I can tell you." He turned to Eve. "Nice night outside and it's devilish stuffy in here. Comin' out for a walk?"

"Eve!" Professor Wiernick's voice rose loudly. "Come over here."

"And that's an order," Eve said to Kemp in an undertone.

She walked away. The major's thick lips made an ugly shape as he looked past her at her husband. The actor-manager saw the smoldering light in his dark eyes.

"Damn attractive woman, Wiernick's wife," observed Tom Paton. "Must be close on a quarter of a century between their ages. Well, it works out sometimes."

Kemp shot a suspicious glance at him, muttered something about getting some fresh air, and stalked off towards the door.

"Charles Kemp seems to have taken a knock," murmured Dr. Tom. "But about tomorrow. What sort of footwear have you got, Mr. Grimmett? All right for a scramble?"

This led to a discussion of mountain equipment, mountaineering history, and mountains in general which lasted until Sir Abercrombie, a little tired after his long journey, announced his intention of seeking his bed. Dr. Tom undertook to obtain Richard's permission for the use of his ice-axe by Grimmett and to order packed lunches for the morning. The inspector did not accompany his host upstairs. When he entered the bedroom ten minutes later Sir Abercrombie, in a pajama suit of a chaste apple-green shade, was preparing to get into bed; or rather, had interrupted his bedward progress to consider with a critical eye a large engraving that hung on the wall above the bed.

"Tell me, Grimm," he boomed. "What circumstances, in your opinion, would lead a maiden of some seventeen summers, with abnormally large eyes and a vacant expression, clad in a modest but excessively unbecoming nightgown, to visit a blasted heath in a snowstorm in order to clasp her arms round a cruciform monument entwined with ivy?"

"Unsound mind and suicidal tendencies," suggested Grimmett absently.

"You are right. You must be right." Sir Abercrombie got into bed, pulled the bedclothes halfway up, and paused. "If it were done when 'tis done, then 'twere well it were done quickly," he added resolutely, and got out again.

Thirty seconds later, having turned the engraving's face to the wall and dived into the blankets once more, he fixed a still critical gaze on the inspector, who was removing his clothes and placing them very neatly on a chair.

"I fancy I can tell *you*, Grimm," he said, "what it is that causes a detective-inspector from New Scotland Yard to wear that preoccupied look while disrobing. Correct me if I am wrong. You have been either detecting or inspecting."

"Right, Sir Ab," admitted Grimmett. "Both, I suppose. Though I've detected precious little, come to think of it."

He draped himself swiftly in flannelette pajamas with a blue stripe and went to the washbasin. Sir Abercrombie, who was inclined to be garrulous for the first five minutes after entering his bed, wriggled his toes on the hot-water-bottle provided by the management and indulged his taste for talking.

"The sleuth-hound expression is unmistakable. Presumably I wear it myself at times. And thereby, Grimm, we defeat Duncan's dictum—'There's no art to find the mind's construction in the face.' Did you know, by the way, that the word 'sleuth' is Middle-English and signifies a slot or track? Pray tell me upon whose slot or track you have been exerting the well-trained mind since we parted in the hall."

"Ugluck whish," began the inspector.

"Tell me when you have finished brushing your teeth, then. That toothpaste of yours has a pleasant aroma, if I may say so. Mine used to have, but now it has been given what the manufacturers assert to be a new and thrilling flavor. To thrill, according to my dictionary, is to pierce or penetrate, as with something sharp, and to some extent my toothpaste performs that function. In this age, Grimm, people much prefer a new and unpleasant thing to an old and good one. Thus progress, instead of bringing comfort in its train, brings annoyance and frustration, to the increasing delight of the Devil and the confounding of earnest seekers of light such as you and I. Have you—as I perceive you can be articulate again—have you found any light?"

By this time Grimmett was getting into bed. He settled himself with a grunt or two before replying.

"The anonymous letter, you mean, of course," he said, his china-blue eyes regarding Sir Abercrombie above the sheets. "Well, there was one thing we didn't ask Mr. Stonor, and one thing I wanted to check on, so I thought I'd tick 'em both off just to satisfy myself."

"My methodical Grimm!" approved the actor-manager. "And these things were—?"

"We didn't ask Mr. Stonor if he drove up to Wales by himself. He didn't say so, and we assumed he did. But there's twenty-five people at this meet and only nine cars, so it's a safe bet some of 'em had lifts. I reckoned Mr. Thripp would know, so I put it to him casual-like in a bit of a chat we had about the long way people had to come to get here. It seems Mr. Stonor gave Mr. Frank Hibberd a lift here from London."

"And why, Inspector, this passion for investigation?" demanded Sir Abercrombie as he paused.

"Just to satisfy myself," Grimmett replied. "I reckoned it was a queer way of delivering an anonymous letter, just dropping it on the seat of a car, no envelope or anything. And now it looks queerer still." He raised himself on one elbow. "Look, sir. Writers of anonymous letters take darned good care their letters get to the right person—otherwise they're in for trouble. Well, *if* that letter was meant for Stonor to see and no one else, this particular writer was mighty careless. Either he didn't bother to find out if Stonor had driven up alone, or else he knew Hibberd was with him. In the second case, how was the writer of this anonymous—"

"Call him X," suggested Sir Abercrombie.

"Right. How was X to know that Hibberd wouldn't be the next person to go to that car after he'd left the note in it?"

"Hum." The actor-manager, who was beginning to feel sleepy, roused himself a little "You know, Grimm, there is one person who could have been sure of that."

"Who's that?"

"Frank Hibberd himself."

"By gum, sir, that's a point! And it'd explain another thing, too." The inspector reached over to his coat, which was hanging on the back of a bedside chair, and fished out the letter. "There's no sign of this thing having been *folded*. Stonor himself told us it was *crumpled up* with part of the message showing. Well, I nipped out to have a look at Stonor's car. It's a Ford Consul, new, and the windows fit so tight up to the framework of the top that you'd never get this paper through unless you folded it flat."

"Stonor might have been mistaken about leaving his windows closed the first time," remarked Sir Abercrombie sleepily.

"So he might. He seems a casual sort of gentleman. But the whole thing's puzzling, so it is."

Sir Abercrombie grunted agreement. Grimmett replaced the letter in his coat and got down under the bedclothes.

"Look at it from another angle," he went on. "Mr. Stonor sticks it out he doesn't know what the letter means or who it's from, and seems to me he wouldn't have brought it to us unless he was telling the truth about that. Now, suppose it wasn't meant for him, who was it meant for? This is what you'd call speculation, I know, but I got a good once-over of your other dinner meet people from Dr. Richard Paton this evening, and I'd say there's one of 'em who might be the target for that letter. And that's Professor Julius Wiernick."

"Uh-huh?"

"Yes. This Professor Wiernick," pursued the inspector indefatigably, "has very few friends, seemingly, and it's long odds he's got plenty of enemies. Some of 'em, probably, in the Foothold Club. What's more, he's writing his memoirs and likely to say some nasty things about a number of people. Remember what the anonymous message said? 'If you persist in taking the job,' it said. I'm free to admit that's a queer way of saying 'If you go on with those memoirs', but it could be."

He paused for comment. None came.

"What d'you think, Sir Ab?"

A snore, gentle but unmistakable, answered him. Grimmett reached out of bed and switched off the light.

Chapter IV

Distress Signal

Sir Abercrombie Lewker, a light sleeper, was dimly conscious of engine noises and heavy vibrations at some period of the night. Later, more fully awakened by footsteps and voices below the window of the bedroom, he glanced at the luminous dial of his watch. It was twenty past five. As he composed himself for another two hours of slumber he remembered the military exercise due to begin this morning; no doubt the earlier rumblings had been the lorries arriving with Major Kemp's officer cadets, and Kemp and Peter Lumley were now setting forth to perform their several parts in the exercise.

Sir Abercrombie's own exercises (a matutinal routine of body-bending and toe-touching) were performed at seven-thirty, to the admiration of Inspector Grimmett, who contented himself with a modest stretch under the blankets and a subsequent splashing of a great deal of cold water over his barrel-like torso. The dark morning was clear and cold, but Lewker was disappointed of his looked-for view of Crib Goch from the bedroom window. Mist hid the snow-sprinkled upper part of Snowdon's shapely outlier, and there was a stir of wind among the rocks on the opposite hillside.

"Looks a bit doubtful for our Horseshoe climb, I reckon," remarked Grimmett hopefully.

Lewker beamed at him. "Not at all, Grimm. The wind has backed to west-south-west, and that is very satisfactory. It will be a little warmer at lower levels and the rock-climbers will find their rock free from ice-glaze. Above two thousand five hundred feet, however, it will continue to freeze, so we shall have good sound snow for our traverse of the summits."

"But the mist up there, Sir Ab. Doesn't that make it a bit tricky?"

"For the inexperienced, yes. For the Original Members of the Foothold Club, no. Abandon hope, Grimm—you are, in vulgar parlance, for the high jump. And if you have finished adjusting that pictorial sweater of yours, let us to breakfast."

Both men had put on knee-breeches and sweaters. Lewker's breeches of lined windproof cloth were obviously a vintage pair and had a patch sewn across their broad seat; his Shetland wool sweater was well-worn and ingrained with the little brown seeds of heather. Beside him Inspector Grimmett, in bluish tweed breeches and a Norwegian sweater with a rank of reindeer displayed across its chest, looked noticeably smart. They emerged into the passage as Mark Stonor came out of the adjoining room, and Sir Abercrombie, greeting him, commented on his early rising.

"I am an earlier bird than you seem to imagine, Lewker," returned the president with donnish geniality as they walked towards the head of the stairs. "I have already been out for my half-hour morning stroll—I never miss it, rain or shine." He lowered his voice. "I shall take your advice about the—ah—matter we discussed last night, and ignore it. It may well be some ass's idea of a practical joke."

"That is possible," Lewker agreed. "At least it should not be allowed to spoil your weekend. Do you propose to climb?"

"Tomorrow, possibly. Today I shall walk up to Glaslyn, I think. I have color film in my camera and I want a picture of Clogwyn y Garnedd in winter conditions."

They entered the lamplit dining-room, where—although it was not yet eight-thirty—a dozen Footholders were already breakfasting. Grimmett noted a more cheerful and less formal atmosphere than that of last night, and dress was certainly informal, ranging as it did from Eve Wiernick's neat ski-suit to Tom Paton's ragged windproof trousers and faded flannel shirt in some unrecognizable clan tartan. The doctor greeted them heartily with his mouth full of porridge.

"Mr. President, good morning. Room for three here. Dick's deserted me for Mrs. Hengist's Horned Crag gang at yonder table. Here's the ice-axe, Grimmett."

The inspector, pleased to notice that the 'Mr.' had been dropped, examined with interest the implement which Dr. Tom picked up from beside his chair and handed to him. It was like a small pickaxe with a spike at the bottom end, three feet long and weighing (he judged) about three pounds. The steel head was about ten inches long, including the adze at one end and the pick at the other, and was stamped with the name 'Aschenbrenner.'

"What exactly are we going to do today?" he inquired, setting down the axe gingerly against the skirting-board.

Lewker and the president had sat down and were discussing Welsh mountain weather past and present. A waitress set plates of steaming porridge before the three newcomers. Dr. Tom chivvied the remains of his own porridge into the shape of a capital C in the bottom of his por-ridge-bowl.

"Having no map," he said, "this'll show you. Snowdon summit"—he put a small dump of white sugar on the C halfway along its curve—"two lakes, Llydaw and Glaslyn"—he poured some milk into the curve—"Lli-wedd on this side and Crib Goch on that, somewhere near the ends of these ridges of porridge. The opening of the C faces east. Crib Goch, on the north arm, is the peak right above this hotel. We start by climbing that, then go right round the C over Snowdon summit, down and up again to get over Lliwedd, and down finally and round the end of the lake here to get back to the hotel. Got that? Show you a map later, if you like."

Grimmett, munching porridge with gusto, nodded. "We go over three summits, seemingly. This one called Lliwedd, that's where there are some rock-climbs, Doctor, isn't it?"

"That's it. Finest precipice in Wales—thousand feet from base to sum-mit. Dick and his lot will be climbing Horned Crag, on the eastern end of Lliwedd, and Wiernick and Ferguson and Flora Massey will be at the other end of the cliff on Slanting Buttress. Both parties intend to get an early start, by the look of it, like us."

The Slanting Buttress party, plus Eve Wiernick, was at an adjoining table, from which the professor's nasal tones rose occasionally in tren-chant comment. At another table Grimmett perceived Reid Cable, the burly Under-Secretary of the Ministry of Fuel, and his wife. With them was Frank Hibberd. The inspector's glance dwelt for a moment on the secondary-modern schoolmaster who had been on three Himalayan ex-peditions—and who had driven up to North Wales with Mark Stonor. Hibberd's lean ranginess, close-clipped mustache, and piercing blue eyes were in keeping rather with the popular idea of an explorer and moun-taineer than with that of a schoolmaster. Grimmett doubted his suitabil-ity as a teacher of youth; there was intolerance in the tight line of his mouth, a hot impatience in the eyes and the deep vertical lines between the brows.

George Thripp trotted into the room, looking more than ever like an anxious tortoise in his gray turtle-necked sweater.

"Will everyone please leave a note of where they are going in this book"—he held up a red-covered exercise-book—"which will be in the hall. Thank you."

He trotted out again. Professor Wiernick was heard to complain of an excess of Thrippery at the dinner meet.

"A damn sound idea of Thripp's," Dr. Tom said loudly to Grimmett. "Might mean the difference between life and death if someone got into trouble."

"In some senior members of this club, my dear Paton," remarked the professor, turning in his chair, "the difference between life and death is already undetectable."

The doctor replied irritably over his shoulder. "You know as well as I do, Wiernick, or should know, that if a man gets seriously injured on a mountain and dies, he dies in nine cases out of ten from exposure following shock—prolonged exposure due to the fact that the search party doesn't know where to look for him. It's the merest mountaineering common sense to leave information of where you're bound for and when you expect to be back."

Professor Wiernick looked as if he was well prepared to pour acid on Dr. Tom's irritation, but Donald Ferguson cut in quickly from his place opposite the professor.

"It's not likely there'll be any search-parties this weekend at least, as far as the club's concerned. I'll not answer for Kemp's army laddies."

"The military passion for wearing camouflaged clothing in the hills," declared the professor, "would baffle any search party. A red windproof could quite conceivably save a man's life in certain circumstances. Don't you agree, Ferguson?"

"That is very true," Stonor said pontifically before Ferguson could reply. "My own anorak is bright green, but the same principle applies."

By this time eggs and bacon had arrived. More people came into the dining room, exchanging good mornings with the earlier birds. Outside the morning was lightening, and a waitress switched off the lights in the room. Ferguson addressed Sir Abercrombie.

"We're making an early start for Lliwedd. Where are you bound for?"

"I have chosen the Horseshoe as being suited to my age and infirmity," responded the actor-manager, helping himself to toast. "I gather you are for Slanting Buttress. Surely a Moderate is small beer for a tiger like you?"

"I'm no tiger nowadays," disclaimed Ferguson. "Besides, the chimney pitch of Slanting Buttress is no' as easy as all that."

"Uncle and Professor Wiernick are being very kind and taking me up

Slanting Buttress," put in Flora Massey; she had a contralto voice, pleasant to listen to. "I think they're going to climb something harder when they've finished hauling up their poor novice."

Richard Paton came across the room to them, and Grimmett took the opportunity of thanking him for lending his axe.

"The spike's pretty sharp," Richard said. "Use it for prodding Dad if he keeps stopping to admire the view. He has a tendency that way."

"Better than the modern tendency to swarm up overhangs and ignore the view altogether," growled his father.

Richard addressed himself to Miss Massey. "When you've finished your climb, Flora, you might like to stroll along over East Peak and meet us at the top of ours. We could walk back together."

"I will, if I don't see Peter first. He's going to be somewhere about up there after this exercise business, and I promised I'd look out for him."

"Oh," said Richard. "I see."

From the other side of the room came Mrs. Hengist's klaxon tones commanding her party to prepare for action. Richard strolled away.

"One up to Mr. Lumley," murmured Dr. Tom. He rose to his feet. "Come on. What did the president of the Alpine Club say in 1899? 'Nothing, after a good guide, is so conducive to a successful expedition—' "

" 'As an early start,' " Lewker finished for him. "Grimm, remove your avid gaze from the toast-rack and look to higher things. Excelsior is the word."

Mark Stonor rose with them and they left the dining room, the inspector narrowly avoiding a collision between the spike of his borrowed ice-axe and the presidential stern. Fifteen minutes later, having duly recorded their intentions in the red exercise-book, they were out in the brisk mountain air. Above the craggy shoulders that rose darkly opposite the inn the sky was overcast but bright, the clouds that still hid the upper peak of Crib Goch, two thousand feet above, were faintly luminous, and Stonor, in red woolen cap and green anorak, opined that there might yet be light enough for color photography by noon. Inspector Grimmett, handling his unaccustomed ice-axe and staring up at the apparently sheer precipice that fell out of the clouds a long mile to westward, found it incredible that he was about to try and climb up there.

"All set?" grunted Dr. Tom, shouldering his rucksack. "Come on, then."

He led the way through a gap in the wall on the other side of the road and up the stony turf of the mountainside. On their left, winding up the other side of the mountain-shoulder above them, the broad ribbon of the old Pony Track started on its way towards Llyn Llydaw and the base of

Lliwedd; Ferguson and Flora Massey and the professor were already some distance up the track, and as Grimmett followed his leaders along a smaller path to the right he saw Mrs. Hengist's Horned Crag party emerge from the inn and start up the Pony Track. The gaunt figure of the president, hung about with cameras and exposure meters, ambled more slowly in their wake.

"Good fellow, Stonor," remarked Tom Paton as they passed out of sight of these persons. "Nurses this club like a baby. Don't think he likes the idea of Ferguson being next president, somehow."

"Doesn't the president choose his successor, Doctor?" Grimmett asked.

"Not in the Foothold Club. Committee nominates him. Special meeting, end of November. The retiring president has no say in it. Ferguson's all right, senior mountaineer, Alpine climber and so on, but he's a bit of a vulgarian. That wee Glasgow accent of his—Stonor's a frightful stickler for what he considers correct speech."

"Anti-non-U, so to speak," suggested Grimmett.

"That hits him off nicely. Of course, Ferguson's well on his way to a knighthood. Wiernick was expecting one, I gather, in the last Honors List, but it didn't come up and he's been sore about it. But damn it all, let's forget 'em. Mountains are greater than men. Lewker, where's your apt quotation for the climber's setting-forth?"

" 'Now for our mountain sport; up to yond hill,' " boomed Sir Abercrombie promptly from behind him. "*Cymbeline*, Act Three, Scene Three," he added with precision.

"That'll do nicely," grunted the doctor.

The path mounted steeply across a slant of boulders much scraped by generations of nailed boots, and conversation ceased as breath became scarce. In front went Dr. Paton's bearlike form in a stained brown anorak topped by a deplorable hat with a switchback brim. He carried his ice-axe Alpine fashion, with its head in the bottom of his rucksack and the spike sticking up behind his head, and a coil of rope was slung round his broad shoulders. Next came Lewker, who had thrust his axe through the waist-loop of nylon line that was secured round his ample waist with a snaplink. Grimmett brought up the rear in a new double-texture shooting jacket and a tweed hat. He had begun by carrying his borrowed ice-axe like a lance or spear, with its two-inch spike swinging to all points of the compass, but the actor-manager had tactfully hinted at the danger to anyone walking in front on a steep path and the inspector, blushing for his ignorance, had adopted the customary method of tucking the shaft under his arm with the pick hooked behind his shoulder.

The path, sometimes rocky, sometimes boggy, climbed steadily along the massive flank of the ridge that rose steeply on their left hand. On the right, beneath the falling mountainside, the cleft of Llanberis Pass dropped ever more deeply into the winter haze, with the vast shoulders of Glyder Fawr sweeping up into the clouds on the opposite side. Each time they topped one of the shaley rises of the path the abrupt face of Crib Goch loomed more dark and gigantic above the rock-strewn slopes ahead. They had been going for half an hour before Dr. Tom, puffing slightly, called a halt—to admire, he explained, the view. The Pen-y-Pass Hotel was a dim white speck far down behind them. In the purple distance of the valley below a pale glimmer of water showed between the knees of the hills.

"Llyn Peris," panted the doctor; he pointed to a dark crag some distance down on the farther side of the pass. "Dinas Cromlech—the tiger's playground."

Sir Abercrombie nodded grimly at Dinas Cromlech; for him that columnar mass of rock held grim associations.

They went on again. The path climbed steeply, rounded a rocky corner, threaded between small crags and emerged on a narrow grassy saddle in the ridge.

"Bwlch Moch," announced Dr. Tom breathlessly. "Take a—breather."

Inspector Grimmett, coming up last to the saddle and puffing mightily, had yet breath enough for an exclamation.

"By gum!" said he.

He stood on the narrow threshold of a gateway between two realms of space. On his left the ridge rose in abrupt crags; on his right it merged in the pyramidal rock-face of Crib Goch, huge and forbidding. From his position between these giant gateposts Grimmett looked out across a gulf a mile wide, walled by precipices and roofed by the clouds, with a long sheet of water gleaming dully, like a pewter dish, in its bottom five hundred feet below. Opposite him, on the farther side of the lake, the wall of the cwm was formed by a massive rock-face whose top vanished into cloud; this awesome cliff, thought Grimmett, must be nearly half a mile long. Only the white specks dotting the crags just below the fringe of the clouds—tiny ledges on which the snow still lay—gave any indication that the sweep of precipice was not sheer and unclimbable.

"That'll be Lliwedd, I reckon?" he ventured.

Sir Abercrombie, squatting on a rock and contemplating the view with benign satisfaction, nodded.

"Lliwedd it is, Grimm. If the clouds were two hundred feet higher you would perceive that it has two summits, East Peak and West Peak. On East Peak, at the left-hand end of the precipice as we face it, is Horned Crag route—Mrs. Hengist and company are bound thither."

"You can see some folk on the Lliwedd track down there," interjected the doctor.

"I see them. That will be Wiernick's party, I fancy. I can just discern that red cap of his. They will have to go right round above the farther shore of Llyn Llydaw, Grimm, in order to reach the foot of Slanting Buttress, which is on West Peak at the extreme right-hand end of the cliff."

Dr. Tom, who had extracted some chocolate from his rucksack, broke the slab into three pieces and offered two of them to his companions.

"Carbohydrates," he said. "We'll need plenty of 'em higher up."

The inspector turned to stare up at Crib Goch as he munched. The huge craggy face with its dark slabs and darker clefts looked most intimidating. Very high up near the hidden summit there were patches of snow. He shivered slightly.

"Always a chilly breeze on Bwlch Moch," remarked Dr. Tom, picking up his rucksack. "Let's get at it."

There was a steep and rocky track at first, twisting up the ridge over humps of yellowed winter turf and occasional slabs where Grimmett had to use his hands for the first time that day. Shaley terraces brought them to the place where the wall of rock towered uncompromisingly above their heads. Here they halted for a moment while the inspector, by Sir Abercrombie's instruction, put his ice-axe head downwards in his rucksack like Dr. Tom's.

"You'll need both hands for this bit," grunted the doctor.

He was already a dozen feet up on the rocks on a slanting ledge, clinging his way (most precariously, in Grimmett's view) round a vertical corner on the left. The inspector felt an inward quaking as his worst fears were realized—this was going to be rock-climbing, not walking.

"I reckon I'm not up to this, Sir Ab," he muttered.

"You are, laddie. Pray take my word for it." The actor-manager urged him gently towards the ledge. "Up you go like a good detective-inspector. For the honor of the Yard, Grimm!"

Thus adjured, Inspector Grimmett blew desperately through his mustache and launched himself at the corner. The ledge was smooth and slanted steeply upwards. The drop on his left—a bare twenty feet down to the top of a scree-slope—seemed enormous because of the lake so far down below his scraping boots. Comforting, grabbable knobs on the wall on his right got him up somehow, the spike of his ice-axe rasping along the rock, to a nook in the broken flank of the wall above. Dr. Tom's face peered down from a higher platform.

"Don't clutch and struggle, Grimmett," he said severely. "Stand up straight and watch where you're putting your damn feet."

He vanished, and the scraping of clinker nails as he climbed merged with a melodious booming, as of a musical bumblebee, that accompanied Sir Abercrombie's approach from below. Grimmett, an amateur of the easier classics, recognized the opening tune from the first movement of Beethoven's Pastoral Symphony. Breathing heavily, he tackled the splintered rock-face that now confronted him. It was easier than the first bit and brought him to a crest, a backbone of nubbly reddish-tinted rock that sprang straight up above him into the clouds like a Jacob's ladder. Twenty feet overhead a large gray rump decorated with a patch of Royal Stewart tartan cloth was all that could be seen of Dr. Paton who was scrambling upwards at a most reassuring speed. The ridge, Grimmett told himself, could not be as steep and hard as it looked to his unaccustomed eye.

Five minutes later and a hundred feet higher he realized that it was as easy as walking—if you ignored the empty space on three sides of you and kept your nose to the rock. After ten minutes, Inspector Grimmett was almost enjoying himself. This was genuine mountaineering, and there was excitement in it for a staid detective-inspector who had never in his life grasped a rock handhold until today. Down on the path it had been moderately warm, but up here it was cold, freezing, and whenever the mounting ridge leveled itself for a yard or two he trod on a narrow path of snow. There was a ribbon of snow twisting down the gully on the right of the ridge, too, giving the place the ferocious look of those pictures in books of Alpine adventure. A few feet higher up there was snow in every hole and corner of the rocks.

A sudden waft of colder air touched his face. They were entering the clouds. He halted on a narrow platform floored with hard snow to put on his woolen mitts and rub his cold hands together. Looking down under the trailing fringes of the mist he could see the inn like a white pebble in the dark trough of the valley, the path they had climbed a brown thread flung carelessly on the gray-green quilt of the lower slopes.

The strains of the Pastoral Symphony (Simplified or Lewker Version) grew upon his ear, and a brown woolen balaclava rose above the rim of the platform. Sir Abercrombie, heaving himself on to level ground, inquired how his friend liked Crib Goch.

"Grand!" returned the inspector. "Perishing cold, though. I was thinking it must be a bit like the Alps."

> " 'O, who can hold a fire in his hand
> By thinking on the frosty Caucasus?' "

intoned the actor-manager. "On, Grimm, on. There are better things than this higher up."

Grimmett scrambled on. The cold mist enfolded him and the downward view was lost. The rocks were furred with tiny crystals of frozen mist now, and even through the woolen mitts his hands were chilled. Where the snow lay on places more or less level, it was so hard that Dr. Paton's fifteen stone had scarcely printed any evidence of his passage upon it. The doctor himself was out of sight in the grayness overhead—a grayness that varied strangely in intensity, being dark one second and the next much lighter, like a symbol of human fears and hopes. When the inspector had climbed for another five minutes the mist around him was like white cotton wool; fifty feet higher it was luminous, filled with blinding white light. Grimmett found the angle of the ridge easing in front of him. He was traversing a sort of gangway of snow with a drop into hidden depths on either hand when a joyful roar from Dr. Tom, above him, came so loudly that it almost overbalanced him. Thirty seconds later he was standing beside the doctor on an attenuated point of rock in brilliant sunshine, speechless with combined lack of breath and excess of admiration.

They had climbed through the roof of clouds and now were above it. The roof had become a white sea, undulant but nearly motionless, in which their summit was islanded beneath a sky of deep, gentian blue with other sunlit and snowy summits gleaming far and near like icebergs on a frozen ocean. The contrast between the cold and gloom of five minutes earlier and this sudden brilliance of light and color and warmth was extreme.

"We're damn lucky," observed the doctor. "This sort of thing turns up maybe one day in the year."

Sir Abercrombie's woolen balaclava bobbed up beside them. For a few seconds he stood looking round him and breathing deeply.

"O, Iago, the pity of it, Iago!" he exclaimed at last. "O that Shakespeare had been a mountaineer! What epitomes of magnificence he would have left us!"

"Well, it's damn wonderful, Shakespeare or no Shakespeare," growled

Dr. Tom. "Look at our shadows on the clouds down there."

The two mountaineers began to point out the various emergent summits for Grimmett's benefit: the peak of Moel Siabod sticking out to the eastward, the twin Glyders in the north floating like atolls on the foam. Two whaleback slivers just emergent above the level cloud-sea south of them were the east and west peaks of Lliwedd a mile away across the hidden depths of Cwm Llydaw. Westward lay the finest sight of all, the conical summit of Snowdon itself, robed in glittering snow, its mere three-and-a-half thousand feet meaningless in conditions that made it fully as imposing as a Himalayan giant. Grimmett saw that the summit of Crib Goch, where they now stood, was the tip of a long peninsula rather than an island, for a ridge, snow-plastered and extremely narrow, ran westward from it towards Snowdon; a ridge that rose and fell in great spikes and humps of rock for rather more than a mile, curving round to the left to rise finally to the highest summit in England and Wales. The inspector's attention focused itself on the part of this ridge that ran from where he stood towards the nearest rock-spike, two hundred yards away. For the first few feet the crest was level and flat, a path of snow a yard wide with a steep slope falling from its left edge into the frothy vapor that lapped along the crags fifty feet below. On the right (all the way along the ridge, as far as Grimmett could see) there was a vertical drop into the invisible depths. But beyond the short level section all semblance of footing disappeared—the ridge became a knife-edge, partly of snow with a glisten of ice about it, partly of rock where the edge thrust reddish-brown teeth above the top of the white wall. To the inspector's possibly exaggerative eye it looked perilous in the extreme. His apprehensions were increased when he saw Dr. Tom uncoiling the 120-foot rope.

"I'm damn glad I haven't carried this up for nothing," the doctor observed, positively licking his lips with anticipatory pleasure. "We'd better use it on the narrow section, Lewker, don't you think?"

"It would be as well, perhaps. Twenty-foot intervals should suffice."

The doctor tied one end of the rope round his waist; it seemed to be tacitly agreed that he should continue in the lead. Sir Abercrombie made two overhand loops at intervals of twenty feet, one for Grimmett and one for himself, explaining as he did so that the snow on this flank of the ridge had been regulated and they would probably need to cut a step or two.

"Those Boy Scouts you talked about must be tough lads," commented the inspector as he tightened his waist-loop.

"In summer, conditions are very different," the actor-manager returned.

"On any fine Saturday or Sunday you will see a veritable procession of youths and maidens skipping along the crest. To traverse it today in safety is the prerogative of seasoned mountaineers, Grimm."

Inspector Grimmett, who was feeling far from seasoned, nodded and tried not to think of a film he had once seen wherein three roped climbers fell shrieking to their deaths from a snow-ridge in the Alps. In imitation of Dr. Tom, he got his ice-axe out of his rucksack.

"*Now*," said the doctor, with a wink at Lewker, "for our mountain sport!"

He walked along the narrow snow-path to its end and kicked with his boot at the steep slant of snow beyond, making little or no impression. His axe came into action. A couple of deft slashes with the adze end of the head carved a short groove or nick in the slope, just large enough to take the edge of his right boot sole. He trod firmly upon it, cut another farther on, and swung his left boot across, to stand upright on these two rudimentary steps while he cut the next one. Grimmett, under Sir Abercrombie's direction, paid out the rope as the doctor alternately slash-slashed and stepped, balancing along the steep tent-roof of the snow-slope with a grace and lightness strange to see in a man so large and heavy. Grimmett noticed the chips of snow-ice hewn out by the axe sliding and scuttling away down the white precipice to vanish in the clouds. It made him feel slightly sick to watch them.

"Come on, Grimmett," grunted Dr. Tom.

He had reached a place on the snow-wall where the rocky edge protruded from the crest just above his head, and had hitched the rope over a notch in the edge. Grimmett restrained an inclination to blow through his mustache and gritted his teeth instead. As soon as he set his nailed boots in those immature steps he felt their inadequacy and leaned inwards towards the slope, trying to dig his gloved hand into it.

"Grimm!" called Sir Abercrombie gently from behind him. "Hold your axe horizontally across your body, spike towards the slope. Now stand upright. Excellent. Now walk, balancing yourself with the spike against the snow."

The inspector's sense of balance was good and he was as physically fit as any man at the Yard. With every step he gained confidence, not unaided by the realization that Dr. Tom had the rope safely hitched in front of him while Sir Abercrombie held it behind him.

"Good man," observed the doctor when Grimmett reached him. "He's all right," he added more loudly, to reach the actor-manager's ear. "We can move all together. Give me a shout if he slips."

Before Grimmett could protest he was chipping his way onward again.

When he had gone twenty feet Grimmett perforce had to follow. Sir Abercrombie, a few coils of rope held in his hand, was moving across the snow-wall close behind him. The inspector gulped. The party was in the very position for the fatal accident of the film he remembered so damnably clearly—one slip, and all would go hurtling down to death!

A few seconds after this solemn thought had crossed his mind the inspector, treading incautiously, slipped and slid helplessly on the hard steep surface.

"Hold!" boomed from behind him. In front, Dr. Tom stood fast with the rope in some miraculous way looped over his axe, the spike of which he had plunged into the snow. Grimmett, suspended gently fore and aft, clawed up for three feet or so with the aid of his axe-pick and regained the line of steps, feeling both frightened and apprehensive of reprimand from his companions.

"Upsadaisy," said Dr. Tom cheerfully. "If you'd stuck the axe-spike in as soon as you felt yourself going you wouldn't have slid an inch. By God, Lewker, Wiernick and Ferguson don't know what they're missing, messing about on dirty wet rock down below!"

"They climbed together in the Alps, did they not?" Sir Abercrombie said, beaming reassuringly at the inspector.

"Yes. Years ago." Dr. Tom was once again cutting methodically along the snow-slope. "Stonor used to climb with them. And John Lumley, young Peter's father. We'll take to the crest for a bit here."

Grimmett's relief at finding himself treading a backbone of solid rock instead of edging along a sort of upended skating-rink was short-lived. On his right the rock fell away from his boot nails in a vertical wall, and through a gap in the clouds he momentarily espied a small lake so directly beneath him that he was convinced that a man could leap into it from this crest—a leap of a thousand feet or so. He was actually relieved when the crest narrowed into a knife-edge of snow and the doctor led down on to the hard white slope again.

Inspector Grimmett, indeed, found himself passing through the same spiritual metamorphosis he had experienced on the rocks lower down. The sparkle of snow and sky, the glitter of far summits in the blue, the sense of being uplifted above the cares and burdens of the lower world— these things worked upon him in partnership with his growing confidence until he was really and positively enjoying himself, in a manner and degree that was entirely new to him. The narrow section of Crib Goch took them less than fifteen minutes to traverse, and in that time

George Grimmett became the latest recruit to the sport or craft of mountaineering.

The crest ended in a snowy nook below an upstanding column of rock with a crack in its side—the first of the Snowdon pinnacles.

"We can do without this damn rope now," declared Dr. Tom, untying his waist-knot and glancing at his watch. "Just eleven. Should be on top by half past twelve. Hup!"

With this self-encouraging monosyllable he launched his bearlike figure at the crack, which was vertical but short, and hauled himself neatly to the top of the pinnacle. Grimmett—ready to follow anyone up anything now—stepped out of his loop and swarmed up after him, leaving Sir Abercrombie to add the forty feet of rope to the coil he carried before climbing the crack in his turn. Over great red pillars that seemed to float in mid-air they clambered, clinging round pointed obelisks poised above the mists, treading gingerly along sun-warmed cockscombs of rock, lowering themselves into the blue shadow of clefts where the cold gripped ear and cheek and volutes of snow-ice jutted over forbidding chasms. As they topped the last pinnacle the inspector became aware of a change in the surrounding atmosphere. The cloud-sea that surged sluggishly just below them was heaving into slow-motion breakers, sending up translucent towers and columns that were like genii rising to challenge the unclouded heavens. Close behind him as he lowered himself cautiously down a splintered rock-face he heard the melodious humming alter its theme.

"You're on the Fifth Symphony now, seemingly," he remarked as the actor-manager joined him on a broad ledge. "That's the 'Fate-knocks-on-the-door' theme."

"Right, Grimm. It is more conformable to our imminent plunge into the shades."

Afterwards, and in spite of Sir Abercrombie's denials, Inspector Grimmett was confirmed, by this small circumstance, in his old conviction that his friend possessed a sixth sense which gave him premonition of coming disaster.

Less than five minutes later, when Dr. Tom's burly shape was almost down to a broad saddle not far below the pinnacles, Lewker's voice boomed commandingly.

"Listen!"

They halted, all three of them. A mist-wraith drifted up from below to come between them and the sun. There was at first no sound but the multitudinous murmur of a hundred faraway streams. Then, faint and shrill as a bird's cry, they heard the note of a whistle—a single blast, lasting for perhaps two seconds.

"Kemp's damn cadets, probably," the doctor called from his perch on a boulder just below. "They ought to know better than—"

"Wait," said the actor-manager sharply.

And the whistle-blast came again, fainter on the varying wind but unmistakable.

"I heard it once, before I called to you," Lewker said rapidly.

Dr. Tom nodded and cocked his ear towards the southward; he appeared to be counting under his breath. Again the distant whistle shrilled.

"Four," he grunted, frowning heavily.

Grimmett, puzzled, looked from one to the other of his companions. Their expressions were grave, even anxious. There came a fifth blast, and a sixth. Then silence.

"Ten-second intervals, all right." The doctor glanced at his watch. "Should be a minute's pause now."

They waited. No one spoke. The mist-fingers were now stretching over the saddle of the ridge below, and the sun was a pale disc struggling in their grasp.

"One minute," said Dr. Tom.

As he spoke the thin high call came again, and after ten seconds again, and again.

"Lliwedd?"

"It could very well be Lliwedd, Doctor. The sound comes, I fancy, from the neighborhood of West Peak."

"What is it?" Grimmett asked, as he and Sir Abercrombie joined Dr. Tom.

The doctor answered him. "Mountain Distress Signal. Never used unless someone's in serious trouble, usually a climbing accident." He looked at Lewker. "We could get down from Bwlch Goch and cut across between Glaslyn and Llydaw, couldn't we? I'm not too clear about the route myself."

"I fancy I can find it."

"You'd better take the lead, then. And we'll go fast. Wiernick's party might have had trouble."

Sir Abercrombie nodded and turned to the inspector.

"Keep close behind me, Grimm, and tread exactly as I tread. We are going to travel fast."

He started down the short scree-slope that separated them from the level saddle below. An edge of old snow ran along the saddle on the left.

Lewker, driving his nailed heels well into the bank of snow beneath, led them to the left over the edge and down into the gloom of chilly mist.

Chapter V

On Slanting Buttress

In the mile-and-a-quarter of high and narrow crest that runs westward to form the northern side of the Snowdon Horseshoe, there is only one pass; that is to say, there is only one place where the ordinary mountain-walker can cross it from side to side, or descend from it into the deep valleys on either hand. This is Bwlch Goch, the Red Pass. From here a steep and rugged gully, laborious but not a rock-climb, drops into Cwm Glas on the north, while on the south side a man who knows the route can make a zigzag way down the craggy flank of Crib Goch to reach the shores of Glaslyn nine hundred feet below. This latter way Sir Abercrombie had taken some years before. Not for the first time, the remarkable gift of memory that had helped him to the solution of many problems of crime proved useful in mountain route-finding. He had made no conscious note of the terrain on that previous descent, but now, as though the pressing of a button had set in motion a cinematographic record, every detail of rock and scree and turfy ledge that had then passed before his eyes recurred to him with absolute clarity. Although the mist into which they had plunged limited visibility to fifty or sixty feet he led downwards without hesitation.

He went fast. On this southern flank fronting the sun of past days, very little snow remained, and that was generally confined to deep-cut gullies whose enclosing sides had shadowed the white ribbon that curled in their bottoms. Lewker almost ran diagonally down a slope of rubble, swung to the right on shaley ledges, and picked a way down a bottomless slant of boulders. Behind him Grimmett slid and clattered gallantly, keeping up so well that the actor-manager could hear, every so often, the "*Phooff!*" as he blew through his mustache—invariable sign that Inspector Grimmett was not easy in mind. Without pausing in his rapid stride he boomed advice over his shoulder.

"Unstiffen the joints, Grimm. Crook the pregnant hinges of the knee.

India rubber, not iron, is your material for rapid descent."

The inspector had not enough breath for reply but he strove to obey. Sir Abercrombie had retained his ice-axe in his hands and held it ready to use for a balancing touch here or a passing support there; his short legs seemed almost to twinkle as he sped downwards, his body slightly crouched and bent forward, his eye ever on the place two steps ahead where his boot would rest. Grimmett did his best to imitate him, and found that the crumbling steeps down which they sped like three falling stones became slightly less frightening and certainly less tiring. Behind him Dr. Tom lumbered bearlike as ever, with a bear's extraordinary lightness in crossing rough ground. The mist swirled slowly above and below, and through it came at intervals that urgent sequence of whistleblasts from the invisible distance.

As he rushed smoothly downwards Sir Abercrombie speculated. Allowing for the wind, which was southwesterly and had lately become stronger, the distress signal was coming from the south. Lliwedd's West Peak, whereon lay the Slanting Buttress climb that Wiernick and Ferguson and Flora Massey were doing, was due south from Bwlch Goch. But Wiernick and Ferguson—the former especially—were good and experienced rock-climbers to whom Slanting Buttress was an easy scramble climbed primarily for the amusement of their girl companion, and Flora could hardly have come to grief when they were continuously safeguarding her with the rope. It was unlikely that the leader, whether it was Ferguson or Wiernick, would have fallen on such a climb. There was, however, another who could by this time have reached a spot not far from the foot of the West Peak if he had followed his avowed plan: Mark Stonor. Stonor had proposed to walk up to Glaslyn, the crag-encircled lake at the foot of Snowdon's summit precipice. And Stonor had yesterday received an anonymous letter threatening his life.

They were down to the lower fringes of the mist now. The grayness at their feet formed into darker or lighter shapes of mountainside or lake. The last trailing wraiths of vapor shredded away above their heads as they scurried down to the verge of a steep little drop and saw Glaslyn two hundred feet or so below them. The *llyn* was a dark eye gleaming in the huge vague features of Snowdon. The craterlike walls that almost encircled it dropped out of the mist-shroud on the mountain's head. The contrast between the gloom of this sunken hollow and the brilliance of the upper world they had quitted fifteen minutes earlier was startling, and the eye found relief in the greener hillsides lower down, which were just in sight on the left beyond a jutting shoulder of mountain. The western half of Llyn Llydaw curved round into view here, with the immense rock-face of Lliwedd rising from its farther shore. And the whistle signal came to their ears again and more clearly, though they were still too far away to be able to make out anyone on the precipice.

Sir Abercrombie had paused for an instant on the brink of the crag. His memory recalled the descent of a stony gully on the right here, but today there was no stony gully—a hundred-foot strip of old snow floored the cleft, lying at a steep angle.

"Glissade, Grimm!" he called. "Observe. So!"

On the word he sprang down into the cleft, alighted on the ribbon of snow, and went sliding down it. His ice-axe, gripped by the middle of the shaft with his right hand while the left grasped its head, acted as a brake, its spike furrowing the snow beside him. Grimmett, hesitating to follow, was overtaken at once by Dr. Tom, who leaped past him and went sailing down the gully in a great flurry of snow. The inspector set his teeth and followed as best he could, managing surprisingly well for the first seventy feet but ending in a series of somersaults which landed him at the bottom unhurt but with the breath knocked out of his body.

Lewker and Dr. Paton set him on his feet and started down again immediately. Easy terraces of grass and bog brought them very quickly down to the lakeside at the point where the stream left Glaslyn to begin its 500-foot fall into Llyn Llydaw.

"Eighteen minutes from the ridge," puffed the doctor. "Not bad. Do we go up the Gribin?"

He jerked his thumb at the massive nose of mountainside that rose opposite them, forming a flying buttress of the high ridge connecting Snowdon summit to the crest of Lliwedd. Grimmett, observing a rough track starting up it, perceived that a man might make his way up the Gribin and gain the ridge of Lliwedd at the top of the rock-climbs on that face.

"No," returned Sir Abercrombie, mopping his pouchy face with his handkerchief. "To the foot of the climb is our way. We have first to find out what has happened and where."

Without waiting for a reply he set off again, heading down the track towards Llydaw for some distance before striking off to the right across the tumbling stream and the evil slope of loose scree beyond it. At its farther side, still high above the lake's end down on their left, he led them at the same level round the curve of a very steep mountainside where broken tongues of gray rock plunged down towards the lake and only the undulating ribbons of grass between them offered a route. In front, the bare rock of Lliwedd soared ever higher in gray buttress and slab. The whistle signal sounded again, startlingly close.

"You can see 'em now—Slanting Buttress!" jerked Dr. Tom.

The others, stealing brief upward glances from their precarious footing, spotted the two tiny figures high on the rock-face and nearly half a mile away. They were a short distance apart and seemed to be quite motionless. One of them was a dot of sky-blue; Flora Massey had been wearing a windproof of that color. Of the third climber there was no sign. There was no doubt in Sir Abercrombie's mind that some sort of accident had taken place and that one of those two had been sending out the distress signal. Without pausing in his stride he took his own whistle from his anorak pocket and sounded the correct reply—three blasts at intervals of twenty seconds.

"There's someone coming up from the lake shore down there," Grimmett panted, pointing. "Might be the president."

"It's Stonor all right," said the doctor. "Green anorak, red cap."

Stonor was climbing the slopes above the lake from the opposite direction to that followed by the Crib Goch party, plodding doggedly up towards the foot of the precipice. It was evident that he was making for the origin of the distress signal, for a moment later he saw the party crossing the mountainside higher up and waved to them with a gesture that indicated the two figures high on the immensity of the crag.

"Meet him—bottom of Slanting Buttress," gasped Dr. Tom. "That's— four of us."

He had scarcely finished speaking when there was a sharp hail from behind them. A tall man was literally racing across the broken slope by the way they had come. Grimmett, who had imagined that Sir Abercrombie was leading his party at the fastest speed humanly possible on such terrain, was amazed to see that this newcomer was fast overtaking them. He caught them up just as Lewker gained a rocky knoll, and the inspector recognized the lean face and piercing eyes of Frank Hibberd, the explorer-schoolmaster.

"Party on Slanting Buttress in trouble," Hibberd said without preamble; he did not seem at all out of breath. "Saw them from the Gribin—I've a Ross glass with me. Leader's fallen, I think."

The four men halted and Hibberd slipped off his rucksack and got out a Ross monocular glass, which he handed to Lewker. Through its tremulous circle the actor-manager scanned the upper part of the towering wall of rock whose foot they were approaching. From its face a rock buttress, much broken into ledge and nook, projected to fall steeply and splay out

at the bottom on a glacis of shaley ledges. Where the top of Slanting
Buttress merged in the steeper face above he picked out the figures of
two climbers: Flora Massey's blue-clad form perched motionless in a
shallow cleft and her uncle, less conspicuous, some thirty feet to the
right of her and slightly higher up, beyond a vertical corner. There was
nothing to be seen of Professor Wiernick—until the glass showed the
tenuous white line of the rope, hanging vertically from a point five or six
feet to the right of Ferguson in line with a wide and steep chimney which
rose on the precipice above. About sixty feet of the taut rope was in view,
but its lower end and whatever dangled from it was hidden by a mass of
intervening rock.

He passed the monocular to Grimmett, who raised his eyebrows and
then scanned the cliff in his turn. Sir Abercrombie addressed the others.

"It appears that Professor Wiernick fell from the chimney pitch. Ferguson is belayed and is holding him on the rope, but of course he cannot
pull him up or move from his own position."

"The girl's waving to us," Grimmett put in, with the glass to his eye.

A thin cry floated down to them. Hibberd waved his long arm and sent
back a reassuring bellow.

"Miss Massey is a novice," pursued Lewker rapidly, "and will be badly
shaken by the accident. No doubt Ferguson has told her to stay where
she is until help comes. Wiernick must be unconscious or he would be
making some attempt to help himself."

"Let's get on, damn it!" growled Dr. Tom impatiently. "Wiernick may
be—"

"No." Hibberd cut him short. "Plan here. When we get below the face
we shan't be able to see them. What's your rope—one-twenty? I've a
hundred feet of line in my sack. We can lower Wiernick. I'll go up with
one man, the rest stay below to receive him. Someone had better go straight
down to Pen-y-Pass to get a stretcher party."

"Mark Stonor," suggested Lewker.

"What about Ferguson and the girl?" demanded the doctor.

"We'll bring 'em down when we've lowered Wiernick," Hibberd said.
"The climb's only a Moderate. They won't want to go on up the pitch
their leader fell off. Right?"

Without waiting for a reply he turned and set off again across the mountainside, his long stride making it difficult for the three who jogged and
clattered behind him to keep up.

Far above them, on their right as they traversed the awkward slopes of
scree and grass and boulders, hung black crags fledged with moss and

brown reeds. The skyline above those crags, Grimmett recalled, must be the saddle called Bwlch-y-Saethau, between Snowdon and Lliwedd. The ceiling of gray clouds had lifted from the higher crest of the great precipice ahead, but away on their left, across the wide wild cwm that held the sunken length of Llyn Llydaw, the opposing crest of Crib Goch was still shrouded in mist. Mark Stonor's red woolen cap bobbed energetically among the rocks down below, between them and the dark waters of the lake, as he toiled up to join them.

They climbed the sliding scree coming down from a gully in the crags above and reached the steepening foot-rocks of Lliwedd's West Peak. The rock-face was now towering immediately overhead, so steeply that the climbers were hidden from those below. Hibberd led on upwards without a pause. It was hand-and-foot work and the inspector felt far from safe, but since his companions seemed content to manage without the protection of a rope he set his teeth and scrambled on up rugged slabs and turfy ledges flecked with little dabs of snow. Up on the left a massive nose of rock took shape; that, he guessed, would be the Slanting Buttress. Hibberd was leading them into the tilted chaos of outcrop and corner that flanked the buttress-nose on its right. The outcropping crags continually masked the upward view.

There came a sudden sharp exclamation. Hibberd, clambering round the base of a little bluff, had gained a wide grassy bay inset between rock walls and had halted there, staring upward with his head tilted far back. The others joined him and saw what he was looking at.

Professor Julius Wiernick dangled at the end of a rope three hundred feet above where they were standing. He hung head downwards—his foot seemed to have been caught in a loop of the rope—and with his limply-drooping arms and red-capped head he resembled some grotesque tropical spider resting at the end of its long white thread. And then Grimmett saw that he was no longer wearing the woolen cap. The crimson blob of his skull was not red wool.

"Stretcher wanted in any case," Dr. Paton growled.

Hibberd nodded. "I'd say a doctor's no good to him, poor devil, but you'd better stay down, with this chap." He indicated the inspector. "Lewker and I will go up the Buttress. Right?"

"Good enough." The doctor unslung the rope from his shoulders and handed it to Sir Abercrombie, who began at once to uncoil it. "I've got bandages and a noggin of brandy in my sack. Also about thirty feet of line. Any use?"

"To you, maybe. Look." The explorer stabbed a finger at the crag overhead. "Get up to the right by those ledges. Then you can step back to the left, on to a pretty broad terrace right below Wiernick. That's easy enough. Then we've only seventy feet or so to lower him to you. Get him down to here if you can."

He took the end of rope handed to him by Sir Abercrombie and tied it swiftly round his waist. The two members of the climbing-party gathered up some coils of the long rope and started at once to cross the steep glacis towards the bottom of the Buttress, moving both together. Halfway across they halted while the actor-manager raised his booming voice at its full pitch.

"Ferguson! We are coming up! Stand fast!"

A moment later he and Hibberd had disappeared round a corner of rock. As they did so a man's high-pitched voice called from below. Dr. Tom turned and looked over the edge of the grassy bay and Grimmett, dragging his fascinated gaze from the gruesome figure dangling overhead, did likewise. Mark Stonor had reached the bottom of the footrocks within earshot of their perch. The doctor answered a question that had been inaudible to Grimmett.

"It's Wiernick. I'm afraid he's done for. Fell from the chimney pitch."

The president's reply sounded squeaky and amazed. "Wiernick? But that is incredible, Paton! On Slanting Buttress, of all places! I can hardly—"

"Well, there it is," interrupted the doctor brusquely. "Listen, Stonor. We are coping here and we want you to go down for help. Go to Pen-y-Pass and phone Pen-y-Gwryd. They'll send up stretcher and equipment in a Land-Rover—and stretcher-bearers too, if there are any climbers there. Rope in all the people you can for a rescue-party. Got that?"

"Yes."

"They can get the Land-Rover as far as the east end of Llydaw. The stretcher's to come to the foot of Slanting Buttress. If you meet any competent types send 'em up here. No need to tell you to get a move on."

The president's colorful headgear bobbed in agreement. He raised a hand in farewell and passed from sight below the bulge of the slabs. A few moments later he reappeared, his lanky knickerbocker-suited figure hastening with long strides diagonally down the mountainside in the direction of the more level ground above the shore of the lake. Dr. Tom sat down heavily on a tuft of heather below the steep wall of the grassy bay.

"As for us, Grimmett, we can rest a while," he grunted. "Seems a bit callous with poor Wiernick suspended overhead, but there's nothing we can do for him. Even if he's still alive—and from what I can see it's a million to one against—we can't get near him."

"No." Grimmett sat down with his back to the precipice and looked at his watch. "Eleven-fifty. How long will it take Mr. Stonor to reach Pen-y-Pass, Doctor?"

"Might do it in under the hour. He's a damn good mover for an old un. Say Briggs at the Pen-y-Gwryd gets the phone message at one, he'll have the Mountain Rescue van up at Llydaw by half past."

"We can start looking out for the stretcher party at half past one, then, seemingly. What time d'you reckon Hibberd and Sir Abercrombie will get up to Ferguson?"

Dr. Tom, rummaging in his rucksack, appeared to make mental calculations.

"We can give 'em half an hour," he replied at length, opening a packet of sandwiches. "They've at least four hundred feet to climb, and though it's easy enough it's steep and they've got to watch their step. Fifteen minutes for lunch. Better have a snack now, Grimmett—you may not enjoy your food after we've dealt with Wiernick."

The inspector saw the sense of this and got out his own lunch packet. For a minute or two they munched in silence, gazing out through gray space to Crib Goch whose snow-patched pinnacles were beginning to appear below the lifting clouds. Then Dr. Paton spoke in gruff commiseration, with his mouth full.

"Bit damn hard on you, getting landed with this business on your first climbing day. You're a detective-inspector, I gather. Probably seen a few cases of violent death before."

"I shan't faint when we're getting Professor Wiernick down, Doctor, if that's what you're getting at." Grimmett flicked crumbs from his mustache. "Still, an accident like this isn't the same as a crime of violence. It makes you feel sad more than angry, so to speak."

"And pity doesn't produce the invigoration that anger does. Quite. For my part, I'm sorry but not sad. I never liked Wiernick. What puzzles me is how the deuce he managed to fall off a climb as easy as Slanting Buttress."

"He was a good climber, so I've heard."

"He was. Wizard Wiernick, he used to be called in the years before the war, and he still had more than ordinary skill on rock." The doctor took in half a large slice of fruitcake at one mouthful. "Stone falling from above might have knocked him off balance. It does happen, though it's damn rare in Snowdonia."

They were silent again for a while. Grimmett's was a silence both startled and reflective. The doctor's remarks had blended with his own knowledge to produce a sequence of thoughts which could be made to lead to a speculative but possible conclusion. Wiernick's fall and death (there was no doubt in Grimmett's mind that the professor was dead) were odd and inexplicable, for the present at least. One man's life, Mark Stonor's, had been threatened in an anonymous letter; another man, Wiernick, had died on the following day. And Grimmett himself had suggested that Julius Wiernick was a much more likely recipient of anonymous threats than Mark Stonor. '*Stone falling from above might have knocked him off balance*'—yes, and where would you find a neater way of murdering a man? The victim had first to be a rock-climber leading a climb. You found out what climb, picked a ledge or niche somewhere within range of the top pitch, and waited for his head to come up into view. Then you bunged a stone. Or used a catapult—

Grimmett pulled his thoughts up sharply. This kind of speculation was woolly, amateurish. And there were points against any such unlikely tale. The intended victim was roped to the man below him, who was securely belayed to the rock. That was one thing. Another was that the murderer had to see his victim clearly before he bunged the stone and the victim might very well see and recognize him before he fell, so that if the rope held and the victim survived the fall the murderer would be in a tightish spot. It was too much of a risk. True, Wiernick had bashed his head in on some obstacle in the course of his fall—or had he? Suppose—

"Better get on with it, I suppose," said Dr. Tom with a sigh; and the inspector's wild train of thought went off the rails.

There had been neither sign nor sound of Hibberd and Lewker, for they were beyond the overhead horizon that limited the vision of those below. As he lit his pipe Dr. Tom, for the first time in fifteen minutes, raised his eyes to the limp and dreadful figure hanging overhead. A slabby cliff, slightly concave and glistening with wet, formed the skyline over which the hanging rope first appeared from above, and Wiernick hung against its wall. Below him there were more glistening slabs at a less steep angle ending in a rim of heather which could be the edge of a shelf; this was some seventy feet below the fallen man's dangling hands. From the grassy bay to this possible shelf (which Hibberd had optimistically called 'a pretty broad terrace') was a vertical distance of about two hundred feet, and the intervening precipice of slimy rock and loose-looking vegetated ledges was most uninviting to Grimmett's eye, although its angle was little greater than that of the average house-roof. He did not hesitate when the doctor, extracting thirty feet of nylon line from his rucksack, inquired whether he would prefer to be on a rope.

They left the grassy bay by a crack in its right-hand corner, the doctor going first and drawing in the line as Grimmett struggled up. Above this they moved together, Dr. Tom holding a coil or two in his hand and the inspector following him like a dog on a leash. It was easy enough, but always beneath Grimmett's scraping boots was the rooftop slope down which one could roll for several hundred feet before pitching on to the scree below.

It took them a good quarter of an hour to reach the terrace below Wiernick, for the doctor, seeing his companion's nervousness, took care to work out a route that provided belays every twenty feet or so, rock spikes or boulders over which he could hitch the thin line for greater security.

"Come in useful when we lower him down," he explained for Grimmett's greater reassurance.

To the inspector's great relief, the terrace proved to be a heathery shelf four feet broad and a dozen long, with a thin carpet of old snow lying beneath the dark twigs of heather. The doctor, however, was better pleased to find upon it a large boulder firm enough to be used as a belay. As he looped their tenuous rope round it he declaimed cheerfully:

> "Come one, come all! This rock shall fly
> From its firm base as soon as I!

—Walter Scott, in case you don't know," he added, and struck a match for his pipe, which had gone out during the ascent. "Now for diagnosis."

Puffing deliberately, he stared up at the man who hung vertically over-head. His big face was grave and placid beneath the twisted brim of his ancient hat and his gaze was keen and steady. Grimmett looked up also, but only for a moment. Julius Wiernick's face, a stone's toss above, was towards them; but he had no face. His red woolen cap had fallen on the heather a few feet away, and the inspector bent to pick it up. It was sticky with blood. He let it fall again.

"Any hope, Doctor?" he asked as he straightened himself.

"Never was any," Dr. Tom growled. "Ten-fifty-five when we heard the whistle first. He's been hanging like that for an hour and a half. Even if the frontal bone hadn't been crushed—which it has—he wouldn't have lasted long."

There was a pause. The doctor squatted on the verge of the terrace and peered frowningly down the broken steeps below, apparently conning the route by which Wiernick's body would have to be lowered. Grimmett got a packet of cigarettes out of his rucksack and lit one.

"Funny we can't hear them up above," he remarked. "Mr. Ferguson must be only thirty or forty feet beyond where we can see the rope coming over."

"It's like that on a steep rock face," said the doctor, standing up and untying his waist-loop. "If we were over on Crib Goch we'd hear their voices, likely as not. Got a knife?"

Grimmett produced a penknife and the doctor cut off six feet from their thirty feet of line. He was engaged in knotting this into a loop when a series of short sharp blasts on a whistle came faintly down to their ears. Although the unseen whistle-blower could not be more than two hundred feet above them the sound was scarcely louder than the first signal they had heard from a straight mile away.

"Stand by to receive cadaver," said Dr. Tom grimly.

He hastily retied the cut end of the line round his waist and sent a stentorian bellow up the cliff in reply. The dangling figure overhead jerked grotesquely and began to descend towards them, its head and arms flopping in a hideous mockery of human gestures.

"I'll take him," the doctor said. "Hold the line in case he bowls me over."

The dead man checked momentarily on a mossy ledge, lolloped over it, and slithered down the last twenty feet of slab. The doctor stepped to one side and guided the body so that it lay on the narrow strip of heather at his feet.

"Hold!" he roared; and the rope above checked its downward motion.

The doctor used Grimmett's knife to cut through the rope close to the tightened waist-knot and shouted "All clear!" As the rope snaked upwards to vanish over the rock-rim he knelt and examined the body.

"Made a damn thorough job of it," he growled. "Broke his neck as well."

He raised the disfigured head and waggled it about. Grimmett looked away hurriedly.

"Fell headfirst, pitched on the first ledge, smashed in the frontal bone and dislocated the cervical vertebrae." Dr. Tom stood up, wiping his hands on the tartan seat of his breeches. "Let's get him down. All right, Grimmett?"

"Fine," returned the inspector resolutely.

The doctor unclipped the snaplink that secured a double loop of rope round his waist and handed it to him. "Fasten that round you. Now hitch this line loop to it. You'll go down first, as far as that spike of rock straight below. Secure yourself to the spike, unrope from the long line, and stay put while I pull in the line and lower it again with Wiernick on the end. Got that?"

"Yes."

"You'll have to support him or hitch him to the spike until I come down to join you. Then we repeat. I shan't slip, and you'll be perfectly safe. Let's hope he doesn't get stuck on the way down."

This program was duly carried out. It was a lengthy business and far from pleasant, but the major unpleasantness was, for the inspector, somewhat obviated by the continuous necessities of finding hold for hand and foot and maneuvering so that he would be directly below the doctor for each bout of lowering. When at last they brought the dead man down into the grassy bay and the doctor had covered that dreadful mask with a handkerchief it was ten minutes past one by Grimmett's watch. The doctor took off the line and coiled it up.

"No point in trying to get him farther down," he said. "They'll bring the Thomas stretcher and it'll be a damn sight easier with that. If they've collected enough helpers we'll be let off any stretcher-carrying."

"I reckon we've earned it," Grimmett said feelingly; some of his muscles were already beginning to complain of their unaccustomed hard usage. "The survivors'll be down soon, I suppose?"

"They've had forty minutes now. May take 'em an hour—depends what sort of trim Ferguson and the girl are in."

They went to the outer edge of the bay and sat down to smoke. The clouds had lifted and compacted in an even blue-gray ceiling, and the snowy ridge of Crib Goch was clear. The somber winter's afternoon held not so much as a whispered hint of the brilliance and exaltation that had been theirs three hours earlier. Down on the shelving foot-rocks below them sounded the scrape of boots, and they looked down to see a man climbing up. He wore a round khaki cap and an anorak with camouflage whorls of green and brown, and when he glanced upwards at a shout from the doctor they could see that it was Charles Kemp.

When the major joined them a minute or so later his glance went at once to the recumbent figure at the back of the grassy bay.

"Who is it?" he demanded sharply. "Wiernick?"

The doctor nodded. "Dead. Came off on the chimney pitch. Crushed skull and broken neck."

"God! Poor devil." Kemp cast himself down beside them; his sallow, mustached face was beaded with sweat. "What about the others?"

"All right, far as we know." The doctor gave a rapid and succinct account of what had been and was being done. "All over bar the stretcher party and the inquest," he added grimly. "Made a bit of a mess of the dinner meet, hasn't it?"

"Someone'll have to tell Eve," Kemp muttered.

"Um. Where was Mrs. Wiernick going today? Any idea?"

The major pulled off his khaki woolen cap and loosened the neck of his anorak before replying.

"No. I pushed off at oh-five-two-oh with Lumley, y'know—to keep a check on my lads. It was devilish dark and Lumley didn't get 'em up on to Bulky Thingumjig until nearly oh-eight-double-oh. I went on after 'em, keepin' out of sight, to see how they got on, and came back with Lumley after we'd seen 'em nearly to the other pass—I forget its name."

"Bwlch Cwm-y-Llan," suggested the doctor.

"That's it. Seen anythin' of Lumley, by the way?"

"No. Why?"

Kemp shrugged. "Just wondered. We separated, down in the valley over the other side of Lliwedd. I wanted to go back over the east end of Lliwedd and down into Cwm Dyli. Peter said he'd go on up to Bulky Whatever-it-is, the way we came. My own idea is he thought he might meet up with the Massey girl. I gathered she was climbin' on Lliwedd and he's devilish smitten with the wench."

"How did you know there'd been an accident, Major?" Grimmett asked, offering him a cigarette. "Did you hear the whistles?"

"Not me. Too far away." Kemp struck a match, held it to his cigarette, and inhaled deeply. "No—I was comin' down the slopes and saw the president on his way down, afar off. He yelled at me and waved his arms. All I could hear was 'accident' and 'West Peak', but I changed direction and ambled up here toot sweet. I suppose Stonor was goin' to fetch—"

"There they come," interrupted Dr. Tom, pointing.

Below and rather more than a mile away a little cloud of black dots had appeared at the farther end of Llyn Llydaw. They were moving quickly, and as they strung out on the thread of path that climbed towards the base of Lliwedd it could be seen that there were seventeen men and that two of them carried what might be a stretcher.

"Good for the president," Kemp said.

Dr. Tom fumbled in a pocket of his rucksack and produced a whistle. "Better let them know where we are," he remarked, getting to his feet.

Before he could put the whistle to his lips a long shrill blast sounded from close at hand, somewhere near the base of Slanting Buttress. It reached the ears of the approaching stretcher party, for several of them waved their arms in reply. A few minutes later Sir Abercrombie Lewker came into view as he stepped round the rocky corner east of the grassy bay. Behind him, roped together, came Flora Massey, her uncle, and Frank Hibberd; a large figure in a faded red anorak who followed Hibberd proved somewhat unexpectedly to be Peter Lumley.

The doctor took a deep breath. "Afraid Wiernick's dead," he called gruffly. "We've got him down, in the bay here."

Sir Abercrombie halted his party on a ledge halfway across the glacis and they unroped. Then he came on with Hibberd and Lumley, leaving Ferguson and his niece sitting on the ledge. When they had joined the three men in the grassy bay a brief conference was held. Donald Ferguson, Hibberd reported, was pretty steady, though the shock of the accident (which had happened without warning) and the strain of waiting for help to come had told upon him; his hands had been burned by rope friction. Flora was somewhat shaken but bearing up nobly. It was decided that both of them should go down as soon as possible, escorted by Dr. Paton, to Pen-y-Pass. The doctor supported this plan and prepared to depart.

"How did you come on the scene?" he asked Peter Lumley as he tied the strings of his rucksack.

"Heard whistles," Lumley muttered. "Poked about on the ridge and got down the top pitches."

"Lumley had arrived at Ferguson's stance when we reached him," Hibberd added; he, like the others, avoided looking into the back of the grassy bay where Wiernick's body lay.

Dr. Tom grunted a farewell, departed on his escort duty, and was presently heard encouraging his charges as they descended the easy rocks to the lower slopes. Sir Abercrombie addressed Hibberd.

"The stretcher party will be here in fifteen minutes. There are seventeen of them, and if you and Lumley and Major Kemp lend your aid there will be twenty."

"Count me in, of course," Kemp nodded.

"I will suggest, therefore," Lewker continued, "that Mr. Grimmett can be spared from the carrying work. He is not a mountaineer and he is my guest, and I do not doubt that this sad affair has tried his nerves severely."

"He's done his stuff damned well," said Hibberd. "Twenty's more than enough for the carrying. You two push off and leave the rest of the job to the big battalions."

"My nerves are all right," protested Grimmett. "If I can be any help I'd rather—"

"We shall return over Lliwedd, then." Sir Abercrombie's booming tones drowned the inspector's words easily. "Come along, Grimm. Dr. Paton has left his rope with me, but your climbing education has proceeded so rapidly that I hardly think you will need it for the descent of these slabs."

With a wave of his hand to the others he started to scramble down the foot-rocks. Grimmett followed, frowning. This abrupt departure puzzled him, and the withdrawn and meditative expression he had noticed on the actor-manager's pouchy countenance made him suspect that solicitude for his guest's nerves was not the prime cause of it. Before they reached the easier ground at the foot of the slabs, however, he had decided to say nothing of his wild speculations about Wiernick's inexplicable fall and the threat contained in the anonymous letter to Stonor.

Dr. Paton and his party were already some distance away down the shaley slope to the right, making for the lake shore. Sir Abercrombie turned left-handed at the bottom of the rocks and began to mount the scree, following the base of the crags in a northwesterly direction. Grimmett put on a spurt and overtook him.

"What's the idea, sir?" he demanded breathlessly.

Lewker halted and eyed him quizzically. He had removed his woolen balaclava, and the hair on either side of his large bald head stood out in tufts and tails.

"The general idea, laddie," he replied, "is to go up an easy gully at the end of the crags and get to the top of Lliwedd, descending thence to Pen-y-Pass and the aftermath of an unfortunate—accident." His pause before the last word was slight but not negligible. "The immediate idea, now that we are out of sight and sound of our late companions, is that you shall describe to me, in detail, what happened while I was translated to higher station. In return I will discourse of my adventures aloft."

He glanced round him. On the left of the narrow scree-slope and a few feet higher up a jutting crag overhung a flat slab that might have been placed there to rest weary climbers. Opposite it on the scree a massive cube of rock offered another seat.

"To you the throne, Grimm, to me the footstool. You shall talk while I eat, for, like Jaques in Arden, I have eat none yet." He seated himself on the boulder and waved the inspector to the slab. "Proceed, Grimm. Discourse, I prithee."

Grimmett seated himself, set a hand on each knee, and directed a searching glance at his friend.

"Sir Ab," he said slowly, "it's the first time this trip you've called me 'laddie,' so it is. The last time was on that Murdered Owl case. What's up?"

"You shall call me Eric, and I will always call you laddie," murmured the actor-manager, opening a sandwich packet; he seemed to be in an unsuitably sprightly mood. "I will tell you what is up—to return your neologism—when I have heard what Dr. Tom said about the body of Julius Wiernick, and not before."

Thus encouraged, the inspector gave an account of the happenings on the lower rocks while Lewker was absent on the buttress above. His police training enabled him to be brief but his slow utterance made the tale long in the telling, and Sir Abercrombie (who listened without interruption) had consumed four ham sandwiches and a slice of cake before he had finished. Grimmett had then to wait while he lit his pipe.

"Wiernick," he said at last, expelling blue smoke, "was out of sight of both his companions when he fell. Neither of them can offer any explanation why he should fall, except that Donald Ferguson says that he was attempting a variant of the chimney pitch and may have found it too hard for him. In view of the professor's reputation as an expert rock-climber I think that unlikely. I told Ferguson I would examine the place if it was possible to do so."

"What's a variant, Sir Ab?"

"I will explain that later. Here is the nub of my story. At the instant of falling off Wiernick was heard to utter a loud cry. Ferguson calls it 'a frightened exclamation,' but Flora Massey goes a little further than that. A nice girl, Grimm, and has what is, or are, vulgarly called guts."

"Yes, sir," Grimmett said patiently. "And what does Miss Massey say?"

"She says that Professor Wiernick shouted, or screeched as she puts it, a word. It sounded to her like the name 'Jack.' "

Chapter VI

Detectives' Holiday

"Jack!" repeated Grimmett.

His blue eyes gleamed. The wild surmises that had crossed his mind and had been banished returned again, forgetting their shame.

"By gum!" he said. "It could be—but who's Jack? There's Frank, Charles—"

He checked himself and looked slightly sheepish. Sir Abercrombie had taken his pipe out of his mouth and was regarding him with mingled surprise and reproach.

"Grimm, Grimm!" he boomed severely. "This is very unbecoming. More. It is out of character and not in your part. To me, the eager amateur of crime, should fall the crude speculations and the jumpings to an apparently unwarranted conclusion. To you the honest, plodding insistence on material evidence and the scornful repudiation of guesswork. Yet here you are—and I do not fail to note that you have twice addressed me as 'sir'—considering who might have pushed this unfortunate professor off the cliff when there is every probability that he fell."

"Why did he fall?" persisted Grimmett doggedly.

Lewker shrugged his shoulders. "Rock-climbers have been known to fall, and without obvious cause, though I grant you it is a very rare occurrence. Overconfidence, a molded rubber sole slipping on greasy rock, a sudden muscular cramp, a loose hold, a stone-fall from above—any of these could have caused Wiernick to fall. One of them probably did."

"Probably," echoed the inspector obstinately; he thrust his gloved hands between the seat of his breeches and the rock slab, which was very cold, and looked accusingly at the actor-manager. "Look here, Sir Ab. Knowing you, and knowing what we know, I'll wager you've had ideas, same as me. Aren't I right, now?"

Sir Abercrombie glanced at his watch, stood up, and packed the remains of his lunch into his rucksack.

"It is five minutes past two of a winter afternoon, Grimm," he observed, "and too cold to sit speculating here. Let us stiffen the sinews and summon up the blood by gaining the crest of Lliwedd before we discourse further." He shouldered the rucksack. "It would be well to have your ice-axe ready. You will need it shortly, I fancy."

"Just a minute, Sir Ab. If this crest's another knife-edge like Crib Goch you can count me out. I'd rather go down after the stretcher party."

"Away with apprehension, Grimm. I do assure you, the crest of Lliwedd is broad and entirely non-perilous. There will be snow upon it and in the short approach gully, but we shall not meet any serious difficulty." Sir Abercrombie paused to twinkle at the inspector. "I have a reason for wishing you to come over Lliwedd with me."

Grimmett nodded reluctantly and grasped his axe. When they began to climb again he was grateful for the exertion, for the ten-minute halt had chilled him, and the laborious plod up the scree loosened the stiffness that had gripped his middle-aged joints. As they mounted, skirting the base of steep rocks, the crags on their left lessened in height and showed patches of snow on their ledges. Snow appeared on the scree, at first in frozen flecks, then in wide bands, and finally in a continuous hard slope narrowing into the jaws of a short gully that opened in the steep rocks below the ridge. Sir Abercrombie kicked steps in the steepening surface until they reached the foot of the gully. Here he decided to put on Dr. Paton's rope, explaining to the anxious Grimmett that this was merely a safety precaution. The inspector found the short ascent sufficiently exciting and was glad to emerge at the top on to the broad snow-covered saddle at the eastern end of the almost level Bwlch-y-Saethau, where they took off the rope. A cold wind blew across the snow. Lewker paused to point out the gap of Bwlch Cwm-y-Llan rather more than a mile away beyond the deep and gloomy cwm on the south side of their saddle, and then led the way up the easy rock and snow of the ridge on their left.

A well-trodden trough in the snow showed that a number of other mountaineers had passed that way. Little rock-steps, free from snow and much scratched by boot nails, opposed them and were easily passed. On their right hand the snowy slant of boulders that fell towards the blue depths of the valley was not steep enough to fall down, but on the left of the mounting ridge the verge of the precipice was abrupt—an edge of snow and then nothing for a thousand feet. It was to this side, Grimmett noticed, that his leader's glance was frequently directed.

They had not climbed far above the bwlch when, turning a corner below a projecting rock, they came face to face with Dr. Richard Paton, breathless with the haste of his descent and looking anxious.

"What's happened?" he demanded instantly. "I saw that gang down on the scree. Looked like a rescue-party."

The actor-manager explained briefly. "Miss Flora Massey," he added, "is quite unhurt. Your father is escorting her down to Pen-y-Pass with Ferguson."

Dr. Richard looked his relief. "Good. But—Wiernick, coming off on Slanting Buttress! One can hardly believe it. And how very annoyed he must be, if one can be annoyed after death! How on earth did it happen—and why didn't Ferguson hold him on the rope?"

"Wiernick seems to have been attempting a variant of the usual chimney pitch. But there has been no opportunity so far of discussing the matter."

"No, of course not," Richard frowned. "Ferguson would be pretty shaken—and Flora too. I was deucedly worried when I spotted that horde coming across towards Lliwedd. We were just finishing the climb then—the Penberthys are like a couple of snails on a rock-pitch—and as soon as we got to the top I left them and came over to West Peak."

"The others of your party have gone down?"

"Yes. The Hengist ordained that they should call it a day." He stepped to the edge of the cliff with a casualness that made Grimmett gulp nervously, and peered over. "Flora and the others aren't down to the track yet. I think I'll nip down the easy gully and catch them up. One might be of some use. See you later."

He swung himself down the rocky corner and disappeared.

"They all think it's queer the professor fell off that particular climb," Grimmett remarked as he and Lewker recommenced the ascent. "And why, if climbing-ropes are used as a safeguard, was the rope no safeguard for him?"

"That," returned Lewker over his shoulder, "I will explain within the hour, Grimm, together with other matters that may interest you. For the present—ah! This is what I have been looking for."

He pointed to a single line of footprints in the snow on the left of the trampled track. There were only five prints in sight, for they went straight to the edge of the cliff as though the maker of the tracks had dived off into space.

"Notable big feet this chap had," Grimmett commented as they halted close to the nearest of the prints. "Molded rubber soles and size eleven, I'd say. Would this be where the Slanting Buttress climb ends, now?"

"It would, Grimm. And these, as you were about to remark, are probably the footprints of Peter Lumley. The angle of the first two prints suggests that he approached from the same direction as ourselves and turned off here to go to the edge."

"The major said Lumley was going to this Bwlch-y—Bwlch-y-Sa-ethau, if that's how you say it."

"A good effort, Grimm. So Lumley, hearing ominous sounds below, went a little way down the cliff—it is quite easy—to find out if he could help. He exchanged shouts with Ferguson, and then, being a very capable climber, descended the chimney pitch and joined Ferguson a few minutes before Hibberd and I reached him."

As he spoke, the actor-manager was once again uncoiling Dr. Paton's rope. Noting the inspector's very obvious apprehension, he beamed reassuringly at him.

"No more perils for you, Grimm," he said. "I want you to indulge my whim and assist me in a little investigation which will not take long and which will probably have a negative result. Pray stand a little nearer to this large boulder."

He had tied one end of the rope round his waist. Now he knotted the other end round Grimmett, made a loop in the rope a few feet from the inspector, and placed the loop over the boulder.

"It is barely one hundred feet down to the top of the chimney," he continued, "and, as I have said, easy climbing. I, however, am not Peter Lumley. I require you to safeguard my descent. Pay out the rope as I go down, and when you hear my shout be ready to draw it in as I come up."

"You've got some idea in your head about this business, Sir Ab," said Grimmett accusingly as he grasped the rope.

"I have a dozen, laddie, and not one of them makes sense. Farewell. I go with all convenient speed."

With which presumably Shakespearean exit-line Sir Abercrombie disappeared cautiously over the brink of the precipice.

Grimmett, left alone on the crest with a cold wind blowing at his back, had the spark of a growing excitement to counteract his discomfort. It was plain that Lewker, like himself, thought that there was at least something odd about Julius Wiernick's fatal accident, though he was not going to voice any of his suspicions until he had some backing for them. The inspector was well enough acquainted with his friend's scrupulous code to know that he would not keep a single discovered fact to himself, and took comfort from the fact. If there was to be an investigation, he had been literally in at the death and had an assistant who was at home in this unfamiliar setting of crags and climbers.

The rope rustled steadily over the few feet of snow until about half its length had run out. Then it checked for a second or two and started to move down more slowly. There was only ten feet of it left, and Grimmett was wondering whether he should try to convey this information to the man below, when it ceased to move. In less than a minute more a *basso profundo* shout came faintly to his ears and he began to take in the rope as the actor-manager climbed up again.

Sir Abercrombie had resumed his balaclava for this operation and his woolen-helmeted head bobbed up above the rim of snow like that of some grotesque Jack-in-a-box. He pulled himself rather stiffly up the last few feet and brushed the snow from his breeches and stockings. There was a reflective but not unsatisfied expression on his pouchy features.

"Well, sir?" demanded Grimmett eagerly. "Did you find anything?"

"I found no visible sign of anyone, other than Peter Lumley, having climbed up or down the final pitches of Slanting Buttress today," replied Lewker, unroping. "That, I fancy, answers the question that was uppermost in your mind, Grimm. Pray undo your waist-loop. Thank you. For the rest, the rock-pitch from which Julius Wiernick fell was dry and free from ice. It was impossible to say with certainty that none of the holds upon it had been broken away, but I could see no mark indicating a recent fracture."

"Then—"

"Hold or cut bowstrings. Discourse you shall have, Grimm, but not in a cold wind at two thousand seven hundred feet. Let us, in the barbarous but sufficiently apt phrase, make tracks."

He slung the coiled rope over his shoulders and set off up the crest at a fast pace—only to halt again a few yards higher at a place where the snow on the very edge of the cliff had been well trampled by passing walkers and climbers. Sir Abercrombie peered over the edge.

"But," he said as though he were continuing a sentence, "any good climber could have climbed down here to come within reach of the Slanting Buttress chimney pitch. And he would have left no trace, for all is rock."

He stumped rapidly on again before Grimmett had a chance to say anything, and in a few minutes the inspector had no breath left for comment. Past the cairn on top of West Peak, down and up again over East Peak, down the lumpy ridge beyond, at first on trodden snow and soon on a shaley path. Down and down now, almost flying through the purple afternoon, until the broadening ridge flattened out into the withered yellows and russets of a marshy saddle. The eastern end of Llyn Llydaw lay eight hundred feet below them still, and a stony path slanting steeply down off the ridge led in the direction of the lake. As they started down the path amid a clatter of stones Grimmett caught sight of the stretcher party, groups of dots moving near the lake's end; then he saw, just beyond them, the shape of a covered van which must be waiting on the broad track that ran down from the lake to Pen-y-Pass.

Sir Abercrombie halted some distance down the path at a spot where they were out of the wind and where slabby rocks offered seats.

"Fifteen minutes' rest," he announced, sitting down and getting out his pipe. "I have it on the authority of Dr. Thomas Paton, Grimm, that a halt of anything less than fifteen minutes does not allow the red corpuscles sufficient time to renew themselves. Or it may be the white corpuscles—I am but an indifferent physiologist. In either case, we shall rest and talk. Allow me, pray, to light my pipe before you open the discussion."

Grimmett waited while this was done. The orange flame of the match seemed unnaturally bright against the purple brume of the mountain spaces, and he realized suddenly that evening was almost upon them. Across the valley the rim of snow on the crest of Crib Goch, which had dazzled him with its diamond-sparkle when he had crept gingerly along it little more than five hours ago, had taken on a ghastly pallor beneath the darkening clouds. Nearer and homelier clouds from his companion's pipe drifted across his vision and he turned to find the actor-manager regarding him with one eyebrow raised and his little eyes twinkling amusedly.

"I've just the one question, Sir Ab," he said. "What makes you think Professor Wiernick's death might possibly not have been an accident?"

"A nicely-turned question, Grimm, involving more answers than one. I will begin with a subjective answer, if you will allow it."

He settled his rucksack behind his back and gazed meditatively out over the valley. The stretcher party had reached the waiting van and were clustered round it.

"Less than a dozen people," began Sir Abercrombie, "are killed in climbing accidents in the British Isles every year. Compared with the thousands who are slaughtered on British roads in the same period the figure is negligible, and the publicity accorded to such deaths absurdly disproportionate. In spite of that publicity, however, I have often thought that the circumstances of rock-climbing offer to an intending murderer an excellent chance of committing his crime and escaping undetected.

Given, as a victim, one of the ten thousand or more men and women who take mountains for their recreation, and—"

"And a murderer who's also a mountaineer," put in Grimmett eagerly, "and you've got it. Means and opportunity all nice and handy, and if it's neatly done there's a right good chance of getting away with it even if—"

"Grimm! I beg that you will not interrupt."

Sir Abercrombie's deep and measured tones had become severe. The inspector, abashed, apologized and remained silent during the remainder of the actor-manager's exposition.

"Ten years ago, Grimm, I encountered my first crime of this sort. The circumstances were such that it never came to the knowledge of the police, but the premises were strangely like those of today's fatality. An expert rock-climber, leading a novice up the Milestone Buttress—a climb suitable for absolute beginners—fell and was killed. I established to my own complete satisfaction that he had been murdered. The murderer had descended the climb, unobserved, to a place where he could lie in wait armed with a large splinter of rock. When his victim's head appeared within reach he struck and the climber fell. At the inquest the fatal head injury was naturally attributed to the climber's striking his skull against a rock ledge in his fall."

He paused. From far away came the faint hum of a car engine, slowly diminishing in the distance. The van and the human figures had vanished, leaving the darkening mountainscape lonely in the gathering twilight.

"Add this experience to my previous consideration of mountains as a murderer's weapon," continued Sir Abercrombie, "and you will see, Grimm, why I tend to regard with suspicion such unexplained fatal accidents as the one which took place this morning."

"Fair enough, sir—but that's all general, so to speak. What about the particular? What about Wiernick? And what about that yell of 'Jack!' when he fell off? If that murderer of yours ten years ago got away with it, why shouldn't Wiernick have been killed in exactly the same way? His skull, what I saw of it, was so bashed about a doctor couldn't say whether he'd been slugged with a rock or done it when he fell."

Lewker wagged his head at the inspector. "This is unlike you, Grimm. You are endeavouring to make bricks without straw."

"I don't care," Grimmett said recklessly. "I'm on holiday. Can't a detective officer have a holiday from evidence now and then? Let's have a bit of free speculation and slander. It'll do me good, so it will."

"I doubt it. However, speculate away. Speak—I am bound to hear."

"As Hamlet said to his father's ghost," nodded Grimmett. "But Wiernick's ghost won't give us a line like the one in the play did, and the Yard doesn't take much stock in spook stories anyway. Seems to me we've got more to go on than Hamlet had before the ghost spilled the beans."

He settled himself less uncomfortably on his stony seat and leaned forward with his hands on his knees, his square ruddy face both earnest and excited.

"Look, now. Start with the two facts, both queer. One, Mr. Stonor shows us an anonymous letter which includes a threat to his life. He don't seem much worried and says he knows nothing about it, but if observation's anything to go by I reckon he knows more than he told us. And if that's true, why did he show us the letter at all? Because the threat meant something to him and he was scared, that's why."

"Yet, Grimm," interposed Sir Abercrombie gently, "he went off by himself today, thus according any potential murderer an opportunity of dealing with him in lonely surroundings."

"Well, that adds to the puzzle but the fact's there. The second fact is that Wiernick, not Stonor, dies the day after Stonor got that letter. And Wiernick dies by falling off a climb where there's no reason for him to fall. Right so far, Sir Ab?"

"Perfectly. I have a little to add to your last statement, but it can wait."

"Those are the queer facts, then. I don't know if we can take the last shout of 'Jack!' as a fact."

Lewker took his pipe out of his mouth. "Miss Massey's actual words were 'I heard him give a screech—it sounded something like *Jack!*' "

He replaced his pipe. Grimmett rubbed his mustache frowningly.

"All right," he said. "Let that go for the present. Wiernick—as I said last night, only you weren't listening—is a more likely bloke than Stonor to have his life threatened. You said yourself you doubted whether he had any friends. He's got a tongue like a dagger, a mighty attractive young wife, and he's writing his memoirs, which look like coming near libel. I dare say I'm coming near slander myself now. I'd say Mrs. Wiernick and Major Kemp were pretty thick."

"I will join you in slander, Grimm. I saw them both last night in the Pen-y-Gwryd, and I would say that they are old friends and possibly something more."

The inspector's blue eyes narrowed. "There could be what they call an understanding between them, eh? It's not unlikely they'll be glad to have the professor out of the way. Then there's Frank Hibberd. Didn't I hear Dr. Tom Paton say Hibberd and the professor had a bust-up on some Himalayan expedition and weren't on speaking terms? Hibberd turned up very pat after the accident, didn't he? On his own, too. I wonder where he'd been. It might be interesting to find out where Mrs. Wiernick was today, too."

"Grimm, you amaze me," boomed Sir Abercrombie, regarding his friend with some amusement. "As Glendower could call spirits from the vasty deep, so you call suspects. Peter Lumley, Frank Hibberd, Major Kemp, Eve Wiernick—so diverse in age, sex and character, and all capable of smiting Julius Wiernick with a lump of rock, according to Inspector Grimmett."

"You know very well, sir," Grimmett said tolerantly, "that I'm only looking at motive, so to speak. Coming to means, it needn't have been a lump of rock."

"What, then, my ingenious quidnunc?"

"A pebble. I don't know what a quidnunc is, but I've used a catapult when I was a boy. Give me one made with doubled strands of that thick square-section rubber, and I'd guarantee to stand thirty yards off and bung a stone hard enough to make Professor Wiernick let go his—"

"No, Grimm, no!" The actor-manager threw up a hand in protest. "I refuse to picture Kemp, Hibberd, Lumley or Mrs. Wiernick—or, for that matter, Uncle Tom Cobley—practicing daily with a sling or catapult in order to be sure of hitting Wiernick on the small portion of his head that was not protected by a thick woolen cap."

"The cap had fallen off, anyway," Grimmett said. "I found it on the ledge below him—and left it there, incidentally."

"Was the cap damaged or torn?"

"Not that I noticed. Only bloody. You're thinking it might show signs of being hit with a rock?"

"I am not thinking at all, Grimm. I am simply participating in your delightful holiday from rational detection."

"Well, sir," Grimmett said ruminatively, "the catapult idea's unlikely, but it's not impossible. Peter Lumley wouldn't have needed a catty. He don't show the ghost of a motive, but he could have bashed Wiernick with a rock, right enough."

Sir Abercrombie sucked loudly and ironically at his pipe. "So he could. He could have waited there in exceeding chilly ambush—an ambush that exposed him to the view of anyone viewing the West Peak from the track up Snowdon, which passes on the other side of Llyn Llydaw. He could have struck his blow and then waited there for another hour and a half—it was that long, Grimm—before climbing down to the assistance of the survivors."

"All right, then." The inspector stuck out his jaw obstinately. "So he could. It was his best cover-up, seeing that if he cleared out after the blow his footprints were there to give him away if anyone happened to take a look."

"His name, however, is not Jack."

"Let's work on that, now," said Grimmett imperturbably. "Wiernick sees his assailant the instant before the blow falls. He recognizes him. He screeches his name. Is there a Jack among the folk staying at Pen-y-Pass, by any chance?"

"Some of them you already know, Grimm. Rossiter's name is Henry, Reid Cable's is Maurice. Lord Rendall, I happen to know, was christened Ulric Larkworthy Randolph. No Jack, nor even a John."

"Frank could sound a bit like Jack," Grimmett was beginning, when Sir Abercrombie interrupted him.

"It occurs to me, however," he said slowly, "that I have encountered one Jack since I arrived in these parts. He is Jack Jones-Griffith, a local rock-climbing guide."

"Any link with the professor?" demanded the inspector quickly.

"He has climbed with Julius Wiernick, probably more than once. And for your further excitement, Grimm, Jones-Griffith has been out on these hills today, probably passing within a few hundred feet of the scene of the accident."

"By gum!" Grimmett blew through his mustache. "Anything more on him? Let's have it, Sir Ab."

Lewker did not at once reply. He seemed to be pondering some matter that had just crossed his mind.

"Jones-Griffith," he said absently at last, "is taking part in Major Kemp's training exercise. As I understand Kemp's arrangements, Lumley and Jones-Griffith were to act as guides to the cadets, taking them over Bwlch-y-Saethau at an early hour this morning."

"And they didn't come back together," said Grimmett, "because when we were talking at the bottom of Slanting Buttress Kemp told us he'd been with Lumley and Lumley had left him—on the way back from where these cadets were going to, that was. He didn't mention Jones-Griffith at all. Now then, sir—"

"Enough!" boomed Sir Abercrombie firmly. "Light thickens, and the crow makes wing to the rooky wood." He stood up and tapped out his pipe. "In less magical words, it is getting late, and we must be on the homeward track before dusk."

"But there's a couple of things I'd like you to explain, Sir Ab."

"We will talk further, Grimm, when we reach the level path. But I advise abstention from further airy speculation."

Grimmett got stiffly to his feet. "Don't know whether I can help it now," he said with a grin. "I've sort of got the taste for it."

"Then here is more grist for your unprofitable mill. What color was Professor Wiernick's anorak?"

As he spoke, the actor-manager was already recommencing the descent of the shaley path. The inspector, stumbling on the loose surface, hastened after him.

"I'd call it olive-green, I reckon," he replied. "Why?"

"Add two anoraks and two woolen caps, Grimm, with their respective colors—"

"By gum!"

"—and you may tell me the answer when we reach the track," ended Sir Abercrombie. "For the present, let us save our breath and watch our footing."

Watchfulness, Grimmett discovered, was indeed necessary. The descent was exceedingly steep, his leg-muscles were tiring, and an early twilight had already begun to veil the huge folds of the mountainsides. Llydaw lay like a long pale lizard between darkling shores below them on the left. They came down and down towards its level, leaving shaley rock for boulder-strewn hummocks of grass and slithering down these to gain marshy slopes close above the lake shore. Beyond the head of the lake, rising from the hidden circle of Glaslyn, the precipice of Snowdon loomed, a dim vastness topped with a glimmer of snow where it merged with the darkening clouds. A narrow path—the climbers' way to Lliwedd, which Julius Wiernick had trodden for the last time that morning—took them along the sides of ancient moraine-humps and across boggy patches to the track, broad and roughly metalled, by which the ambulance-van had come up from Pen-y-Pass. They had seen no one, not even a sheep, during their descent, and the track was lonely and deserted.

"Twenty-five minutes to Pen-y-Pass—and, I trust, several cups of tea," announced Sir Abercrombie as their boots rang on the solid surface. "A pity, Grimm, that Shakespeare could not sing the excellences of tea. 'Tea, thou soft and sober, venerable liquid!' That, I believe, is Colley Cibber. But have you the answer to my little equation?"

"I reckon so," Grimmett answered cautiously. "Mr. Stonor's life was threatened. He went out wearing a green anorak and a red woolen cap. Wiernick was killed. He was wearing an olive-green anorak and a red woolen cap. Therefore a murderer could have mistaken him for Stonor. But—"

"But it would have to be a murderer who was not aware that Wiernick, not Stonor, was leading the Slanting Buttress climb."

"This Jack Jones-Griffith wouldn't know that, I reckon."

"I think not. And Jones-Griffith, Grimm, is as tall as Peter Lumley, though not as massive. I should say he takes size tens at least."

Grimmett plodded on in silence for some little time. He was feeling the effects of an unusually strenuous day. The winding track had rounded a corner above a glimmering lake in a hollow on their right before he spoke again, glumly.

"Seems to me you're not taking this business seriously, Sir Ab. Maybe you're right about making bricks without straw."

"My dear Grimm!" said the actor-manager soothingly. "Pray forgive me if I seem to treat your enthusiasm lightly. It is merely that I am tired of speculation. As to bricks, I see about me some scattered dabs of clay insufficient to make one solid brick. Our holiday from logical detection has been entertaining—even, in some ways, edifying—but it is time, I feel, that evidence came into its own."

The inspector's sigh might have been a sign of weariness or of regret for his vanished freedom of thought.

"All right," he said rather more cheerfully. "Talking of evidence, there's two things I want to know. What was that you were saying about Wiernick doing a variant? And why wasn't he saved by the rope when he fell? I thought that was the idea of a climbing-rope."

"I will answer both your questions here," replied Lewker, halting. "Ocular demonstration is worth a thousand words."

They had reached a place where a large rock stood close to the track, its flat perpendicular face suggesting that it had been cut away to make room for the road. Sir Abercrombie rested his fingertips against it so that his arm slanted down at an angle from the rock-face.

"Conceive my arm to be the Slanting Buttress and this rock to be the main cliff of Lliwedd, Grimm. The route goes straight up my arm until it reaches my fingertips. Here the main cliff is too steep to climb, but seventy feet away to the right a wide and shallow groove—an open chimney, in fact—offers a way. It is out of sight round the corner of a vertical rib some distance above the top of the buttress represented here by my fingers. Is that clear?"

"I think so, Sir Ab. When Wiernick and Ferguson and Miss Massey got to the top of the buttress they'd have to go diagonally up to the right for seventy feet, and round a corner, before they got to this chimney."

"Precisely. Narrow ledges make this traverse, as we call it, possible. The ledges are easy, with convenient rock spikes here and there for hitching the rope, but they take the climber out above a very steep rock-face broken by few ledges—the face at the foot of which you and Tom Paton waited. The chimney, as you realize, rises directly above this. Wiernick, if he had climbed by the usual route, would have gone up the chimney for thirty feet only, at which point he would have stepped over to his right, out of the chimney and into a safe and roomy nook. In other words, he would have run out only thirty feet of rope from where Ferguson was belaying him."

"And if he'd fallen just as he was stepping into this nook," Grimmett frowned, "he'd have gone down for sixty feet. He'd have hung thirty feet below Ferguson. Actually, I reckon, he was hanging seventy feet or so below him. So he must have climbed seventy feet above him before he fell, and that makes it a fall of a hundred and forty feet."

Lewker nodded. "A very steep fall, striking two or perhaps three projecting ledges on the way down, with tremendous force. Ferguson had little chance of drawing in the rope."

"I see that, yes. And Ferguson did hold him in the end. The rope tearing through his hands must have damaged them pretty badly, I reckon."

"They were somewhat burned by the friction, but the physical shock Ferguson had to withstand was not so great as one might expect. As I will explain to you, Grimm, *ambulando*."

They left the rock of ocular demonstration and walked on along the track. It curved to the left, crossing the low moorland ridge that separated them from the dip of Llanberis Pass. On the right hand the giant knees of the mountains curved over in purple masses to their hidden feet in the twilight depths of the Vale of Gwynant.

"Wiernick's party climbed on two ropes," pursued Sir Abercrombie. "A hundred-foot nylon, full weight, linked Flora to Ferguson and there was a hundred-and-twenty feet of nylon medium weight between Ferguson and Wiernick. This was because—as I guessed and Ferguson has confirmed—the professor wanted to try a variant to the usual route. Perhaps you remember, Grimm, that he and Ferguson were consulting a massive volume in the lounge after dinner last night."

"I remember Ferguson getting a book from the bookcase and taking it across to the professor."

"Yes. I recognized the book, for I possess a copy myself. It was the Abrahams' *Rock Climbing in North Wales*, published in 1904, and contains an account of the first ascent of Slanting Buttress. From that account it is possible to infer that the pioneers did not step out to the right from the chimney but climbed straight on up the face above. That was what Professor Wiernick proposed to attempt, and did attempt."

"That'd be a deal harder than the ordinary way, I suppose," Grimmett remarked despondently. "And that could be the reason why he slipped and fell off."

"It could be, Grimm. But allow me to conclude my detailed exposition. When Wiernick began to ascend the chimney Ferguson was not immediately below him but a few feet round the corner, securely belayed to a rock projection. Thus he could not watch the professor's movements. Still less could Flora Massey see what happened, for she was safely placed on a lower ledge thirty feet away. The rope running from Ferguson to the professor passed over some quartz knobs at the foot of the chimney, and when he fell the main shock of his fall came on those projections, fracturing one strand of the rope but fortunately not breaking it. Ferguson, therefore, had to withstand only a small part of the actual strain." Sir Abercrombie paused. "You will have noted, I hope, that the professor must have climbed about forty feet *above* the nook at the side of the chimney—the nook on the ordinary route by which the maker of those large footprints descended."

Inspector Grimmett nodded his head dumbly. Fatigue was upon him now. The ache in his plodding legs, the prospect of a much-needed cup of tea, were beginning to occupy his mind to the exclusion of his late eagerness to smell out a crime. When they tramped round a last downhill corner of the track and saw the lit windows of the Pen-y-Pass Hotel close at hand he emitted a deep grunt of relief.

A shiny hospital ambulance stood on the car park close to the corrugated-iron shed, and a uniformed policeman who was chatting to the driver turned to look at them as they trudged past. Lewker went straight to the porch of the hotel without halting and they passed into the hall, where half a dozen young men clad in anoraks or sweaters (presumably some of those who had helped with the stretcher party) were drinking tea and talking in lowered voices. The only familiar face was that of George Thripp who gave them a worried nod as he hurried across the hall towards the little room beside the bar which was used as the hotel office.

The actor-manager seized upon a maid who emerged into the hall on some errand and requested that tea and buns should be sent up to their room.

Fifteen minutes later, having washed and changed, they were drinking a third cup of tea when someone thumped on the bedroom door. The visitor proved to be Dr. Richard Paton, still in his climbing clothes and with a grave expression on his large and normally cheerful face. Sir Abercrombie pulled a bedroom chair in front of the electric fire and inquired how the two survivors of the accident were faring. Dr. Richard declined the chair, explaining that he had only popped in for a moment on his way to have a much-needed wash.

"Flora and Mr. Ferguson are in their rooms," he added. "Slight shock, but nothing more. Ferguson, in fact, insisted on helping us to get the body fixed up in the shanty across the road, where we've put it for the time being. He used to climb a lot with Wiernick when they were young men, according to Dad."

"There is an ambulance waiting, I see," Lewker remarked.

"That's George Thripp's work," Richard nodded. "He organized everything—phoned the police and so forth. They've got electric light in the shanty and the police surgeon's examining the body now. One imagines George already arranging for the inquest. I haven't heard yet what's going to happen about the dinner and the rest of the weekend."

He paused uncertainly, fidgeting with one hand in the pocket of his climbing-breeches. The actor-manager glanced keenly at him.

"You have, I fancy, something else to tell us?" he inquired gently.

"Well—yes. It's damned odd. Anyway, Flora—she's a trained nurse, you know—gave me a hand tidying up the body a bit. We got his anorak off and she emptied the pockets. In the bottom of one of them there was this, screwed up into a ball."

He took his hand from his pocket and held out a crumpled slip of paper. Grimmett, getting up to read it in obedience to Sir Abercrombie's gesture, had a sudden feeling that he had lived this moment before, for the paper bore three lines of uneven typewriting:

"You thought youd got away with it but its catching up with you you dirty skunk your not fit to live and wont if you persist in taking the job so watch out."

Chapter VII

Poison Typewriter

"By gum!" said the inspector under his breath.

Lewker said nothing. He sat quite still, holding the creased paper in his hand but not looking at it; his little eyes, narrowed until they were scarcely visible, gazed at the uninspiring red bars of the electric fire, and his pouchy face was creased in a villainous scowl. He looked like the Emperor Nero planning a holocaust.

"Well, there it is," Richard said uncomfortably. "Dirty business, that sort of letter. I've had a few—one does, you know, in my profession— but I've always burned 'em and nothing's ever come of it. This is rather different, I suppose. Anyhow, Flora said I'd better bring it along to you." He moved towards the door. "She seemed more upset about finding it than about the accident."

"One moment, Doctor." Sir Abercrombie came out of his abstraction. "Does anyone know about the finding of this letter other than yourself and Miss Massey?"

"Not a soul, far as I know."

"Then I suggest that you say nothing about it for the present. Perhaps you would ask Miss Massey to keep silence also."

"Flora won't talk, I know. I certainly won't." Richard, with one hand on the door-handle, turned; he looked worried. "One doesn't want to make trouble, things being as they are, but—well, it might be an idea to find out something about that letter. You see, Flora looked very strange when we found it. I'll swear she's afraid of something."

"We'll look into it, Doctor," Grimmett promised gravely.

"Good. Well—better go and get cleaned up."

He went out. Grimmett blew gently through his mustache and looked at the actor-manager who had resumed his Neronic fire-gazing.

"Things are coming our way, seemingly," he remarked, his china-blue eyes gleaming. "Take it the first anonymous letter got to Mr. Stonor by mistake, being intended for Professor Wiernick. That one you've got in your hand reached the man it was intended for. And he's dead. *Your not fit to live and wont if you persist.* I reckon that's grounds enough for a serious investigation into Julius Wiernick's death, Sir Ab."

Sir Abercrombie handed the second anonymous letter to the inspector and rose to his feet.

"It may be instructive, Grimm," he murmured absently, "to compare this with the missive presented to us by Stonor."

He walked restlessly to the window, opened it and stuck out his head, withdrew his head and closed the window. The engraving of the young lady clasping a cross in a snowstorm caught his eye again; it had been returned to its original position. He appeared to consider it critically for some seconds before once more turning its face to the wall. Finally, and still frowning reflectively, he returned to his chair by the fire. Grimmett, meanwhile, had taken the letter received by Stonor from his wallet and was comparing it with the other.

"Wording corresponds exactly, likewise spelling," he announced. "Same sort of paper—Woolworth unruled notepad, I'd say—and I'm pretty sure they were typed on the same typewriter."

"Indeed?"

"Yes. A Remington, and an old one at that." The inspector glanced keenly and with suspicion at his companion. "Did you expect the Wiernick letter would have been typed on a different typewriter from the other, Sir Ab?"

"I thought it possible. Why, pray, do you ask?"

"The way you said 'Indeed' sounded as if you were surprised."

Sir Abercrombie sighed. "Surprise, Grimm, is born of incongruity or the unexpected. In this business, so far, nothing appears congruous nor is there anything to expect, so I find nothing at which to be surprised— except, of course the fact that Julius Wiernick fell where in theory he should not have fallen."

"All the same, sir," persisted Grimmett stubbornly, "I reckon it fitted in with something you thought up just now. I'd be glad, so I would, if you'd put me in the picture, because I still feel this is going to burst into a fullblown murder case before long."

"My dear Grimm!" boomed the actor-manager reproachfully. "If by 'put me in the picture' you really mean 'put the picture before me,' I would do so were it in my power to the smallest extent. But our picture cannot even be likened, in the well-worn simile, to a jigsaw puzzle. We have, in effect, two or three pieces of jigsaw, each of which could quite possibly be part of a different puzzle. I can imagine other pieces to fit, but there is no linking piece."

"A man threatened with death and a man killed—if there isn't a link there, Sir Ab, I'm a Dutchman."

"The threat of death, Grimm, was conditional, remember. Was Professor Wiernick persisting in taking a job? If so, what job? What was it that he thought he had got away with and that was catching up with him?"

"Mrs. Wiernick might be able to tell us." Grimmett leaned forward eagerly. "Look, sir, this letter in Wiernick's pocket gives us a break, as the Yanks say. We don't have to mention foul play at all—just start an inquiry about the anonymous letters, quietly. Limit it to Mr. Stonor's, perhaps. He'd probably give us permission."

"You think more relevant facts might emerge? You may be right. But I fail to see what line of inquiry we can pursue in the matter of Stonor's letter, and if we cite Wiernick's we are bound to reveal to everyone—including, possibly, his murderer—our ill-grounded suspicions about Wiernick's death."

Grimmett scratched his head. "It's a puzzle where to start, so it is. One thing's plain—we must have more hard facts."

"The hardest facts we have are one death and two anonymous letters. If we renew our consideration of the death we shall merely talk in circles, as it were. Let us consider the letters again."

They bent over the two crumpled papers together. After a moment the inspector got up to rummage in his suitcase and return carrying a pocket magnifying-glass, with which he scrutinised the two letters. Sir Abercrombie was the first to speak.

"As far as the literary content is concerned," he said reflectively, "it is quite clear that we have to look in the past for the origin of the affair. Let X be the sender of the letters and Y the intended recipient. Then we infer that some considerable time ago Y did something which may have been of a criminal nature, something at least which would harm him if brought to light. X has discovered this, and is attempting to use his knowledge to prevent Y from taking some job that X does not wish him to take." He paused and frowned at the glowing bars of the fire. "The odd thing is, Grimm, that X is not content with implying a threat to reveal this shameful something if Y 'persists.' He goes further and states positively that Y will not continue to live if his persistence continues."

Grimmett looked up from his magnifying-glass. "Take it this way, sir. X isn't at all keen to reveal the something. He thinks Y might guess he isn't keen, so he puts in a definite threat against his life to make Y properly windy."

"That is rather subtle of you, Grimm," beamed Lewker. "I do believe you have moved us forward a fraction of an inch along our laborious trail. What have you seen with your additional eye?"

"Not as much as our department at the Yard would see, but enough to be some use, maybe. This typewriter—the old Remington—shows two definite faults at least." The inspector passed letters and magnifying-glass over. "The t's all have a small break in the left-hand part of the cross line, and the r's have got a chip off their bottoms. You can see the defective r's without the glass. That'll identify—" He broke off as someone knocked on their door. "Better slip those in your pocket, Sir Ab. I'll see who this is."

It was George Thripp, armed as always with a paper bearing a list of names. The deepened furrows of anxiety on his brow made him look more than ever like a hopelessly questing tortoise. He murmured apologetically to Grimmett as he came into the room, and addressed himself to Sir Abercrombie.

"Sorry to intrude, Lewker. I hope you're not too tired after your efforts in getting poor Wiernick down?"

"At least I am not too tired to render further assistance, if it is required."

"Good, good. A bad business, though, a bad business," added Thripp hastily, evidently feeling that expressions of approval were hardly the thing six hours after a fatal accident. "We are holding an impromptu meeting," he went on, "to decide upon our procedure for the remainder of the dinner meet. The president would like you to attend, if you'd be so good."

"Of course. When is the meeting?"

"In five minutes' time, at six o'clock. It will be in the small office next door to the bar. We have three members of the club committee at this meet"—Thripp glanced automatically at his list—"Donald Ferguson, myself, and the honorary secretary. We are asking Mrs. Hengist, Dr. Thomas Paton and yourself to join us."

"I will be there," promised the actor-manager, rising.

"Good, good. With the president, we shall be seven—a suitable number if a vote has to be taken."

Thripp was trotting towards the door when Sir Abercrombie stayed him with a question.

"Mrs. Wiernick has been informed of her husband's death, I presume?"

"Oh, yes. Yes." Thripp hesitated. "She took it very well, very well indeed. She'll keep to her room—I'm arranging for dinner to be sent up to her."

"Where did she go today?" asked Grimmett; there was a warning frown on Lewker's face but he ignored it and persisted in his collection of a fact. "I mean," he added, "did she meet someone out on the hills and learn of the professor's death like that?"

"Oh, no," replied Thripp. "She was out walking by herself—in Cwm Dyli, I understand—and returned to Pen-y-Pass just after the president brought the sad news down. He broke it to her himself."

He departed. As the door closed behind him Grimmett swung round to face the actor-manager.

"Cwm Dyli," he said. "Where's that?"

"It is the wild lower valley through which runs the stream from Llyn Llydaw."

"Well, Major Kemp mentioned it too. He said he'd left Lumley on the other side of Lliwedd and came back by another way meaning to cross Cwm Dyli. Then he saw Stonor and came up to the bottom of Slanting Buttress. So he might have joined up with Mrs. Wiernick before then—"

"Precisely, Grimm," Lewker interrupted gently. "But I am bidden to a solemn conclave and must away. I will, however, concede that Cwm Dyli is an excellent place for lovers' meetings, though a little chilly at this time of year."

He made a stately exit before the inspector could reply, and went down the passage to the stairhead, where he paused for a moment. Below him, just inside the front door, Charles Kemp was talking to a tall man in motorcycling kit. He recognized Jack Jones-Griffith. The guide turned a solemn face to him as he reached the bottom of the stairs.

"A very shocking affair this, Sir Abercrombie," he announced. "I heard of it from the local postman late this afternoon, and came up at once on my motorbaike."

"Jack went straight down Cwm-y-Llan to his cottage in Nant Gwynant after our show this mornin'," the major explained, "so he wouldn't know what had happened."

He had changed into a dark suit, presumably in anticipation of the dinner, and his breath smelled of whisky. Sir Abercrombie, espying Donald Ferguson in grave conversation with George Thripp on the other side of the hall, decided he had a minute to spare before the meeting.

"You were well acquainted with the late Professor Wiernick, I believe," he said with casual politeness.

"Our relations," replied Jones-Griffith ponderously, "were those of professional gayde and clayent, but I think I may say we were old friends. Not a year passed, Sir Abercrombie, but Professor Wiernick requested my services to lead him up the hardest claimbs in North Wales. This sad accident has touched me—here."

He laid a hand on his chest and then coughed to hide his manly emotion.

"Quite so," said Kemp with a faint irony. "You were askin' about the rifle, Jack. The drill now is that I issue you and Peter with your rifles tomorrow. You'll be up here at oh-seven-double-oh, won't you?"

"All raight, Major. You've got to carry on, in spaite of the tragedy—I quaite see that."

"Good-oh," nodded Kemp; he seemed to conceal a grin. "I'll be waitin' for you. I've got the six spare rifles and the ammo stored in the tin shanty on the car park—which reminds me." He raised his voice. "Thripp! Is the shed—er—unoccupied now?"

Thripp, frowning reproachfully, came across the hall followed by Ferguson. Ferguson's hands were lightly bandaged across the palms; his face was rather pale but stolidly unemotional.

"The body, Major, was removed in the ambulance some time ago," said Thripp in pointedly lower tones.

"Oh, good. I want to check my stuff. Like to come over, Jack?"

He took a large key from its hook beside the door and went out with Jones-Griffith.

Thripp glowered after them resentfully. "Major Kemp appears to be more concerned with his armaments than with Wiernick's death," he said.

"Aweel, he has his duty to do," said Ferguson. "The president's just gone into the office, by the by," he added.

"Oh, has he? We had better follow, then. Come along, come along."

They went towards the office. Sir Abercrombie was about to follow when someone touched his arm and he turned to find at his elbow a young man in a raincoat, who spoke rapidly but respectfully.

"Sir Abercrombie Lewker, I believe? I knew you from your pictures, sir. I suppose you wouldn't give me something about this climbing accident? It was a professor from one of the universities that was killed, wasn't it?"

The actor-manager surveyed him benignly. "You, of course, are the Press," he said. "And if you are not given a story you will concoct one out of your own lurid imagination."

"Oh come now, sir—"

"I will make a bargain with you. Remain here, question nobody, restrain your morbid curiosity, and within fifteen minutes I will give you a written statement of facts, which your paper may use."

"Thanks very much, sir—but just one thing. I'm told you were on the rescue-party yourself. A personal story—"

"No," said Sir Abercrombie with finality.

He followed Thripp and Ferguson into the office. The other members of the impromptu committee were already present, arranged with what formality the somewhat cramped accommodation allowed. Mark Stonor sat with the honorary secretary, Richard Paton, at a small table. A large desk bearing an aspidistra in a pot and a small typewriter took up most of the remaining space, but a venerable armchair in one corner contained Dr. Tom's massive figure while Thripp, Ferguson, Mrs. Hengist and Lewker sat on smaller chairs and tried to avoid the scorching heat of an electric fire at short range.

The president opened the meeting without preamble. The furrows of his long face had deepened and he looked old and worried. In view of this most tragic accident, he said, they had to decide whether to go on with the dinner meet or whether they should cancel all further activities. He had seen Mrs. Wiernick, who was facing the tragedy with great courage, and she had asked that the dinner and other arrangements should go on as planned, as far as possible; she was sure her husband would have wished that. As the dinner was due to start in an hour and a half, added Stonor, a decision must be made quickly.

"Well, of course the dinner must go on," said Mrs. Hengist trenchantly. "It's a regular club function and the death of one member shouldn't stop it. Eve Wiernick's perfectly right. I never liked Julius Wiernick—nor did anyone, for that matter—but he never had any use for sentimentality."

The president looked mildly shocked. Ferguson shifted in his chair and a tinge of color appeared on his cheeks.

"I think Mrs. Hengist's remark's a wee bit uncalled for," he said. "I'm no' saying Wiernick wasn't a prickly character—he was. But I respected him, and—well, today we'd renewed a climbing partnership that began a quarter of a century ago."

"I'm sorry," said Mrs. Hengist shortly.

Dr. Tom leaned forward impatiently. "Whether we liked Wiernick or not isn't the question," he growled. "Do we go ahead with the dinner? I say yes."

"We'll vote on that," the secretary suggested with a glance at the president. "A show of hands, please—those in favor of the dinner taking place as originally planned. Thank you. All in favor, Mr. President."

"Very well," Stonor said. "Do you know whether there will be any absentees?"

"I've sounded most of them," Richard replied. "Mr. and Mrs. Reid-Cable, the Rossiters, the Penberthys, and George Sheldrake and his niece, are all planning to leave tomorrow morning. The rest, one assumes, will stay on until Monday. They'll all be present at the dinner, I should think. Except, of course, Mrs. Wiernick."

Stonor nodded. "Thank you. As far as tomorrow's activities—if any—are concerned, there will be no formal organization." He cleared his throat portentously. "I need hardly say how much I deplore this sad happening. The Foothold Club has hitherto maintained a fine reputation for good mountaineering and freedom from serious accident. That this should happen at an annual dinner—and," he added rather hastily, "to a respected senior member, is—ah—highly regrettable."

Dr. Tom caught Sir Abercrombie's eye and winked. The president looked inquiringly round the circle of faces.

"Since we are unanimous that the dinner should proceed," he said, "it appears that our business is at an end. Has anyone anything to add?"

"I have, Mr. President, if you will allow me," said the actor-manager. "In my opinion a brief statement of the circumstances of Professor Wiernick's death should be prepared now for issue to the Press."

"The Press!" Stonor repeated the words as he might have said 'the bubonic plague'. "My dear Lewker, any sort of publicity is most undesirable. It might do the club a great deal of harm."

"Yet," said Lewker mildly, "the newspapers will report this accident, whether we like it or not. There is a reporter in the bar at this moment, and no power on earth can stop him from sending in his story. Whether that story contains the basic facts of the matter or is merely a garbled invention of his own depends on us. A bare statement of the facts should be given out. The honorary secretary, perhaps, could prepare one."

"Quite right," barked Mrs. Hengist. "If we don't, you'll find the papers saying a Professor Wierdlock fell off a rope while he was swarming up the notorious precipice of Mount Snowden, with an E."

"And the Foothold Club," added the doctor, with an eye on the president, "might fill up the paragraphs in place of proper information. With potted biographies of its more famous members."

Stonor almost wrung his hands. He looked helplessly at Richard Paton who nodded apologetically.

"It's the only thing to do, sir," he said. "In these cases one has to make the best of a bad job." He hesitated. "For my own part, I'm not yet perfectly clear how the accident happened. Mr. Ferguson, if he feels like doing it, could perhaps give us a short account and I'll make a note or two. Afterwards I'll type out a statement, Mr. President, for you to approve."

"Very well, then," Stonor frowned reluctantly. "How do you feel about that, Ferguson?"

Donald Ferguson passed a bandaged hand across his chin. His blunt features expressed mingled distaste and resignation.

"All right," he said. "Forbye there's no' verra much to tell. Wiernick had been reading Abraham's account of the original Slanting Buttress ascent and wanted to try going straight on up the chimney pitch instead of stepping out to the ledge on the right. He was a verra good rock-climber, as you all know, and the variation would make the climb a bit more interesting for him. Well, at the end of the traverse I took a belay just round the corner below the chimney—I couldn't see Wiernick after he'd started to climb. He ran out about seventy feet of rope. Then there was a loud shout and he came off."

"You had little or no warning, then," the president murmured sympathetically as he paused.

"None," Ferguson said. "The fall was simultaneous with the shout. He went straight down past me. I heard—I heard him strike a ledge. Then the jerk came on the rope. It was running over a quartz projection so the strain was no' verra great." He lifted his hands slightly and let them fall. "I held him. There was no movement on the end of the rope. I shouted but he did not reply. He'd fallen a hundred and forty feet and I thought it likely enough he was dead."

"Couldn't pull him up, I take it?" Tom Paton grunted.

Ferguson shook his head. "I managed to hitch the rope and then brought Flora up to my stance—she was out of sight on a ledge farther down the traverse and didn't know what had happened. We both pulled, and got him up a bit, but we couldn't do any more. There wasn't much room on my stance and Flora went back again. I'd got a whistle, so I started blowing the distress signal."

Dr. Richard, who had been scribbling in a notebook, looked up.

"You've no idea why he came off, Mr. Ferguson?" he asked.

"None at all."

With a word to the president, Richard took his notebook and a sheet of paper to the desk and started hammering jerkily at the aged typewriter.

George Thripp leaned towards the president.

"You'll deliver your speech as planned, I take it?" he murmured.

"Yes," Stonor said; he took some typewritten sheets from his breast pocket. "I must add some—ah—phrases of condolence and amend a jocular expression here and there, when the secretary has finished with the typewriter."

Thripp turned to Ferguson. "You'll be wanted to give evidence at the inquest, I'm afraid. I'm not yet certain whether it will be on Monday or Tuesday."

"Yes, of course," Ferguson said rather irritably.

Dr. Richard pulled his sheet of paper from the typewriter with a loud rasping sound and placed it before the president who read it carefully and then announced that the meeting was over. Sir Abercrombie, going out with the rest, was buttonholed by the secretary.

"One gathers you spotted this reporter chap," Richard said. "Would you mind slipping him this? You can vet it if you like." He glanced over his shoulder at the president who was already fumbling with the typewriter. "I think," he added in a low voice, "I'll see if the Old Man wants any help with his speech. He's badly shaken up by this business, you know, though one wouldn't think it."

Lewker took the paper and went out of the room. There was a bracket light in the corner of the hall near the 'office' door and he paused beneath it to read Richard's inexpert typing. The secretary had been concise and accurate. "*Julius Wiernick (57) Professor of Anthropology at Morchester University, was killed by a fall while climbing ...*" His eye stopped there and went back to the beginning. In the first eight words the letter *r* occurred seven times, and the repetition of a small defect had attracted his attention. The defect was the lack of part of the letter's tail.

He found the reporter and handed him the statement, nipped in the bud a further request for a 'personal story,' and went in search of George Thripp.

Ten minutes later he was sitting in front of the bedroom fire and giving Inspector Grimmett a report of the meeting. He also told of his brief encounter with Kemp and Jones-Griffith in the hall.

"Nothing much to go on in Mr. Ferguson's account of the fall, seemingly," Grimmett commented when he had finished.

"No, Grimm." Sir Abercrombie wrinkled his eyes at the fire. "I think perhaps two things may be worthy of note. One, that all three climbers were out of sight of each other when the fall occurred. Two, that Mark Stonor is apparently more concerned about the reputation of the Foothold Club than about the death of one of its senior members."

"Hallo, sir!" said the inspector sharply. "You on to something? You're not seeing the president as the villain of the piece?"

"Villain and he be many miles asunder," returned the actor-manager sonorously. "And yet—Joan of Arc put innocent men to the sword, and is a saint. I have something for you, however, of a more concrete nature. The typewriter in the room they call the office downstairs is an old Remington and the small *r* is defective."

"By gum!"

"The defect, so far as I could judge, corresponds exactly to the defect in the typewriter on which the two anonymous letters were written. I was unable to discern whether or not the *t* also had a corresponding defect—"

"We can easily check that, and we will, what's more!" In his excitement the inspector had forgotten Sir Abercrombie's dislike of interruption. "But I reckon it's as good as proved with that *r*. Find out who's had access to that machine—"

"Revenging myself, laddie, with this interruption," boomed Lewker, "I will add what I was about to tell you. I have had some conversation with the busy Thripp under cover of an inquiry about using that typewriter myself. It appears that the hotel people have made the office available for the use of the Foothold Club. Any member could have had access to the typewriter at any time in the past twenty-four hours. Thripp has typed names for his seating arrangements and the inevitable lists. Mark Stonor typed his speech for tonight's dinner there yesterday evening and is there at this moment amending some jocular remarks in that speech—jocular, I should say, being something of an overstatement when applied to Stonor's remarks. Major Charles Kemp annoyed the good Thripp by using the typewriter for making out orders when Thripp wanted it. I am much afraid, Grimm, that identification of the typewriter is not going to help us a great deal."

The inspector looked glum; then he brightened a little.

"Still, it's something," he said. "We know now that both letters were typed by someone staying in this hotel. And Stonor found the letter in his car at six yesterday evening, so it must have been typed by someone who arrived before then."

"Your latter point is a good one. No doubt Thripp can tell us which of the hotel guests arrived before six, and on the basis of the same evidence we may eliminate the two Doctors Paton as writers of the president's anonymous letter."

"Not that they needed eliminating."

"Scarcely. And elimination, Grimm, is a damnably slow process."

Sir Abercrombie got up from his chair and began to stump about the bedroom, pausing at various points in his constricted tour. Grimmett watched him, frowning. 'Damnably' was strong language for the actor-manager, who never used an oath except in a Shakespearean sense.

"What's bothering you, Sir Ab?" he demanded. "Seems to me you've put something together out of the little we've got. Is that it?"

Lewker turned from scowling contemplation of a bedside lamp.

"Grimm," he said solemnly, "I have put one and one together and made four. That is what is bothering me. And yet I think the final total is eight, after all."

He looked at his watch, and forestalled the goggling inspector's comment with a sudden change of manner.

"Time and the hour, Grimm, runs through the roughest day, as Macbeth remarked at the beginning of his own troubles. In little more than half an hour we dine, and I have yet to shave. I fear the dinner will not be as joyous a feast as we anticipated, but to the philosophical mind neither good food nor good wine should lose their taste, whatever the circumstances."

He was plugging his electric razor into a lamp socket as he spoke, and a moment later the resultant whir rendered him deaf to any words of Grimmett's.

The twenty-three Foothold Club members who assembled for the dinner which was the core or nucleus of the dinner meet found formality established by the placing of a hollow square of three long tables, and seated themselves thereat under the observant eye of George Thripp and in accordance with the neat cards he had typed bearing their names. The president, at the top table, had Lady Rendall on his right and Flora Massey (as niece of the president-elect) on his left. Lord Rendall and Donald Ferguson, with old George Sheldrake and the honorary secretary, made up the company of 'nobs,' as Dr. Tom termed them. Dr. Tom was seated opposite Lewker, who was pleased to find that Thripp had decreed that the inspector should sit beside him. It did not escape the actor-manager's notice that Grimmett, after casually examining the name-card on the table in front of him, toyed with it for a moment and then slid it absentmindedly into his pocket.

A very subdued murmur of talk accompanied the serving of dinner. At times, indeed, a somewhat gloomy silence prevailed in some quarters, and on one such occasion Sir Abercrombie took it upon himself to end the pause by asking Charles Kemp, who was sitting next but one to Dr.

Paton, how his cadet exercise was progressing. Kemp replied shortly that it was going all right.

"I find it interesting," boomed Sir Abercrombie, trying again, "that there should be a Nepalese among your officer cadets. Do you find him as intelligent as your other trainees?"

The major apparently decided to respond. "Oh, quite," he said, suspending his attack on a leg of Anglesey chicken. "Devilish bright lad, considerin' he comes from a godforsaken village called Khamche about a gunshot from the Tibetan frontier. Difficult in some ways, but far better than the usual Shorehurst type in others."

"Indeed?"

"Things like takin' cover, gettin' over rough ground and so forth. That lad could give points to any cross-country runner if you threw a lot of boulders and a hillside or two on the course."

Here Kemp's neighbor put in a question about Himalayan shooting, and the buzz of general conversation rose to *piano* again. Lewker took no part in it for several minutes; he had something to think about.

The dinner proceeded quietly towards its end. 'The Queen' and a relaxation with cigars or cigarettes; 'The Club' proposed very briefly by George Sheldrake. The response to this latter toast was the president's speech, which began with a short and solemn reference to the recent fatal accident and went on with a résumé of the club's past doings and future prospects. It did not contain a word that could have been called jocular by the most austere of critics. What it did contain was proof, if ever spoken word and tonal inflection gave proof, that Mark Stonor cared as greatly for the standing and reputation of the Foothold Club as another man might care for his wife and child.

Stonor sat down amid subdued applause and then rose again to announce that the dinner was at an end and that as tomorrow was Sunday, breakfast would not be served until nine o'clock. Upon this the party broke up. Most of the women gravitated towards the lounge and the men to the hall bar, but there was a marked tendency to make for bed without undue delay. Sir Abercrombie found Frank Hibberd in the hall and contrived to get five minutes' chat with him over whiskies and sodas. There were interruptions, for there was a considerable press round the bar hatch, and Lewker observed old George Sheldrake with a hand on Donald Ferguson's shoulder and heard Sheldrake's voice momentarily above the general hum of talk.

"... great days of the thirties, when you and Wiernick, Stonor and poor Jack Lumley, climbed together for three Alpine seasons in succession ..."

Ferguson's somewhat doughy face showed a spasm of emotion at the old man's words; the first emotion Lewker had seen him show since Wiernick's death.

From the corner of his eye the actor-manager saw Grimmett, on the other side of the crowded hall with Peter Lumley, signal with upward-jerking forefinger that he intended to go upstairs and turn in. Lewker acknowledged the signal, turned to find that Hibberd was chatting with Major Kemp, and resolved to go to bed himself; for a middle-aged man who did very little mountaineering these days the past twelve hours had been fatiguing. Mark Stonor, it appeared, had made the same resolution. He came shuffling through the little crowd on his way to the stairs, scattering solemn and benedictory good nights.

"No Alpine start tomorrow, Mark, thank God!" said old Sheldrake as he passed.

"No, George," returned the president gravely, "but I shall be up at seven as usual—my morning walk, you know, to Llydaw and back."

He passed on and went up the stairs a pace or two behind Inspector Grimmett. Sir Abercrombie, about to follow them, was intercepted by Peter Lumley. The large young man looked shaggy and sullen as ever but his glance was keen—even, thought Lewker, anxious.

"Anyone got any idea why Wiernick came off, sir?" he asked bluntly in an undertone.

The actor-manager shrugged his shoulders. "Why does a good climber now and then fall? I doubt if we shall ever know why Professor Wiernick fell, Lumley. Why do you ask?"

"Your friend Grimmett seemed to think it was rum."

"Some accidents are rum. It could have been a rotten hold that came away, or a foot slipping on wet or icy rock."

Peter Lumley stared hard at him for two or three seconds. Then he raised the pint tankard he was holding and buried his face in it. Sir Abercrombie waited for a moment, but as Lumley seemed to have nothing more to say he bade him good night and went upstairs, reflecting rather irritably that Grimmett should have known better than to suggest that there was any special rumness about the accident. As he reached the head of the stairs a girl came along the dimly-lit passage that led to the bedrooms at the back of the inn. It was Flora Massey. Lewker nodded silently to her and would have gone on towards his own room, but she hurried to intercept him.

"I—I've been in to see Mrs. Wiernick," she said.

"Indeed," returned Sir Abercrombie gently, certain that she had started with the intention of saying something else. "And how is Mrs. Wiernick?"

"Oh, she's very brave about it. She made me tell her all about the accident, and who came to help." Flora stopped; she had a handkerchief in her hands and was twisting it nervously. "Sir Abercrombie," she went on suddenly, "that letter—the one we found in Professor Wiernick's pocket. I'm—I'm frightened about it."

"Can you tell me why you are frightened, Miss Massey?"

His deep tones were as soothing and reassuring as he could make them. The girl drew in her breath, came a step closer, glanced at the shadowy passages and the stairs before whispering her reply.

"Because my uncle—Donald Ferguson—has had letters exactly like it."

Chapter VIII

Bedroom Scenes

Sir Abercrombie's hand went to his chin and his small eyes sparkled. The dim light at the stairhead showed him little of Flora Massey's face, but he could see that she was watching him with anxious expectation. Above the subdued babel of talk that came from the hall below there sounded Major Kemp's voice announcing that he was going to turn in.

"Miss Massey," he said rapidly, "this is no place for the exchange of confidences. Will you come to my room? Mr. Grimmett is there to chaperon us."

"All right," Flora whispered.

The actor-manager led the way along the passage and took the precaution of a preliminary look into the bedroom. Grimmett, who had taken off his coat, hastily put it on again at Lewker's command. Flora was hustled gently but swiftly into the room and the door closed behind her. Lewker fetched the most comfortable of the three available chairs, a rather creaky basket-chair, and set it before the electric fire with two bedroom chairs on either side of it.

"Miss Massey has something to tell us," he said to Grimmett, "which bears upon our little problem, Grimm."

The inspector flashed a wary glance at him. "Problem, Sir Ab?"

"The anonymous letters," nodded Lewker.

"Oh!" Flora paused in the act of sitting down. "There've been others, then?"

"There has been at least one other that you do not know of. I think, Grimm, that we should tell Miss Massey of that."

Sir Abercrombie made this decision as he watched the girl sink down, a little wearily, into the chair. Hitherto he had not given his critical attention to the young woman who seemed to have engaged the rival affections of Peter Lumley and Dr. Richard Paton; her dark, high-colored prettiness and youthful plumpness of figure was not likely to impress a man who would always consider Ellen Terry the ideal of feminine beauty. Now, however, he perceived character and charm in Flora's firmly molded face with its big dark-gray eyes and broad brow. It was a charm that would not project itself a hundred feet beyond the footlights (as Eve Wiernick's would have done) but was evident at closer quarters; and a character that betrayed its firmness and patience in the set of lips and chin.

"Very shortly after Mr. Grimmett and myself arrived here yesterday evening, Miss Massey," he went on, "Mark Stonor brought to us a letter which was similar to the one found by you and Dr. Paton in Professor Wiernick's pocket. He told us it had been found on the seat of his car an hour after his own arrival, and declared that he had no knowledge of what it meant or of who might have sent it." He glanced at Grimmett who was frowning dubiously and tugging at his mustache. "I am being perfectly frank with you, Miss Massey, in the hope that you will reciprocate. Mr. Stonor happened to know that Grimm here is a detective-inspector and that I have done a little criminal investigation in my time. We undertook to try to find out the writer of his letter. The more detailed the information you can give us, the more likely we are to succeed."

Flora, who had sat up with a jerk at the mention of Stonor's letter, looked from Sir Abercrombie to the inspector. There was something very like relief in her expression.

"I dare say it's unsympathetic of me," she said, "but I'm glad someone else had one of those letters. You see, if Professor Wiernick had one before he died, and Uncle too—"

She stopped suddenly. Sir Abercrombie sat down beside her and motioned Grimmett to the other chair.

"Just so," he said understandingly. "A threat followed by a death. You would be anxious about your uncle. But, Miss Massey, the letter may have been quite unconnected with Wiernick's death. Have you any reason to think the professor's fall was other than an accident?"

"I don't really see how it can have been anything else. It was just that finding the letter afterwards was—odd and frightening."

"Yes. Knowing what you already knew—that your uncle had received similar letters."

"Has Mr. Ferguson received a letter like that since he got here?" demanded Grimmett penetratingly.

Flora glanced swiftly at him. "He's received two. But perhaps I'd better begin at the beginning. Uncle Donald's not married and I keep house for him and act as his secretary. He has a lot of correspondence and so on in connection with his youth center scheme—you know about that?"

"Of course," said Lewker; Grimmett nodded.

"Well, I usually open the letters. One morning—it was the first week in December but I forget the date—the first of these anonymous letters came. As far as I can remember, it was exactly the same as the one we found in the professor's pocket. At any rate, the wording—the threat and all that—was definitely the same. When I showed it to Uncle Donald he was very worried at first, I think, but after a bit he laughed and said some silly gowk was playing a joke on him. He made me promise not to say anything about it to anyone. I'm breaking that promise now, because I'm scared on his account. I do hope I'm doing the right thing."

Her hand lay on the arm of the chair and Sir Abercrombie patted it reassuringly.

"In my opinion, Miss Massey, you are," he boomed.

The girl smiled faintly at him. "Thank you. And—would you mind calling me Flora? 'Miss Massey' always sounds so comic."

"I will do so, and with gratification."

Grimmett leaned forward. "Did Mr. Ferguson keep this letter, now?"

"No—he burned it, I think. And he told me to hand over any others, if they came, without opening them. It was in the kind of cheap envelope they call buff manila and the address was printed in capitals with a biro pencil."

"Postmark?" frowned the inspector.

"I'm afraid I didn't look at that. I suppose it was awfully careless of me."

"And there were other letters, Miss—um—Miss Flora?"

"There were two more, and I didn't look at the postmarks of those either, Mr.—do I call you inspector?"

"I'd rather you didn't," Grimmett said with a reproachful look at Sir Abercrombie. "I'm supposed to be on holiday. Can you recall what dates these other letters arrived on, Miss Flora?"

Flora considered for a moment, a finger at her lips. "The second one," she said, "came just before Christmas—about the twenty-first of December. The third was on the thirteenth of this month. Those are the ones that came to our London address by post. The letters that came here weren't posted—that was what made it so horrible."

"Horrible?" repeated Grimmett.

"Yes—knowing the person must be here, at Pen-y-Pass. Because the first letter was left in Uncle's car, after we got here yesterday."

The inspector's mustache rustled like a grove in a stiff breeze, and he shot a meaning glance at Sir Abercrombie. The actor-manager did not see it, for he was sitting with his eyelids lowered and his hands clasped on his ample paunch looking like a lounge-suited Buddha endeavouring to contemplate his own navel.

"About what time would that be?" Grimmett asked.

"It must have been put there some time after six," said Flora. "We got here quite early—before five, anyway—and put the car in one of those barns. Uncle just takes the ignition key and doesn't bother to lock it. We had tea and he went out to the car about six to fetch his suitcase, and if it had been there then he'd have seen it. I popped out later on—it was a quarter to seven or thereabouts—to get a powder-compact I'd left in the dashboard shelf. There was an envelope on the driving-seat."

"An envelope," Grimmett echoed, frowning; Sir Abercrombie unclasped his hands and looked up.

"One like the others, with 'Donald Ferguson' on it in biro capitals. I took it to Uncle. I didn't like to worry him, but he had to know, didn't he? He just said I was to forget it and stuck it in his pocket. That was one." Flora shivered. "The other was—nastier, somehow. Sort of creepy."

"Just a minute before you go on, Miss Flora," put in the inspector. "Does Mr. Ferguson know about the letter in Wiernick's pocket?"

Flora shook her head. "I didn't tell him. It'd only worry him more, and it was all dreadful enough already about—about the body."

Her involuntary shudder was quickly controlled. The actor-manager patted her hand again.

"We are adding a burden to the load you have borne very bravely for nearly twelve hours," he said gently. "Would you prefer to stop now, and tell us the rest tomorrow?"

"No," she said at once. "I want to tell you the whole shoot. Then perhaps I'll sleep tonight. After that meeting they had before dinner Uncle came up to my room to see if I had his handkerchiefs—they'd been packed in my case. Actually, I'd put them in a drawer of the dressing-table in his bedroom, so I went in there with him to show him. There was a buff manila envelope—just like all the others—on the corner of the dressing-table."

"The bedroom door had been left unlocked?" Grimmett questioned sharply.

"No one locks their doors here," Flora answered. "There aren't any keys anyway. Well—Uncle Donald stood absolutely rigid when he saw the envelope, and then he grabbed it and ripped it open. He didn't let me see the message inside, but I asked if it was the same as the rest and he just nodded and stuck it in his pocket. His back was towards me and I couldn't see his face. I'm sure he was very worried, though. After a bit he turned round and said 'Well, we needn't worry now, lassie, it's one of the men here having a wee bit of fun'."

"You, however, do not believe that," said Sir Abercrombie. "Nor do you believe that your uncle believed it."

"No," she said firmly.

The inspector crossed his knees and folded his arms with an air of concentration.

"This letter, then," he said, "must have been put on the dressing-table between the time Mr. Ferguson was last in his bedroom and six-forty-five, if you see what I mean."

Flora nodded. "He was in there just before the meeting, about ten to six, it'd be. He'd certainly have spotted it if it was there then. So it came between five-fifty and six-forty-five. But there's something else, Mr. Grimmett. My bedroom's next to his and they're both at the back of the hotel. There's a messy sort of yard there and an outhouse roof under our windows. No one seems to go there and it's all out of sight of the kitchens—and Uncle Donald always has his window open. The dressing-table's bang up against the window. So—"

"So it could still be an outsider, Sir Ab!" Grimmett exclaimed.

The actor-manager frowned reprovingly at him behind the girl's back.

"Reverting to the first anonymous letter your uncle received in London, Flora," he said, "the unknown writer—if, as you say, the Wiernick letter was similar—used the words 'If you persist in taking the job'. Applying the words to Donald Ferguson, can you suggest what job that might be?"

Flora hesitated. "Well," she said slowly, "there was a job sort of mooted—still is, I suppose. The idea was he might be director of youth centers for England and Wales. I thought that might be it, and some jealous person was getting at him about it. But now, of course, it's different. You can't apply that to Professor Wiernick and Mr. Stonor."

"You have no other theory about the meaning of the letter? There is mention of the person addressed thinking he had 'got away with it' and that 'it' was catching up with him. That conveys nothing to you?"

"Absolutely nothing." She glanced at her wristwatch. "In fact, I don't think there's anything else I can tell you—and I ought to be going. Uncle Donald will be looking for me. You won't tell him I told you all this, will you?"

"It may be very necessary to question him about the letters eventually," Lewker warned her gravely.

"But not tonight, at least?"

"Not tonight, certainly."

Sir Abercrombie rose to his feet and Flora did likewise. The inspector raised a delaying hand as he got up.

"There's just one thing I'd like to ask, Miss Flora," he said determinedly, "if it won't upset you."

She smiled wryly at him. "I don't think anything could upset me now, Mr. Grimmett. Ask away, please."

"It's about what Professor Wiernick shouted as he fell off the climb—sorry to remind you of it. Sir Abercrombie says you told him it sounded like a name—Jack."

He was going on, but the girl interrupted him quickly.

"I said Jack because that was the nearest I could get to it. Uncle Donald didn't hear anything like a word, you know—I expect that was because I was off to one side and he was tucked underneath a chunk of rock. The sound was a sort of angry screech. Almost as if someone had done something silly and he—the professor—was yelling a furious command at him." She put a hand to her eyes and then dropped it swiftly as though ashamed of the gesture. "I really must go now."

She went towards the door. Lewker was standing immobile, his lips pursed and his pouchy face screwed into a weird grimace. From this curious immobility he started just in time to reach the door before Flora.

"I, too, have a last question, Flora," he said with his hand on the door-handle. "It is a very personal one and you will have a right to resent it. Are you very friendly with Peter Lumley?"

The girl looked swiftly at him and away again. The color had deepened on her cheeks and she was frowning, but after a moment her lips twitched slightly and she turned to regard him with a frank smile.

"I don't resent it," she said softly. "Peter doesn't hide his feelings, does he? I—I like him awfully."

"Thank you," said Sir Abercrombie gravely. "Sleep day out of countenance, my dear, if you will. Leave us to find this anonymous nuisance."

He closed the door behind her and returned, scowling reflectively, to the inspector, who was watching him open-mouthed.

" 'Yelling a furious command at him?' " he repeated interrogatively to himself.

"Gets us nowhere," said Grimmett irritably. "Unless he meant to say 'Jack, drop that rock.' But what was the point of asking her how she felt about young Lumley?"

"I like Miss Flora Massey," Lewker returned absently, sitting down in the basket-chair. "You were talking to Lumley just now, were you not?"

"I was." Grimmett sat down with an air of defiance. "And I got a fact or two. He and Jones-Griffith did their guiding stuff for these cadets and got them over that Bwlch place on Lliwedd—"

"Bwlch-y-Saethau?"

"Yes—at eight or just before. Then they linked up with Kemp, who'd been following to see all was well, and went on down into that valley the other side to watch the cadets carry on. About nine o'clock they turned back, but Jones-Griffith, who lives in a cottage in Nant Gwynant, left them to go straight down to his place—so he said."

"He might well do that, Grimm. If they went nearly to Bwlch Cwm-y-Llan, where—you recall—there was to be a mock ambush by Welsh guerrillas, Jones-Griffith would have a mere three miles, all downhill, to walk into Nant Gwynant."

"All right, sir. But we first heard the whistle at five to eleven, and if I've got the lay of the land right Jones-Griffith could have got up the backside of Lliwedd and had ample time to do the dirty on the professor."

"He could indeed. But what of Lumley and Kemp?"

"Wait a bit, Sir Ab." The inspector's blue eyes were glinting. "The letters in the cars—Jones-Griffith could have put them there. And look at this last anonymous letter, the one left on Mr. Ferguson's dressing-table. It's clear someone could have climbed up from outside and put it there, and that'd be between ten to six and quarter to seven. It was six o'clock, near enough, when you saw Jones-Griffith in the hall and he went out with the major to the shed. What's to prevent him hanging about for twenty minutes afterwards and sneaking round the back to deposit that letter? And his name's Jack, remember."

Lewker nodded. "I concede the possibility, Grimm. But I would like to hear what more you extracted from Peter Lumley in compensation for exciting his suspicion that the accident on Slanting Buttress was, as he put it, rum."

"Dunno about exciting suspicion, sir. I reckon he thought it was rum before I got talking to him. Anyhow, according to him the major pushed off soon after Jones-Griffith, saying he'd like to work his way round the east end of Lliwedd instead of going back over the Bwlch, the way they'd come. Lumley says he didn't go with the major because he'd told Miss Massey he'd look out for her at the top of her climb."

"That, again, is very likely."

"Yes—but look." Grimmett held up a finger. "When they parted it'd be a bit after nine. Kemp had bags of time to double back and be above Slanting Buttress well before ten-fifty-five. As for Lumley, I've had a look at your map and there's a track up to the Bwlch on Lliwedd from the valley where they were, and a chap like Lumley could've covered the distance in half an hour or less. Yet he doesn't appear on the scene, climbing down to Ferguson and Co., until after twelve o'clock—nearly three hours later. What did he do in between?"

Sir Abercrombie, who had been frowning rather sleepily at the fire, sat up and felt in his pocket for his pipe.

"There, Grimm," he boomed, "you have me, as they say. But to swell your rising sea of possible Wiernick-slayers, let me draw your attention to a rather odd coincidence, if coincidence it is. You may recall the Patons *père et fils* mentioning that Wiernick and Hibberd took part in a Himalayan expedition in 1954."

"I remember," Grimmett frowned. "They had a bust-up over something—the professor insulted a god in one of the villages, something like that."

"Just so. The name of the village was Khamche. At dinner this evening Major Kemp informed me that the Nepalese cadet among his trainees—a somewhat unpredictable youth by name Galu Regmi—hails from a village named Khamche in the Himalaya."

"*Eh?* Not the old green-eye-of-little-yellow-god yarn?" The inspector buried his face in his hands and groaned. "I know—the god has to be propitiated. Galu Whatsit is the chosen instrument. He gets drafted to Shorehurst, hypnotizes the major into rigging this show when the professor'll be up here, and bumps him off." He dropped his hands. "No, no, Sir Ab—you'll have to do better than that. How'd the boy get away from the others without their seeing him, anyway?"

"There is excellent cover in the valley for a born hillman. And Kemp tells me that Galu Regmi can cover rough country like a greyhound."

Grimmett waved Galu Regmi aside with a violent gesture.

"Let's get on to these anonymous letters," he said in a fretful tone very different from his usual amiability. "I'm fed up with them so I am, but they're the likeliest lead we've got so far."

The match between Sir Abercrombie's fingers winked in rhythmic flames as he lit his pipe and then died suddenly in futile smoke beneath his blown breath.

"Grimm," he said between puffs, "it grows late. You are tired and I am tired. This my last pipe of the day shall be our hourglass, and since it

contains but a half-pipe of Sweet Briar we have little more than ten minutes for further discussion. Pray begin."

"All right, then, Sir Ab." Grimmett drew a deep breath and seemed to
blow away his temporary irritability. "I'll try and summarize what we've
got about these letters. All of 'em were sent by the same person—that's a
practical certainty, anyway. They were received by three people—Mark
Stonor, Julius Wiernick, and Donald Ferguson. We know Ferguson got
five, three in London by post and two here delivered by hand, so to speak.
They began arriving in the first week of December last year."

"Pray note that date, Grimm," murmured the actor-manager.

The inspector glanced sharply at him but made no comment. "We don't
know how many letters Wiernick received," he went on, taking his table
name-card from his pocket, "but the one we've got was typed in this
hotel. I've checked the two t's on this card and they've got the small
break in the left-hand part of the cross. Memo—Mrs. Wiernick may be
able to tell us of any previous letters received by her husband. The letter
Stonor gave us was also typed in this hotel. It was left in his car and
Ferguson's last-but-one letter was delivered the same way. Stonor says
he's had no other letters, but my own idea is he was lying—and I reckon
you think the same, sir."

"I think the president was not being at all straightforward with us,"
said Sir Abercrombie carefully.

"He knew what the letter meant and who it was from?"

"That is what I think, Grimm."

"You didn't say so when we were discussing it afterwards," grumbled
the inspector.

"At that time I did not think so. I still do not know for certain. But the
conclusion I have drawn is logically sound only if Mark Stonor was perfectly aware of the meaning of the letters and the identity of their sender."

"Then you've got a theory, Sir Ab." Grimmett sat forward in his chair
and fixed an accusing gaze on the actor-manager. "Let's have it, now, or
I won't sleep tonight."

Lewker hesitated, drawing thoughtfully at his pipe. Then he shook his
head resolutely.

"No, Grimm. It is too rash, too unadvis'd, too sudden. It is not even a
theory, being merely an explanation that fits some of our facts. And even
if it were the correct explanation, it would still leave the greater problem
unsolved."

"Is it good enough for us to put it to Stonor?" Grimmett demanded.
"We can come the official over him and have it out—we've got to have it

out now. Ferguson's got the wind up and I don't blame him. Miss Massey's scared. If Stonor knows what it's all about he'll have to tell us or we'll make it a police inquiry."

Sir Abercrombie considered behind a cloud of smoke. "Very well," he said at last reluctantly. "We will tackle the president tomorrow. We will also ask young Mr. Lumley to answer a few questions." He frowned into the thinning wreaths of tobacco smoke. "I wonder if Peter is very like his dead father in appearance."

"Why?" snapped the inspector. "Another theory? Of the murder this time?"

"At best, Grimm, I may only call it the ghost of a theory. And since I cannot believe in it myself I shall not ask you to do so. Instead, and with these last smoldering grains of the Indian weed for warrant, I will finish your consideration of the anonymous letters."

He sucked hard at his pipe, which was nearly out, and succeeded in reviving it. Grimmett, who knew his man, pricked up his ears almost visibly.

"We waste time chewing—in the Shakespearean phrase—the food of sweet and bitter fancy," began Lewker ponderously. "I will be brief. First, the letters. Three men receive them, yet the wording can surely have point for one recipient only. That is curious. Next, the recipients. How do they behave? Ferguson destroys them and bids his niece keep silence about them. Stonor brings one letter to us, for no apparent reason except to call our attention to it."

"If he knew who wrote it and what it was about, that's curious, too," Grimmett put in.

"Perhaps. Pray do not interrupt, laddie. Julius Wiernick, who presumably received his letter here at Pen-y-Pass, screws it into a ball and keeps it in his anorak pocket. To my mind that also is curious. Now consider the whole. These three men are linked by the receipt of similar anonymous letters. We look for a further link, and what do we find? That in their youth they did a good deal of climbing together, especially in the Alps. I overheard George Sheldrake talking to Ferguson in the hall after dinner. He spoke"—the actor-manager's voice took on the very tones of Sheldrake's—"of 'the great days of the thirties, when you and Wiernick, Stonor and poor Jack Lumley, climbed together for three Alpine seasons running.' "

" 'Poor Jack Lumley,' " repeated Grimmett, staring at him. "That'd be Peter's father. He's dead. Poor *Jack* Lumley! By gum, sir—"

"Just so, Grimm." Sir Abercrombie got up abruptly. "My pipe is out, I

have never liked ghost stories, and it is within two minutes of eleven
o'clock. Not one word more, unless it be—good night!"

Inspector Grimmett knew better than to contravene an order issued in
iambic pentameter. He was also physically tired. He performed his turn-
ing-in routine in what may have been record time for him, and his methodical procedure made him a mere thirty seconds later than his less
careful friend in clambering between the sheets. He did not lie awake for
long; but his last reflections, somewhere between thoughts and dreams,
concerned the ghost of a long-dead mountaineer that prowled in broad
daylight on the snow-rimmed crags of Lliwedd.

As for Sir Abercrombie Lewker, his precious gift of falling instantly
asleep when he wished to do so did not fail him, nor was he troubled by
dreams. When he woke he expected to find that it was eight in the morning, or later, but his watch told him it was five minutes to seven. Somewhere outside the soft *thud-thud-thud* of a four-stroke motorcycle engine sounded for a few moments and stopped; doubtless it was the arrival of the motorcyclist that had awakened him. The front door of the
hotel creaked open and was shut. Footsteps sounded below his window,
moving away, and a murmur of men's voices. He remembered the arrangements for the second day of Major Kemp's officer-cadet exercise;
Jones-Griffith had come up from Nant Gwynant and Kemp and Lumley
had gone out to join him. There came very faintly the sound of another
door being opened—that would be the door of the corrugated-iron shed
on the car park, whence Lumley and Jones-Griffith would be issued with
rifles and blank ammunition for their mock guerrilla ambush on Bwlch-
y-Saethau. A pause, the footsteps of one man coming back to the hotel,
the front door opening, short pause, door closing, footsteps going away:
the major had hung the key of the shed in its place again. The actor-
manager, lying snug and comfortable in his bed, listened for the sound of
three pairs of boots trudging up the track leading to Llydaw and Bwlch-
y-Saethau, but he heard nothing. A little odd, he decided sleepily, and
prepared to drop off for another hour's sleep. It was not to be.

Almost at once the gurgling of the washbasin in the adjoining bedroom—Stonor's—apprised him that the indefatigable president was rising at his usual hour. More wakeful now, he amused himself by deduc-
ing the stages of Mark Stonor's dressing from the faint noises that followed, noting a smothered grunt now and again that seemed to indicate
that Stonor was finding his joints stiff and aching from yesterday's exertion—understandable enough when one considered that he must be over
sixty and had covered the distance from the foot of Slanting Buttress to

Pen-y-Pass at top speed. Sir Abercrombie's own leg muscles, when he stretched them under the bedclothes, were not devoid of stiffness. He reflected philosophically that twenty years ago he would have thought it excellent fun to get up in the dark of a January morning and carry a rifle up to Bwlch-y-Saethau; of that, at least, age had relieved him.

The sound of the door of the next room opening returned his thoughts to Mark Stonor. The morning seemed abnormally dark; Stonor's constitutional would have to be along a track if he wished to avoid breaking his leg on a boulder. He was more wakeful now, and on an impulse got out of bed and went to the window, without switching on a light to disturb Grimmett. When he pushed open the casement and put out his head the familiar smell of mountain mist came at once to his nostrils, and he knew why the outside noises had seemed muffled and why he had heard no footsteps on the Llydaw track. Mist filled the darkness of the morning and sprang into local visibility below him as the light in the hall was switched on and the windows irradiated the mist with a blur of brightness. The air was mild, though clammy, which probably meant the passing of the snow—and of those footprints above Slanting Buttress.

The hall light went out and the front door opened and closed. He could just discern the gaunt figure of the president below him. Stonor paused outside the porch for nearly a minute, evidently allowing his eyes to become accustomed to the half-darkness. Lewker opened his mouth to bid him good morning and then closed it again without making the greeting; after breakfast Stonor was going to be treated with some severity, to make him divulge the whole truth about the anonymous letters, and though Lewker himself was doubtful whether the treatment would produce results he considered it better not to begin the day with friendly salutations.

Stonor coughed and started out across the road towards the Llydaw track. The mist swallowed him up before he had gone half a dozen paces from the inn. Sir Abercrombie left the window half an inch open and got hurriedly back into bed, where in spite of his expectations he dropped off to sleep again and did not wake until a quarter past eight.

The mist, he observed as he sat up and threw off the blankets, was as thick as ever, though it was now milk-white in the growing daylight. The stone wall across the road was a wall's ghost, and the shed on the car park, fifty or sixty yards distant, was completely invisible.

"Morning, Sir Ab." Grimmett's face emerging from the folds of a towel was like a red sun beaming through the clouds. "Slept well, seemingly. You look as if you'd solved our problem in your sleep."

"But I have not, Grimm."

Sir Abercrombie sprang incautiously out of bed and groaned as his stiffened limbs took the strain.

"I need a third leg this morning," he declared, supporting himself by the bedpost. "And that," he added reflectively, "is what we need for our solution. Two legs we have, albeit creaky ones—the anonymous letters and Wiernick's death. With a third leg, Grimm, I fancy the problem would stand up and explain itself."

Chapter IX

The Third Leg

It was not until Sir Abercrombie came down the stairs into a deserted hall, where an energetic Welshwoman was sweeping and dusting, that he remembered that it was Sunday morning and there would be no breakfast until nine o'clock. He was hungry. For that very reason he had hastened his washing and dressing, and there was now half an hour to wait before the oldest enemy of man could be defeated with porridge and coffee.

"*Bore da*," he boomed gloomily to the maid, who returned his greeting with tolerant good humor; visiting Saxons who thought they could speak Welsh were no strangers to her.

Sir Abercrombie went upstairs again and, encountering Grimmett as the inspector was emerging from the bedroom, broke the bad news to him.

"I suggest we emulate the presidential promenade, Grimm," he added. "It will unstiffen our limbs and stimulate those little gray cells of which a distinguished amateur in your line of business is so fond."

Grimmett readily agreed. "Give us an appetite, too," he remarked.

"Thus, in the words of melancholy Jacques, giving its sum of more to that which had too much," said Lewker sadly. "But we must remember, after all, that there are unfortunates in the world who have never known what it is to be hungry."

They put on windproofs and went out into the wet-cotton-wool opacity of the morning. The road past the inn ran steeply downhill in both directions, and a morning milk-lorry could be dangerous on such a day. Sir Abercrombie therefore chose the Llydaw track, known as the Pony Track since the days when tourists ascended Snowdon *à cheval*.

"Stonor went this way," he remarked as they crossed the stony level of the car park. "We may encounter him returning. If so, Grimm, no mention of our investigations unless Mark himself opens the subject."

"Right, Sir Ab."

They trudged on in silence for a few moments. The wall of mist moved with them, revealing a few yards of track in front and behind, a vignette of rocks and grass slanting up on their right, a turfy edge on the left with blank whiteness below it. Grimmett, whose thoughts were busy with certain aspects of Wiernick's death, hesitated to begin a discussion; his companion, he knew, deplored serious conversation before breakfast.

"Mr. Stonor seems fond of walking about on his own," he ventured at length. "In the circumstances that's queer, so it is."

"Circumstances, Grimm?" Sir Abercrombie's thoughts had been elsewhere. "Ah, yes—the threat in the anonymous letter."

"That's it. You said yourself it was queer, him going off by himself yesterday and giving anyone a chance that wanted to deal with him quiet-like. And now look at him—out in a thick mist."

"Mist may hide the hunted as well as the hunter, Grimm. And do you know, I hardly think Mark Stonor is in any danger from the person who typed that letter."

"No, Sir Ab?"

The inspector looked hopefully at the actor-manager, but he was vouchsafed no explanation and stumbled over a large stone.

"There's one thing occurred to me," he went on, watching his footing more carefully, "and that's the time Mr. Stonor took yesterday to get to where we saw him coming up from the lake. He started out from the hotel at twenty past nine, near enough. It was half past eleven when we spotted him, and he was then—I've been looking at your map again—just about two miles from Pen-y-Pass. He was supposed to be walking up to Glaslyn, according to what he said, and two hours to go two miles is a mighty large allowance for a man who did it in under the hour from the foot of Slanting Buttress."

"I wonder." Lewker's remark seemed to appertain to his own thoughts rather than to Grimmett's words. "Stonor? He could very well have taken that long. He travels the fastest who travels alone—but that proverb is seldom applicable to middle-aged mountaineers. You pause here to contemplate a waterfall, there to examine a charming arrangement of moss in a cranny. With a companion you would walk past the little lake in the hollow below the track, but alone you make a detour to look at it." He looked at his watch. "On for another five minutes, Grimm. We should then reenter the Pen-y-Pass portals as the porridge—ah, the porridge!—receives its final stir."

The track had been rising and bending to the left. It now leveled out and swung in the other direction. The mist was as thick as ever, and they heard the tread of nailed boots before they saw the figure walking towards them.

"Here's Mr. Stonor coming back," Grimmett said, and was proved wrong a second later.

"Good morning, Thripp," said Sir Abercrombie, halting.

George Thripp stopped with something of a jolt and pushed back the hood of his windproof. He had been walking with his head sunk forward in seeming meditation and had not noticed their approach until Lewker had spoken.

"Good morning, Lewker—good morning, Mr. Grimmett," he said punctiliously, and took off his glasses to peer at them. "Very thick, very thick indeed. Did you hear the shooting?"

Lewker shook his head. Grimmett stared, and then remembered Kemp's military exercise and the 'guerrillas' on Bwlch-y-Saethau.

"Kemp's cadets, I suppose," Thripp went on mournfully. "I got as far as Llyn Teyrn and was turning back when I heard a gunshot. Spoiling the mountain solitudes—pity, great pity. The president felt strongly about it. He had Kemp on the carpet yesterday for fixing his maneuvers on the same date as the dinner meet. He doesn't like Kemp, I'm afraid."

Lewker and Grimmett had turned and the three were walking back together. Thripp wiped his glasses with a handkerchief and put them on.

"These things are a nuisance in a mist," he said. "A great nuisance. They will keep clouding over."

Grimmett said he had heard it was a good thing to smear a slice of potato over the lenses, but he'd never tried it.

"I believe Jack Lumley used to do that with his snow-goggles," said Thripp. "You never met him, I think, Lewker. A big man, excellent on ice and an Original Member. Killed on the Matterhorn when he was only twenty-eight. A great loss to the club, a great loss."

"I never met Lumley, as you say," Sir Abercrombie's tone did not reveal his satisfaction at being given this opening. "Peter Lumley is his son, of course. Does he resemble his father?"

"Oh, very much, very much. Peter is now the same age as Jack was when he died, though he looks younger than that." Thripp sighed. "A very nice fellow, Jack Lumley, very nice indeed."

"Peter, then, was only one year old when his father died?"

"That would be so, yes. Mrs. Lumley—Jack's wife—died three years ago. Charming woman, quite charming. She was a member."

"And Jack Lumley, I believe, used to climb a great deal with Mark Stonor and Ferguson."

Thripp stubbed his boot against a projecting stone and dropped a pace behind.

"That is so, yes," he agreed, catching up again. "And with poor Wiernick. They used to be called The Quartet, I remember, and prided themselves on their speed. Sheldrake once said they were a quartet with two movements, *allegro* and *presto*."

The actor-manager chuckled politely. "In Alpine climbing, Grimm," he explained, "time is a most important factor, especially when the weather is unsettled. To climb fast becomes as essential to the safety of a party as to climb skilfully and carefully."

"Very true, very true," Thripp agreed. "And they were safe climbers, all four of them. Lumley especially. We saw little of him at our Welsh meets—Alpine climbing was his *forte*—but Donald Ferguson, of course, was always at Pen-y-Pass in those days. He was based in Liverpool then and was conveniently placed." He sighed and took off his glasses to wipe the mist from them. "And now two of the four are gone—both killed in climbing accidents of—I may say—an unexpected character."

"Unexpected?" Grimmett repeated interrogatively.

"Knowing the men concerned, unexpected, Mr. Grimmett. Julius Wiernick was, in his youth, the finest rock-climber I have ever seen. He still retained his skill in late middle-age. I would never have expected him to fall when leading—but then, of course, a loose hold or a falling stone may undo the best of us. The best of us."

"And Lumley?" queried Sir Abercrombie with the air of keeping a moderately interesting conversation going.

"Again unexpected, Lewker. Yes." Thripp replaced his glasses and trod more confidently down the stone-littered track. "He was killed on a traverse of the Matterhorn. I was secretary to the club at the time, and I well remember being stunned, positively stunned, by the brief report Wiernick gave us of the accident. It seems the party were descending to Zermatt in a snowstorm and Lumley, who was descending last, insisted on detaching himself from the rope on the Shoulder. Now that was very unlike Lumley, who was always a stickler for proper rope usage."

"Perhaps he wanted to—um—pump ship," ventured Grimmett.

Thripp peered at him reproachfully. "In a snowstorm at fourteen thousand feet that call of Nature does not normally arise. In any case, a climber would not untie from the rope. However, it appears Lumley would not listen to argument—he could be extremely stubborn—and declared he would rather descend solo at his own pace. The others went on, assuming that he was following. When they reached the Belvedere he did not arrive, but the weather by now had worsened so that they could not go back to look for him. In the morning they went up with a search party and found no trace of him. Obviously he had slipped and fallen."

Thripp's rather stilted utterance could not detract from the plain tragedy of the story. They walked on in silence for a few paces. Out of the mist ahead and below there came the intermittent roar of engines, suggesting that cars or lorries were maneuvering on the car park, but though the hotel must now be only two or three hundred yards away the walkers on the falling track might have been in some other parish of the infinite, hemmed in as they were by the walls of mist.

"Did they not recover Lumley's body?" Lewker asked; he spoke casually, but the inspector was aware of urgency behind the question.

"Not at that time," replied Thripp. "It was thought he would have fallen on to the Matterhorn Glacier, on the west, but a search party two days later found nothing." He hesitated. "The sequel, if it is a sequel, is a little—um—gruesome. Last spring the Furggen Glacier, which as you know falls steeply on the eastern side of the Zermatt ridge, gave up the body of an unidentified man. It might just possibly have been poor Lumley, you know."

"May I ask how you learned of this, Thripp?"

Again Thripp hesitated. "In point of fact," he said at last with apparent reluctance, "it was brought to my notice by Peter Lumley. Peter is a member of the Club Alpin Suisse and receives a monthly magazine published in Geneva, and it seems there was brief mention in the magazine of the discovery. He wrote to me asking what I thought about it. I told him what little I knew about the matter and suggested he might contact the president about it."

"Do you know whether he did so?"

"I don't know—no."

George Thripp's flow of reminiscence seemed to dry up rather suddenly. Sir Abercrombie speculated aloud.

"There have been cases of bodies, recovered from crevasses after an interval of thirty or forty years, being identifiable because of their preservation in intense cold. It is conceivable that it might be so in this case."

"Possibly, possibly. But I gathered that the body in question had not been so preserved. According to Lumley's magazine, moreover, there were injuries that rendered identification of the features impossible. Not, Lewker, a pleasant before-breakfast subject." Thripp peered into the whiteness in front. "However, I believe I see the car-park shed. Breakfast will be welcome, very welcome."

The square shape of the corrugated-iron hut loomed on their right. Just beyond it two big lorries of the hooded military sort were drawn up side by side, and their drivers, who were smoking cigarettes and stamping their feet in the lee of the shed, nodded good morning to the three as they crossed the car park towards the still invisible hotel.

"Kemp's young soldiers should be down shortly, I believe," said Thripp. "And there goes the breakfast gong. We've timed it very nicely, Lewker, very nicely. Good morning, Miss Massey. I hope you were able to sleep?"

Flora was standing in the porch, grave and rather pale. Her glance at Sir Abercrombie as she replied to Thripp's greeting was significant, and he lingered while the others went in through the inner door.

"I wanted to see you," she said at once in a low voice. "I've told Uncle Donald the whole thing—what we talked about last night."

"The letters?"

Flora nodded. "I couldn't sleep. I went to Uncle Donald's room and told him about the one we found and what you told me as well."

"It is just as well," said Lewker reflectively. "How did your uncle take it, may I ask?"

"He was angry first of all because I'd not kept my promise to him. Then he went sort of relieved and anxious both at once, if you can understand that. He said he'd like to have a word with you this morning. And then—"

"Yes?" said Lewker as she stopped.

"Then he kissed me," said Flora slowly. "He doesn't usually. He hasn't done it for years."

"Then you may be sure you have done the right thing," the actor-manager told her reassuringly. "He has something on his mind and he is doubtless grateful to you for precipitating the inevitable revelation. We must arrange a confidential talk as soon as possible after breakfast."

"He isn't down yet. He was really very tired, you know."

"Naturally." He sniffed hungrily; there was a faint but urgent aroma of porridge coming from the other side of the door. "Will you honor Grimmett and myself with your company at breakfast?"

"I think I'll wait for Uncle, thank you very much," said Flora with the ghost of a smile. "You didn't see Peter, did you? I'm just looking out for him."

Sir Abercrombie said he thought it was likely to be at least half an hour before the maneuverers returned from Bwlch-y-Saethau, and followed

Grimmett upstairs, scowling blackly. The inspector was standing in the bedroom with his anorak half off, staring fixedly at the wall.

"Look," he said the moment Lewker entered. "Was there anything queer about Lumley's death, do you reckon?"

"I have no idea, Grimm."

"Well, it could be that's the incident in the past that links the three men who had anonymous letters, couldn't it? And if that's so, it means Stonor, Ferguson and Wiernick all have something to hide about that Matterhorn accident. Now look at this, Sir Ab. Peter Lumley traversed the Matterhorn last summer—the major told you that and you told me, if you remember. Right. So Peter was at Zermatt a month or two after this unidentified body was discovered. It'd be queer if he didn't make some inquiries."

"Off with the rest of that anorak, laddie," Lewker cut in; he had removed his own and was hastily brushing his remaining hairs. "Eat first, think afterwards. One may have food for thought, but that we should ever use thought for food may all the gods forbid!"

"Yes, but just glance at it, sir." Grimmett hung up his anorak and turned with his blue eyes gleaming. "It may be speculation but it fits. Say Lumley found there'd been dirty work of some kind and wanted revenge. He writes the anonymous letters—"

"Why not confront the dirty workers with his findings?"

"There could be a reason for that. Anyway, he goes a step further—maybe brooding over it and getting a fixation. That's common enough. He's the one chap who could easily have knocked Wiernick off Slanting Buttress. He looks like his father, Mr. Thripp told us. Wiernick's yell of 'Jack!' can be explained from that."

"Jones-Griffith being now relegated to the post of understudy, I presume," said Sir Abercrombie; he grasped the inspector's arm and urged him towards the door. " 'Hark! I am call'd; my little spirit, see, Sits in a foggy cloud, and stays for me.' Porridge, Grimm, porridge!"

Grimmett allowed himself to be borne porridge-ward, but not to be silenced.

"Say what you like," he said defiantly, "but I reckon I'm on the right track. I can feel it in my bones, so I can."

"I am inclined to think you are getting warm," replied the actor-manager as they began to descend the stairs. "But on your theory, Nemesis has overtaken one of the three only." He lowered his voice. "A has gone. Are we to expect a similar end for B and C?"

The inspector looked solemn. "If something happens to B or C," he muttered back, "we can say good-bye to speculation. It'll be that third leg you were talking about, all right!"

They entered the dining room. The tables were once more separate and there were only seven people in the room besides a waitress who was distributing bowls of steaming porridge. At one table Dr. Richard Paton sat with Mrs. Hengist and the Penberthys, at another was George Thripp with Mr. and Mrs. Reid Cable. Lewker and Grimmett made for the table where they had first been seated and had hardly settled themselves before Dr. Tom Paton arrived and joined them.

"Not much pleasure going out in this muck," he remarked when they had exchanged subdued greetings. "More like a damn London fog than a proper mountain mist. You got any plans?"

Lewker replied that he and Grimmett did not propose to go far from the hotel. Dr. Tom grunted.

"Applies to most of us, probably. I'm all against hypocrisy and all that, but it doesn't seem decent to enjoy oneself with this damn business hanging over the place."

Porridge arrived and conversation lapsed. George Sheldrake and his unattractive daughter came in with Frank Hibberd and took their places. Dr. Tom, the first to finish his porridge, laid down his spoon and looked frowningly round the room.

"President not down yet?" he demanded. "That's unusual for Mark Stonor. Never knew him to be late for breakfast yet."

"He is down," said Sir Abercrombie, "in the sense that he is up. I witnessed his setting-forth for the customary morning walk at twenty minutes past seven."

"In mist and dark? That's like Stonor, anyway. The ordered life though the heavens fall. But twenty past seven"—the doctor glanced at his watch—"and it's now nearly quarter past nine. Where would he go for two hours on a morning like this?"

"He went across the road, at least," Lewker said, dodging a plate of eggs and bacon that hovered by his ear before being placed on the table before him. "It is unlikely, I should say, that he took any route other than the Pony Track, and I heard him say last night that he intended to walk to Llydaw and back."

Dr. Tom was embarking on an account of an occasion when he had lost himself in the mist on familiar ground when he checked himself in some surprise. Grimmett, who was being served with eggs and bacon, had put a question to the waitress.

"Have you see Mr. Stonor this morning, miss? Number six is his room."

"No, sir," said the girl briefly, and hurried away with a pile of empty porridge bowls.

The doctor raised his eyebrows. "The Case of the Lost President, Grimmett?" he inquired beneath his breath.

The inspector did not return his grin. "Just curious, Doctor," he said rather lamely, and attacked his eggs and bacon.

"Stonor wouldn't get lost in a mist," Dr. Tom said positively. "Let alone up the Llydaw track which he knows like his own solemn old face. Incidentally, he wouldn't get more than a couple of hundred yards beyond the end of the lake, because the causeway's under water. He wouldn't want to paddle. Well—this time I was telling you about, I'd left the damn compass behind—"

He interrupted himself again to greet Charles Kemp, who was asking if he could join them. The major was in sweater and windproof trousers and his dark jowls were unshaven.

"Seen Eve Wiernick this mornin'?" he inquired as he sat down.

The three others had not. Kemp muttered something about makin' sure she was all right after breakfast and started to deal seriously with his porridge. He seemed preoccupied and in no very good temper. Sir Abercrombie asked him if his exercise was proceeding satisfactorily.

The major shrugged. "Might be worse. The guerrilla stuff was a flop this mornin' because the lads were comin' down the Gribin by the time we got there. That was ten to eight, so they must've started out devilishly early from the other side."

"Tricky going in this mist," remarked the doctor. "It would be dark, too."

"They'd done it the day before and there's a track a good bit of the way. Incidentally, the causeway over Llydaw's under a foot of water. Lumley and Jones-Griffith and I had to off boots and roll up our breeks. Melting snow's raised the lake level, I suppose."

"There was no shooting on the Bwlch, then?" Lewker frowned.

"No. Took the rifles for a walk. Lumley and Jones-Griffith went down again. I stayed at the foot of the Gribin to collect the lads. Left 'em there havin' a ration breakfast, poor boffins." He looked at his watch. "They should be comin' in any time now. Transport's waitin'."

"Do they have to wade across the causeway?" Grimmett asked.

"No. Nor did I, comin' back. Came over Bwlch Moch, and that's what they'll do. I checked the party in as they came down the Gribin, and gave 'em the route. Hope to God they don't miss it in this brew-up of mist—there's one bod astray already."

The waitress who had just brought his plate of eggs and bacon addressed Grimmett.

"About number six, sir, Nellie took a cup of tea up at half past eight and there wasn't anyone in the bedroom. She went up a minute ago and knocked to say breakfast was on, but Mr. Stonor wasn't there again."

The inspector thanked her and she went away. The major eyed him curiously.

"What's goin' on?" he asked. "Stonor reported missin'?"

"Dunno about missing," growled Dr. Tom, "but it's a little rum. Lewker here says Stonor left for his morning walk at twenty past seven—still dark and mist damn thick—heading probably up the Pony Track. He's not been in for breakfast and it seems he's not in his room."

"Oh lord," said Kemp. "Oh well, he'll turn up, I suppose."

He attacked his food with the zest of a man who has been energetic in the open air for two and a half hours before breakfast.

"Did you say that one of your cadets was missing?" Sir Abercrombie asked.

Kemp nodded, with his mouth full.

"Yes, blasted young nuisance!" he said as soon as he could speak respectably. "It seems he pushed off on his own before it was light this mornin'. The lads say he was mad keen to get up a mountain and I'd say the odds are he's gone over Snowdon."

"This'd be the Nepalese chap, Galu Something," Grimmett said shrewdly.

"Galu Regmi it was. I'm not worryin'—yet. He can look after himself on a mountain, that type. But my God he'll find himself in the rattle when he comes down!"

"Bad day for search-parties," growled the doctor, with a side glance at Lewker.

Sir Abercrombie's attention was on the three people who had just come into the dining room. Flora Massey and her uncle were followed by Peter Lumley, whose unusually sleek red hair suggested a wetting with mist followed by a violent brushing. The effect was spoiled by his very dirty white sweater. Ferguson, sturdily grim but rather pale, nodded a general good morning; his hands had been freshly bandaged, and the bandage on his right hand, extending nearly to the fingertips, hinted that the friction-burns from the nylon rope were giving trouble. Richard Paton's pathetic failure to catch Flora's eye did not escape the actor-manager's attention.

As the three passed, the major caught Lumley's sleeve.

"Seen anythin' of the lads, Peter?" he demanded. "Or, for that matter, of Mark Stonor?"

"No," returned Peter briefly.

"You came down the track from Llydaw, didn't you?"

"Yes. Didn't see a soul, though. Mist's like a blanket. Jack got in first. He's in a shed messing with his motorbike."

Kemp lowered his voice. "See here, Peter. Galu Regmi's not with the main gang, or wasn't when I checked them in at the foot of the Gribin. Thousand to one he's all right, but you never know. Be a good feller and tell Jack to hang on for a bit, will you? Just in case we have to get a search party out. I'll be out myself in a minute and you can return your rifles to store."

Peter Lumley nodded reluctantly and went out again. He had hardly reached the door when there came to the ears of those in the room the muffled crack of a rifle-shot fired at no great distance from the hotel.

"Would that be your chaps. Major?" demanded Grimmett quickly.

Kemp jumped to his feet, his face reddening angrily.

"If it is, someone's for it!" he barked. "They've strict orders—by God I'll have his blood!"

He strode hastily from the room. Other sounds came from outside, cheerful voices and the clatter of approaching footsteps. The doctor rubbed the moisture from the panes of the window and peered out. A single youthful voice shouted "Here are the *camions*, chaps!" and there was a ragged but hilarious cheer. In the mist, which was starting to thin before a light westerly breeze, ghostly figures with packs and slung rifles could be made out moving across the car park.

"Let's hope this youngster Regmi turns up," said Dr. Tom, returning to his toast and marmalade. "This mist'll stay on the hills all morning, even if it clears down here. That time I was telling you about, you could see farther than this and I was on ground I knew backwards, but as near as damn it I walked over a precipice. It turned out I'd mistaken the—"

Again his story was interrupted, this time by George Thripp. Thripp must have gone out of the room unobserved, for he came in through the door and straight to their table.

"I overheard what you were saying about the president," he muttered, blinking worriedly at them through his glasses. "As you say, it is odd, very odd. He isn't in the hotel."

"You've been looking for him?" queried the doctor.

"Yes. You see, he makes a point of being on time for all meals. I've had a quick look—naturally I haven't looked in unlikely places—but he isn't in his room or in the bathroom or in either of the lavatories. Nor is he in the lounge. No one's seen him this morning."

"Except Lewker," Dr. Paton pointed out. "He saw Stonor starting out at twenty past seven."

"And rather carelessly assumed," added the actor-manager, "that he would have returned to the hotel before you left for your own walk, Thripp. You saw nothing of Stonor, of course?"

"Well, no, of course not," Thripp stared blankly at him. "I'd have said so when I met you, wouldn't I? I left the hotel at ten past eight or thereabouts and walked up the Pony Track for about a mile, as far as Llyn Teyrn. I turned back there, Dr., and met Lewker and Grimmett almost at once and they turned back with me. I've no idea, naturally, whether or not the president had returned to the hotel before I set out."

Donald Ferguson, who had left his table to join the group, added his voice to the discussion.

"He might well have turned off the track into Cwm Dyli and lost himself in a mist like this."

"Most unlikely—most," Thripp said positively. "I've been out this morning, Ferguson, and you haven't. I assure you it's very thick, abnormally thick. No one but a fool would have done that, and Mark Stonor isn't a fool. It was dark as well, remember, for nearly an hour after he'd started out."

"Oh, aye. I'd forgotten that. It was getting light when I woke." Ferguson rubbed his chin, frowning. "All the same, and granting Mark's no fool, he's no' been quite himself these two days. He seemed to be brooding over something, I thought." His gray eyes held significance as they briefly met Sir Abercrombie's glance. "There was a touch of melancholia in his character, and I know yesterday's tragedy knocked him over."

Tom Paton shifted impatiently on his chair. "Fuss about nothing, isn't it?" He appealed to Hibberd and Richard Paton, who had now arrived. "Stonor goes off for his usual morning walk and is late getting back, that's all. Damn it, it's only twenty to ten. Anyone looked in the sheds to see if he's there fiddling with his car?"

"I didn't look there, certainly," Thripp admitted.

He was turning away when Grimmett spoke, somewhat apologetically.

"You gentlemen know the ground better than I do, and you'll correct me if I'm wrong, but it seems to me we can rule out two possibilities. Taking it that Mr. Stonor stuck to a path or track for his morning walk, there's only two he could take. One's the track up to Llydaw. Mr. Thripp didn't go all the way to Llydaw this morning, but Mr. Lumley came down that track on his way back from the lake, and he saw nothing of Mr. Stonor. The other path's the one up to Bwlch Moch, and Major Kemp's cadets have just come back down that, if I understood him correctly. If they haven't seen him—"

"Good, good," nodded Thripp. "We can narrow down the possibilities. He wouldn't have waded across the causeway, that's pretty certain. I'll go and find Kemp and get him to ask his cadets about the other track."

He trotted away. Hibberd, tugging dubiously at his mustache, regarded the others questioningly.

"Don't want to go into a flap about this yet, do we?" he asked. "It'll only upset everyone, perhaps needlessly, and they're all upset enough as it is."

"Thripp is a bit of a fusspot," Richard Paton said. "But there's the chance that Stonor did go on the hillside and broke his leg over a boulder. One can't just let it slide."

"Give him until eleven, anyway," growled his father. "The damn mist may have cleared a bit by then, and if he's still not turned up we'll organize a search party." He rose to his feet. "I'm going to have a scout round myself. Might find one of the hotel staff who's seen him since seven."

"Right," agreed Hibberd. "If nothing's been found about him by eleven we gather in the hall and get cracking. We can rope in Kemp and Lumley for a start."

He went out with the two Patons. Ferguson lingered, tapping his fingers on the table and frowning at the empty plates.

"I'd better get this over, Lewker," he said after a moment. "Can we talk somewhere? I was hoping Stonor would be present when I said what I have to say, but perhaps it's better as it is."

"Very well," nodded Sir Abercrombie, getting up. "The hotel office should provide sufficient privacy. You will not object, I trust, if Grimmett comes with us?"

"No. But I'm hoping you'll treat what I tell you as confidential."

They went out into the hall. From the still invisible car park came the sound of Major Kemp's voice upraised in severe harangue, loudening briefly as the door opened and Thripp came in.

"The cadets didn't see him," he reported, detaining Lewker as the actor-manager was about to follow his companions into the office, "and he's not in the sheds. We wait till eleven and then organize a search party—I expect Hibberd's told you."

He bustled worriedly away. Lewker went into the little room beside the bar and closed the door after him. It was chilly in there, but Grimmett had switched on the electric fire and pulled three chairs in front of it. They all sat down. Ferguson stretched his bandaged hands to the reddening bars and began to speak at once.

"You've rather forced my hand, you and Flora between you, forbye it will be a relief to tell you, and that's a fact. I'd better say at once I've no idea where these anonymous letters came from or why they should be sent, but I've a pretty good idea what they refer to."

"An incident that occurred on the Matterhorn in 1934?" queried Sir Abercrombie gently.

Ferguson turned to look steadily at him. "Aye, you're that far, are you? How much do you know about it, Lewker?"

"Merely what Thripp told us."

"Thripp was secretary then. We sent in a cooked-up report of Lumley's death. I'm going to give you the true story now—but I want you to understand I wouldn't breathe a word of it if it wasn't for two things. One, you seem to be on the track of it anyway. Two, I'm— well, I'm scared."

"Of what, Mr. Ferguson?" asked the inspector quickly.

"I don't know. That's the devil of it, Mr. Grimmett. There's no valid reason why Wiernick and I should be receiving these anonymous letters, but I am and Wiernick was—and Wiernick's dead."

"Killed," observed Lewker, "by an accidental fall."

"I'm no' saying it wasn't," Ferguson said quickly. "It was an accident as far as I could see, and that's a fact. But Wiernick's dead just the same, and that bluidy letter was in his pocket. I don't like it one wee bit. If what I'm going to tell you helps to straighten the matter out I'll consider I'm justified in telling it."

He paused, staring at the fire. Sir Abercrombie frowned restrainingly at Grimmett, who was showing signs of impatience.

"It was our fourth Alpine season together," Ferguson began abruptly. "In the second week we traversed the Dent Blanche and then went over to Breuil to traverse the Matterhorn. We climbed in two ropes—Wiernick and myself, Stonor and Lumley. The weather broke when we were on the last bit of the Italian ridge. Stonor had been going badly and he and Lumley were well behind as Wiernick and I got to the top. There was a fearful storm on, but there was no reason to suppose the other rope would get into trouble and we went on down the Swiss ridge. The storm got worse—snow, hail, thunder—and we had to waste time in sheltering and go down at snail's pace when we could move at all. We were done in when we reached the Belvedere."

"A hut-hotel at about eleven thousand feet," put in Lewker for Grimmett's benefit.

"We waited for two hours," Ferguson went on, intent on the scenes he was reliving in the glow of the electric fire. "The storm got worse. No sign of the others. Wiernick wanted to go up and look for them, but a guide—he was one of the only two climbers at the Belvedere—restrained us almost by force. It would have been bluidy silly anyway, late in the day and in a *tourmente* of snow."

He stopped and passed his hand across his face. Outside the hotel one of the lorries started sounding its horn in short blasts, presumably inviting the missing Galu Regmi to hurry down. Ferguson's voice went on steadily against the noise.

"I'm going to cut short the rest of it. We went up the ridge again at first light next morning, when the storm was over. There were four of us. The guide and his *patron*, a little doctor from Munich named Zukmayer, made up the party. We found Stonor lying in a sheltered place above the Solvay refuge, alive. He had on Lumley's windproofs and some other clothing of his—it had just about saved him from death by exposure, Zukmayer said. We went on up and saw Lumley. He was lying on a sloping ledge well down on the side of the ridge just below the Shoulder, dead, wearing only a pair of trousers and a shirt. He couldn't have climbed down to the ledge."

Grimmett sucked in his breath with a sharp hissing sound. "But that," he began, "means he wasn't—"

"We could deduce as well as you can," Ferguson broke in harshly. "Lumley collapsed. Stonor thought he was dead. Knowing he had the thinnest chance of survival himself, he stripped the body and put on Lumley's things. But Lumley wasn't dead, you see. He must have recovered, tried to drag himself on, and fallen—"

Ferguson's utterance choked and he bowed his head on his hands for a second. Then he recovered himself.

"I'm sorry. It's a dooms miserable tale. Wiernick saw what had to be done. He told Zukmayer and the guide the report would be simply that Lumley had fallen to his death, which was true enough, and sent them down. When they'd gone I lowered him to the shelf on our rope. There was no hope of Lumley's being alive, of course. Wiernick did what the mountain would have done in a day or two—sent the body down to the Furggen Glacier. It was a sort of burial, in a way." He looked rather uncertainly at Sir Abercrombie, whose pouchy face was grave. "I still think Wiernick's decision was right. Stonor was alive and Lumley was

dead. What difference could it make to Jack if there was an inquiry and
Stonor had to go through life with the stigma of having robbed and deserted a dying companion on a mountain? We knew Stonor. We knew he
must have been convinced that Lumley was dead and that he himself
would die from exposure unless he had the extra protection of the dead
man's things—but would other people believe that?"

"You hushed it up, then," said Grimmett bluntly.

Ferguson nodded. "That's it. We hushed it up. The guide was easy to
square—I doubt he was pretty hazy about what had happened anyway.
The little doctor, Zukmayer, saw our side of it and swore to keep what
he'd seen to himself. The tale we put up for the benefit of Lumley's wife
and the club was no' verra convincing, I'm afraid, but it was never questioned."

"And Mark Stonor?" questioned Sir Abercrombie. "Was he kept in
ignorance of his mistake?"

Ferguson did not answer at once. He was rubbing his fingers through
his bristle of white hair; it was evident from what Lewker could see of
his face that the emotional strain of telling the story had been greater
than his admirably concise manner had suggested.

"Stonor made a remarkably quick recovery," he said at last. "The little
hospital at Zermatt gave him expert treatment and he was up and about
in two days and not even a touch of frostbite. We'd intended to say nothing to him about our discovery, but in the end we had to tell him everything. There was the body, you see. He knew where he'd left Lumley and
there was no way of explaining why we hadn't found the body and had it
brought down. We had the de'il's own job to persuade him to keep quiet
in his own interest."

"But you succeeded?"

"Aye. By showing him what a bluidy awkward business it would be for
Wiernick and me if he broadcast the truth. We made a kind of pact between
us then, to keep the truth absolutely between our three selves. And, Lewker"—
Ferguson straightened himself and looked earnestly from Sir Abercrombie
to the inspector—"I'm relying on you to keep the secret."

"It shall remain a secret," said the actor-manager slowly, "so long as
the cause of justice does not require any part of it to be revealed. But it
seems now that the secret has not been kept, Ferguson."

Grimmett leaned forward. "Exactly. Those anonymous letters—it's a
safe bet the writer knew about this business, because they were sent to
the three men concerned in it. Now, sir. What about this guide who was
there with you?"

"Frido Taugwalder was his name," Ferguson said. "He was killed in an avalanche on Monte Rosa, the year before the war."

"That leaves Dr.—what was it?—Zukmayer."

Ferguson frowned. "I've no' heard of him from that day to this. But the letters, Mr. Grimmett, were being sent to me even up here. Didn't Flora tell you there was one put in my car and another left in my bedroom?"

"Yes. But," said Grimmett impressively, "the letters received here by you and Mr. Stonor could have been placed where they were found by an outsider—someone not at the dinner meet or staying in the hotel."

"You're no' suggesting Zukmayer's in Snowdonia, surely!"

"Would you know him if you saw him again?"

Ferguson stared and shook his head. "It's more than a quarter of a century ago, remember. We were young men then. But—"

The bursting open of the office door interrupted him. Charles Kemp stood in the doorway, tense with excitement or anger. Over his shoulder appeared the large shocked countenance of Dr. Tom Paton.

"Stonor's been found, Lewker," he hissed dramatically. "Galu Regmi found him. He's dead."

"Dead!" Grimmett bounded to his feet. "How?"

"Shot," said Kemp with a kind of savage gusto. "Shot—with one of my own bloody rifles."

Chapter X

Grounds more Relative

The mist was lifting. Its ponderous gray lid was being raised with infinitesimal slowness from the mountain landscape as if some ultra-careful cook was preparing to examine the progress of an overnight jam-making. By contrast with the flat, colorless underside of the clouds the revealed circle of hillside and valley had the dark brightness of tapestry, greens and browns and russet-reds glowing with a compressed brilliance that seemed to have been squeezed into them by the pressure of the mist. The mild and clammy air was full of mingled odors, faint but distinguishable when a feather of breeze brushed lightly beneath the mist-fringe; the scent of sodden pasture and wet rock and peaty moorland, with its lingering memory of the sheep who were now wintering in the valley fields, hung against a background exhalation of melting snow. For on the invisible ridges above the clouds the snow was melting fast, and two thousand feet lower down the little streams tinkled more loudly and the green mosses oozed and overflowed with its distant contributions.

Sir Abercrombie Lewker, as he trudged up the Pony Track towards Llyn Llydaw for the second time that morning, felt a conflict of emotions within him. On the one hand, the mist in which he himself had been groping was lifting now; he saw things clearly for the first time and was glad. On the other hand, a man had been killed (if the report, as seemed certain, was true) and he had been too slow, too lacking in imagination, to prevent it; for that he was sorry.

At his side Dr. Tom's bulky figure strode purposefully, taking two strides to Lewker's three. In front of them Inspector Grimmett plodded at top speed, now and then shooting a panted question at the short, dark young man in Army windproofs who walked smoothly beside him. Galu Regmi's English was excellent and his enunciation clear. His answers were audible above the hurried tread of four pairs of boots.

"… I touched nothing … It was very plain that he was dead … Near this end of the causeway ... I ran all the way to the lorries."

Grimm, reflected Sir Abercrombie as the four of them swung on up the rough track as though they were out to break the record from Pen-y-Pass to Llydaw, must be feeling actual relief now that the case had opened out so dramatically. It had not indeed, been a case at all so far—merely a dubious accident dubiously connected with some rather unusual anonymous letters—and anything like the routine investigation and interrogation for which Grimmett was trained had been impossible. Now there was more suitable grist for his mill. According to Galu Regmi's story (which, at that moment, there seemed no reason to doubt) the Nepalese had determined to return to Pen-y-Pass over the summit of Snowdon, risking the wrath of his superiors for the satisfaction of his love of mountains; he had descended to Llyn Llydaw in thick mist, waded across the flooded causeway at the end of the lake, and found the body of an elderly man lying beside the track with a shocking wound in his head and a rifle lying beside him. It was perhaps natural enough that Regmi should not touch the body or the rifle. He had gone straight down to Pen-y-Pass at the best speed he could muster and had reported to Major Kemp.

The effect of the news on George Grimmett had been to convert him from a slightly embarrassed stranger in unaccustomed surroundings to a masterful embodiment of law and order with the whole power of the state behind him. He had acted swiftly and efficiently. The phone call to the chief constable had caught that official on the point of setting out for morning service and swung him into instant cooperation. Richard Paton had been left with instructions for the local police when they arrived from Caernarvon. A polite but firm order that no one was to leave the hotel under any circumstances had been issued. In less than ten minutes after Regmi's news had been received the machine had been put into gear and Inspector Grimmett, accompanied only by a doctor, a gifted amateur of his acquaintance, and the finder of the body, was on his official way to the scene of the crime.

Speed was desirable because there were other people about. Sunday had brought walkers and climbers to the mountain as usual and three cars had already drawn up on the car park at Pen-y-Pass. Two of the parties (reported the lorry-drivers who had seen them arrive) had gone up the path towards Bwlch Moch and would therefore not go near the body. The third party had taken the Pony Track. Grimmett was anxious to head them off and prevent any possibility of body or weapon being tampered with.

The four reached the place where the track ran level across the steep

mountainside above Llyn Teyrn. This, remembered Lewker, was where
Thripp had turned back from his morning walk. Thripp had spoken of
hearing a shot and had attributed the shooting to Kemp's cadets. The
time must have been about 8:45—and that did not fit in with the new
equation required for this problem (as the actor-manager saw it) by
Ferguson's story of the death of Peter Lumley's father. However, the
shot could just possibly have been unconnected with Stonor's death. He
was speculating ahead of the evidence, and the time for that was past.
The answer to the problem was, he believed, clear and correct in his
mind, but the proof, the setting-out of the steps in the solving of that
problem, was still incomplete. Like a schoolboy who has glanced at the
answer-book before doing his algebra homework, he had now to make
certain that every stage in the solution of the equation would stand scru-
tiny.

"Chaps ahead," remarked the doctor. "I'll deal with 'em, Grimmett."

Three figures had come into sight on the track in front. Grimmett's
party, walking considerably faster, overtook them a quarter of a mile
beyond Llyn Teyrn, and Dr. Tom called a good morning as they passed.
There were two young men and a girl, clad in anoraks and carrying ruck-
sacks.

"The causeway's under water, I hear," he added. "Going that way?"

The leader of the party shook his head. "No. Going over Lliwedd." He
raised his voice as the others drew ahead. "There was a climber killed
there yesterday, we heard. Know if it's true?"

"Yes," grunted Dr. Tom briefly over his shoulder.

They hastened on and in a few minutes were out of sight of the slower
party round a bend of the track. Another two or three hundred yards
brought them to the end of Llyn Llydaw. The dark ruffled water stretched
away between shores that were reduced to mere banks by the truncating
curtain of the mist, and only the white threads of streams tumbling from
the clouds told of the invisible peaks and ridges overhead. Here the metalled track bent sharply to the right, following the lake shore; the boggy
pathway to Lliwedd went off to the left. Grimmett slackened his pace
when they had gone a little way along the track to the right.

"How far now?" he asked the Nepalese.

"Approximately a hundred paces, sir," said Galu Regmi, his round
high-cheek-boned face solemn.

They walked on. Boulders fringed the lake shore on their left, turfy
slopes rose into gray obscurity on the right. Some little distance ahead
the track appeared to run straight into the lake; the causeway built long

ago to carry it across the narrows to the old copper mines was a foot below the surface of the water.

"There," said Galu Regmi, pointing.

"Stop," commanded Grimmett sharply.

Twenty yards from them was a cluster of gray boulders beside the track, a stone's throw short of the beginning of the submerged causeway. From behind the rocks protruded a boot and part of a leg.

"Don't come till I call, please," said the inspector.

He pursued a slow and zigzag course towards the boulder, crouching to peer at the track and the softer ground on either side of it. Apparently he found nothing of interest. When he came level with the boulders he stood six feet away from them and gazed for some seconds at what lay behind them before calling to the others to come on.

"He's not a nice sight," he warned them as they approached.

He was not. Sir Abercrombie was not sorry when the doctor's broad back came between him and the stained and shattered head of Mark Stonor as he knelt to make his examination. The president of the Foothold Club lay on his back with his long legs asprawl and his bony hands resting on his chest. The fingers of one hand were crooked in a clutching position, those of the other hand were open. Both hands, and the breast of his jacket (not the bright green anorak, Lewker noticed, but a thicker coat of olive-green cloth) were reddened with the blood from a hole in his throat just below the chin. Close beside him on the short grass lay a rifle, a weapon rather smaller and lighter than he had expected and with odd protuberances. Stonor's red woolen cap, he saw, had fallen off; Dr. Tom was now examining the top of the skull and making grunting noises as his crimsoned fingers parted the hair near a ragged wound that appeared there.

Sir Abercrombie stepped back on to the track. Grimmett, who had rapidly examined the ground on the left of the body before he allowed the doctor to kneel there, was moving slowly about on the other side with bent head, treading delicately and looking as if he was executing a *pas seul* in slow-motion. Cadet Regmi stood a few yards away watching the proceedings stolidly, and Lewker considered the round expressionless face for a moment. The broad blunt features, the small black eyes with their hint of a slant, recalled the Sherpas he had encountered on his one venture into the high Himalaya; men who would cheerfully face appalling hardship and danger—and as cheerfully kill, if a killing was necessary.

"Is the rifle that lies there the same type as those the officer cadets have been using?" he inquired.

"It is, sir," Regmi said, his little eyes flicking a glance at the actor-manager. "Model L 1-A-1 it is called, seven-point-six-two millimeters."

"A magazine rifle?"

"Yes, sir. Twenty rounds, self-loading."

Dr. Paton turned from his examination and rummaged in his rucksack, which he had taken off and placed beside him. He got out a triangular bandage and some cotton wool and held them out to Regmi.

"Here, soak these in the lake and bring 'em back," he growled; and then, evidently realizing that Regmi was a foreigner, "Soak—in plenty water. Savvy?"

"I understand you perfectly, sir," the Nepalese said gravely.

He took the things and crossed the narrow strip of grass and stones to the lake shore. Grimmett, who had been somewhat oddly engaged in collecting flat rocks and sticking them on end in the ground, ceased his labors and came to stand by the doctor.

"Well?" he demanded.

"Suicide," said Dr. Tom shortly. "He shot himself. No doubt of that. See the entry of the bullet there, in the throat?"

"Yes."

"It went straight up and through the brain. Nothing much to stop it, you know. Then out through the parietal. It had force enough for that and the bullet may have gone a long way afterwards." He wiped his fingers on the turf, frowning. "But why the devil Mark Stonor should have killed himself—"

"Your reasons for the statement, Doctor?" Grimmett interrupted.

"Well, look at the damn wound. How would a man get shot under the chin if he didn't do it himself? As I see it, he must have held the rifle against his chest with the muzzle against his throat, vertical. The barrel's not long and he had reach enough to get his thumb down to the trigger. Died instantly."

"When?"

"Now you're asking, aren't you? I haven't a thermometer and if I had I couldn't tell you any more than you know already—that he died within the last three-and-a-half-hours." Dr. Tom fingered his chin meditatively, leaving a red-brown stain there. "Can I move one hand and one foot?"

The inspector hesitated for a second. "All right. Leave the original attitude just as it was, please."

"I'll try." The doctor took hold of the left hand by one finger and raised it slightly; hand and arm were obviously stiff. "Easy enough to do with that," he said, releasing it and taking hold of the left foot. "This is quite a bit freer, as you see. At a guess—call it an empirical hypothesis if you like—I'd say he'd been dead nearer three hours than one. And that's as far as I'm prepared to go, Grimmett. Thanks, Cadet What's-your-name, I'll have those."

Galu Regmi had returned with the bandage and cotton wool saturated with water. Dr. Paton took them and looked at the inspector.

"You want the face cleaned up, don't you?"

"Yes," said Grimmett. "Might as well go the whole hog," he muttered to Lewker as Dr. Tom began his task. "There's a police photographer with the local C.I.D. men, but Lord knows when they'll get here." He glanced at the Nepalese cadet, who was standing a few yards away, and lowered his voice. "Look here, sir, you don't believe in this suicide theory, do you?"

"Why not, Grimm?" countered Sir Abercrombie. "You recall what Ferguson told us—that Stonor, knowingly or not, deserted Jack Lumley while he was still alive and hastened his death by taking his protective clothing. That is a very unpleasant thing to have in one's memory for twenty-seven years. And that is the thing which, in the words of the letter Stonor brought us, was catching up with him."

"Maybe it was. But I've a thing or two to show you—and I shouldn't wonder if Dr. Paton doesn't find us something else."

He was bending forward as he spoke. Lewker, overcoming a certain squeamishness, looked over his shoulder. Dr. Tom had removed most of the blood with the wet bandage and was now finishing off with the cotton wool.

"Been some bleeding from the mouth," he said without looking round. "Natural enough in the circumstances. Abrasion here, left side of chin— could have been done by the muzzle of the rifle when it went off, I suppose."

"The tendency of all firearms is to kick backwards on discharge," the inspector pointed out.

The doctor grunted. "You're right and I'm wrong. This is a contusion, a bruise with the surface slightly broken. I'd lay a hundred to one it was done before death."

Grimmett's blown-out breath made a noise like a considerable escape of steam as it passed through his mustache. Dr. Paton sat back on his heels and screwed himself round to frown at them.

"I dare say I'm not supposed to know what's going on round here," he growled, "but it feels to me like a damn crime wave. A child could see

you two thought there was something queer about Wiernick's death yesterday. Now poor old Stonor's had the top of his skull perforated by a
rifle bullet he sent there himself and you're out to make it murder. Or are
you?"

The inspector stood up and glanced first at Galu Regmi, standing motionless with folded arms at the other side of the track, and then at Lewker.

"I'm grateful for your help, Doctor, so I am," he said. "But you'll understand that this is a matter under police investigation now and I'm
bound to keep my own counsel. I'll take the liberty of asking your opinion on one thing more and then we'll call it a day as far as you're concerned. You don't mind?"

"Not a bit, but you can't stop me from being curious. I'd have said
Stonor was the last man to commit suicide and about the last man anyone'd
want to murder. What's this opinion you want?"

Grimmett considered for a moment, evidently choosing his words with
care.

"I'd like you to tell me," he said slowly, "whether, in your opinion,
anything about the body or injuries of Mark Stonor is inconsistent with a
sequence of events I'll put to you now. Stonor comes up here in the mist.
It's just beginning to get light. A man could easily conceal himself among
these rocks in those circumstances. This man rises suddenly as Stonor
passes his hiding-place and hits him on the jaw with all his strength.
Stonor goes down and lies as we see him now. The man picks up the rifle
he's brought with him, lays it on Stonor's chest with the muzzle below
his chin so that the bullet will be directed up into the brain, and pulls the
trigger. He then clasps Stonor's hands round the rifle and leaves him
there."

"Having arranged for him to be shot in such a way that any damn goop
of a G.P. would say it must be suicide," nodded Dr. Tom; he stood up and
contemplated the body with his face screwed into a weird grimace. "It
could be—it could be. And look here, Grimmett. If this postulated murderer knew nothing much about rigor mortis he'd probably think the
fingers would stiffen round the rifle. In fact, of course, rigor wouldn't set
in for at least half an hour and might not reach the hands for an hour."

"So the fingers would relax?" Grimmett said intently.

"They might retain the clasp he gave 'em for a minute or two. Then
they'd relax. Either the relaxation or the later stiffening could cause the
rifle to roll off his body and lie where it is."

"And the bruise on the chin could have been caused by the blow of a
clenched fist?"

"It's on the left side, where a right-handed man would probably strike," said the doctor cautiously.

Grimmett nodded, his eyes narrowed and gleaming.

"If Mr. Stonor shot himself," he said, "it's a bit unlikely he'd lie flat on his back to do it. He'd stand up to pull the trigger. What'd happen to the rifle after that?"

"Hundred to one he'd drop it instantly. The shock of the discharge would make him do that, probably."

"Yes. And wherever it fell, it's not very likely it'd fall where it's lying now—a couple of inches from his left side with the butt against his thigh. Thank you, Doctor."

Dr. Tom looked as though he was going to say something else, sighed, and picked up the bloodstained rags.

"I'd like a wash," he said. "I'll nip across to the lake and bury these things on the way."

He departed on this mission. Grimmett turned at once to Galu Regmi and politely requested him to go to the corner of the track, where the path to Lliwedd diverged; in the event of the C.I.D. men from Caernarvon arriving, he was to bring them along to the body. The Nepalese showed white teeth in a brief smile as he saluted and turned away to comply. His heavy face did not look intelligent to a European eye, reflected Sir Abercrombie, but his small black eyes glinted with something that might have been amused understanding.

"Now, sir," snapped the inspector briskly as soon as the cadet was out of earshot. "Take a look at these."

He stepped quickly to the places where he had been sticking bits of rock in the ground. There were three such places. One was between the body, which lay about two feet from the indeterminate edge of the track, and the track itself; the other two were on the other side of the body and close to it. Grimmett had used his flat rocks to protect three marks on the surface of the ground, Lewker perceived. He bent over the first mark. It was a fresh but somewhat blurred scrape six or seven inches long, nearly level with the dead man's right foot.

"A right-handed man striking with all his force has his weight on his left foot," Grimmett said. "His right toe drags as he throws his weight forward in the blow. I reckon that's the drag of the right foot. Nothing more to be got from it that I can see."

He trod lightly round the feet of the corpse to his other miniature cromlechs. Sir Abercrombie, who had crouched to peer more closely at the scrape, was slow to follow. The inspector removed the protective fences and pointed to two indentations about eighteen inches apart and close to the body. One, near Stoner's hip, was a rounded hollow, the other—near his knee—was a deeper semicircular groove.

"Left knee and toe," Grimmett explained. "The murderer knelt here to arrange the rifle in Stoner's hands. There's a very light flattening of the ground where his right foot rested but you can't get much from that."

"And can you get very much from these, Grimm?"

"It's some confirmation of my theory of the murder, I reckon. Don't move the weapon if you can help it, sir," he added quickly as Lewker stooped above the marks, which were only a few inches from the rifle. "This murderer didn't get far with his suicide frame-up, it's true, but I'd say he had brains enough to use gloves. All the same, we'll have the rifle gone over for prints."

Lewker was examining the toe-print, which seemed the only one likely to be useful. The ground from which the sparse blades of grass sprang consisted of very fine grit intermingled with larger fragments of slaty stone with sharp edges, a material which could not take a detailed impression. It was impossible to say whether the print had been made by the toe of a nailed boot, a molded rubber sole, or some other kind of footwear. He said as much to the inspector, who nodded regretfully.

"A biggish sole with a broad blunt toe," he said. "That's about all you can say."

"And you can say it about almost any climbing-boot," added the actor-manager. "However—"

He straightened himself and went back to the first mark. Apparently a crouching inspection was unsatisfying, for he went down on his hands and knees and peered very closely at the scrape. After a moment he picked out of it, with finger and thumb, a tiny wisp of light-brown material and stood up holding it out for Grimmett to see.

"Bit of string," commented the inspector when he had frowned at it from a distance of twelve inches. "Not much to that, sir. It could have been lying about and got trodden in when the murderer struck Stonor."

"That is possible, Grimm. But it is also possible that this bit of string— hardly, as you see, half an inch in length—may hang a man. I suggest, respectfully, that you retain it." Sir Abercrombie twinkled at his friend. "Your expression implies that you have a theory of this murder—or should I say, at this stage, death?—and that my half-inch of string does not fit into it."

Grimmett, fumbling inside the front of his shooting-jacket to get at his wallet, stared very hard at the actor-manager. He knew the signs; Lewker had arrived at his own solution of the problem and was satisfied with it.

"I reckon I know who killed Mark Stonor, Sir Ab," he said slowly, "and I expect to prove it, if the Chief'll give me the case. Major Wightman-Jones is phoning Sir Frederick to ask him to leave me in charge. But I'll admit freely that a wisp of string that looks as if it's been chewed and spat out doesn't help me."

"I fancy it may help you, laddie." Lewker handed it over. "Place it between the folds of a pound note rather than in that envelope, which—by your leave—I will use to contain further evidence."

He took the envelope, stooped, and scraped into it a little of the grit from the ground an inch or two from the scrape whence he had taken the string. Grimmett, folding the string away as he had been instructed, watched him frowningly.

"This fits in with some theory *you've* got, presumably," he commented. "Am I going to hear it?"

Sir Abercrombie straightened himself and gave him the envelope, carefully folded.

"I think not, Grimm," he said gently. "You, I take it, must keep your own counsel until you have clearer proof of your man. I, too, like Hamlet, must have grounds more relative than this. I need not add, I hope, that all my findings shall be placed in your hands at once—as I place the sample of grit and the fragment of hemp—and that my theory shall be yours as soon as I have tested one last link in my evidence."

"All right, sir," Grimmett continued to eye him speculatively as he pocketed his wallet. "But seems to me we must have the same man in mind. On what we've got, he's the only person who could have been responsible for both these deaths. Am I right?"

"Perfectly right, my dear Grimm. But our premises may not be quite—"

He broke off as Dr. Tom approached, carefully skirting the neighborhood of the body. Judging by the shining ruddiness of his large face his ablutions had been thorough and the lake water cold. He glanced keenly from Lewker to Grimmett.

"Got the damn business taped yet?" he demanded. "I liked old Stonor, and if you're right about this and some chap did him in I'd give fifty pounds to see the murderer hanged."

"You'll read about it, anyway, Doctor," promised the inspector gravely.

"Good. I'm asking no questions—not my business. But if there's anything more I can do let me know. What are we waiting for now?"

"Photographs, fingerprints, ambulance." Grimmett turned his head, listening. "That sounds like them. Didn't waste much time, seemingly."

A black saloon car lurched round the bed of the track and came bumping towards them. Galu Regmi loped easily beside it and an ambulance van followed twenty yards behind. They halted as Grimmett walked forward holding up his hand, and five men, three in civilian clothes and two uniformed constables, got out. One of the plainclothes men carried a large leather case and a camera tripod. Grimmett spoke briefly to Galu Regmi, who saluted and immediately set off at a fast stride back along the track, and shook hands with the large pleasant-faced man who seemed to be the leader of the party.

"I fancy we are superfluous here now," Lewker murmured in the doctor's ear. "Shall we depart? I have a small task to perform."

Dr. Tom nodded. "Right. Unless they want any medical details from me."

Grimmett came across to introduce the large man as Inspector Evans of the Gwynedd Police, and agreed that there was no need for the two unofficial helpers to remain. The doctor picked up his rucksack and they walked away down the track. A photographic flashbulb winked behind them as they reached the corner.

The mist was still slowly lifting, revealing more and more of the vast mountain hollow that cradled Llydaw. Already the lowest slabs of Lliwedd, a mile away beyond the broken slopes above the lake, appeared thrusting down out of the gray vapor. The doctor looked at the distant gleaming rocks and then at his companion.

"Don't tell me if you don't want to," he growled, "but does this shocking affair tie up in any way with what happened yesterday? Wiernick's death, I mean?"

"There is, I fancy, a connection," returned Sir Abercrombie cautiously. "Why do you ask?"

"Oh, well—thinking it over last night it occurred to me there was something damn funny about it. When I was going down after the accident with Ferguson and Flora Massey I got the impression Ferguson was scared as well as shaken up—may have been wrong." Dr. Tom hesitated before going on. "You heard me say Wiernick, Ferguson and Stonor used to climb with Jack Lumley? Well, Lumley was killed twenty-seven years ago. Wiernick went yesterday and now Stonor's either killed himself or been murdered."

"Yes?" murmured Lewker gently as he paused.

"You'll think I'm being fanciful. Got no reason for this, but—well, anyway, in the old days those four stuck together a lot. Three of 'em have been killed in more or less peculiar circumstances. There was always a bit of a mystery about Lumley's death, you know. Ferguson's the only one left, and I'm just wondering whether he ought not to be taken care of a bit. Protected. He's definitely scared, in my opinion. Mind you," he added quickly, looking a trifle sheepish, "I've got nothing to go on. I take it you have."

"We have," Lewker told him. "And I think I may say that—while Ferguson is in some danger—the murderer will have little or no opportunity of striking again. If he is not under arrest before teatime today, Doctor, I shall be very much surprised."

"Great Godfrey!" ejaculated the doctor, impressed. "Nice work—and damn quick. How the deuce—But let it go. I'm just the dumb medico who happens to be on the spot when the corpses start arriving. What's this small task of yours?"

"I will tell you when we reach Pen-y-Pass. You may care to assist me."

"Thanks. I will."

They walked on in silence. The corner rounded, the familiar track unwound its coils ahead, brown moorland rolling down into Cwm Dyli on the right and craggy mountainside rising into the drifting fringes of the mist on the left. On the long curve that skirted the dark waters of Llyn Teyrn they caught sight of Galu Regmi's stumpy figure disappearing round a bend far in front. Dr. Tom spoke only once.

"I was just thinking," he said with a wry grin, "how cut up Stonor would have been about all this, if he was alive. The publicity and the reputation of the club and all that."

Sir Abercrombie came far enough out of his own reflections to nod understandingly, but said nothing. They came over the last ridge and saw the white hotel below them, with the two Army lorries still standing on the car park near the corrugated-iron shed. The actor-manager looked at his watch as they tramped down the final stretch of the track. It was a little after twelve and there would be lunch at half past, but there might be time to do what he wanted to do. Whether he would be successful was another matter.

As they reached the wide square of the car park Galu Regmi was standing very stiffly to attention in front of Major Kemp, who appeared to be delivering a severe lecture. Through the open rear ends of the lorries Regmi's fellow cadets could be seen eating an Army-ration lunch. Kemp dismissed the Nepalese cadet when he caught sight of the two Foothold Club members, and came to meet them, his dark face eager and anxious.

"What's happened?" he demanded. "I saw the police car go up. Stonor's actually—dead?"

"Mark Stonor is dead," replied Lewker briefly; and forestalled Kemp's next question with a demand of his own. "Major, may I have the use of your cadets for approximately fifteen minutes? It is a matter of some urgency."

Kemp stared. "Well, I don't know. What's the idea?"

"I would like them to help me in searching this area for a small piece of wire. If we can find it, it may be of some use to the police."

"Oh, ah." Kemp was plainly as puzzled as Tom Paton looked. "If you say so—the lads were supposed to be away by one-oh-three-oh hours and now they've got to wait until the coppers give us the all clear anyway. May as well make 'emselves useful. Corporal! Get your men fallen in here!"

While a stentorian voice echoed the order and cadets poured out of the lorries, Sir Abercrombie picked up a small stone and went quickly to the corrugated-iron shed. The leveled space of the car park had been made by building up the side overlooking the falling hillside on the east, and the short embankment of rocks and rubble had been added to by the clinkers and ashes of the Pen-y-Pass fires. The shed had been erected on this side with its door facing the drop at the edge of the embankment and a few feet from it. He tried the door, and found it locked. Then he behaved rather oddly. Approaching, the stone in his right hand, to the lock, he turned quickly away and flung the stone with a strong flick of his wrist, marking where it landed. It fell near the bottom of the embankment, among the clinkers and rubbish.

He returned to the cadets, who were drawn up in two ranks in front of Major Kemp. There were twenty-four of them with Regmi, who had fallen in with the rest. Sir Abercrombie addressed them without preamble.

"I want you to search for a piece of wire about six inches long. It will probably be bent at both ends. This piece of wire will be lying on the surface of the ground, so there will be no need to move stones or rummage among the clinkers. I would suggest that the front rank men search at the bottom of the embankment on this side of the car park and twenty paces down the hillside beyond it, keeping within a stone's-throw of the corrugated-iron shed, while the rear rank men search the embankment itself and the car-park surface twenty paces behind it. Bring to me, if you please, any pieces of wire you may find."

He stepped back and nodded to the Major. Kemp barked the order to fall out and get to work, and two dozen anorak-clad cadets swarmed along the eastern edge of the car park. Among them here and there a forefinger tapped a forehead significantly, but Sir Abercrombie noted that this natural opinion of his odd request seemed to make no difference to the ardor of the search. He noticed other things. Over by the hotel two police constables made their appearance, plainly uncertain whether or not to come over and investigate these proceedings. Other faces appeared in the porch—Hibberd and Peter Lumley. Jones-Griffith looked over the wall by the barns, a cigarette between his lips and a startled expression on his brown face.

"What the deuce are you up to?" demanded Dr. Tom at Lewker's elbow, in a puzzled whisper.

"You shall see," the actor-manager told him, "if and when we find my piece of wire."

"Ten to one against it, I'd say."

"I would say evens, Doctor. Come unto these yellow sands."

He led the way down the embankment to the litter of clinkers and rubbish at its foot, where his flung stone had landed, and they peered carefully about. Several cadets, among them Galu Regmi, were searching busily a few yards away. One of them came up to Lewker with a piece of thin rusty wire, which was politely rejected. During the next ten minutes several such pieces were found, in addition to sardine-tin openers, a nail-file, three discarded pipe-cleaners, and a brass-mounted pocket compass in good working order. Then Galu Regmi, who had been searching a little farther down the hillside, came up with a piece of stout galvanized wire bent at one end into an odd shape.

"I have thee!" boomed Sir Abercrombie, taking it eagerly.

He waved to the major, who shouted his order for the search to stop, and with a word of congratulation to the Nepalese scrambled up the embankment with Dr. Tom at his heels. Lewker stopped in front of the shed door.

"Be good enough to witness this operation, Doctor," he said, and inserted the bent end of the wire into the lock.

At the third attempt the lock turned. He threw the door open. The interior of the shed was crowded with miscellaneous junk—chairs, old paint-pots, one or two wooden benches. On one of the benches stood two sizeable boxes painted dark green and stencilled with white letters and figures. Near them a much larger wooden case stood on end, its lid leaning against it; the racks inside were made to contain six magazine rifles, and five weapons of the type they had found beside Stonor's body were in the racks. The lids of the ammunition boxes were open.

"Hold on!" snapped Kemp from behind them. "This won't do, Lewker."

Your inspector friend left orders this shed wasn't to be opened."

Sir Abercrombie locked the door again, this time without difficulty, and cocked a listening ear. The distant sound of a car in low gear grew louder.

"I will inform Inspector Grimmett of my misdemeanor now, Major," he said.

Down the track came the black saloon and drew up, with Grimmett's face peering curiously from the window at the twenty-four cadets streaming across the car park to clamber into their lorries. The actor-manager walked to the car and held out the piece of wire.

"Pray add this to your collection, Inspector," he said. "Dr. Paton is my witness that it was found about thirty yards from the door of the shed over there, and that it will unlock the shed door."

Grimmett took it gingerly. His frown gave place to a pleased smile.

"Thanks, Sir Ab," he muttered. "That completes the case, I reckon."

"Let us call it the penultimate clue," said Sir Abercrombie.

The ambulance van, bumping down the track, slowed up behind the black saloon and the police car moved on. The body of Mark Stonor went on its way to the mortuary. The hotel gong, a well-timed tocsin, summoned the remaining members of the dinner meet to lunch.

Chapter XI

Inspector Grimmett Interrogates

The waitress brought a sealed envelope to Sir Abercrombie Lewker as he was finishing his lunch. It was addressed to him and marked PRIVATE AND CONFIDENTIAL. The note inside had a list attached to it and was from the absent Grimmett.

Dear Sir Ab,

The matter you know of prevents me from joining you at lunch. As this is so, I am writing you. I have been on the phone to Sir Frederick and he has approved my taking the case. Inspector Evans is a good chap and does not object. He is up to his neck in a dance-hall stabbing affair which cropped up last night, but is lending me Sergeant Price and three constables. Sergeant Price has instructions to warn the persons on the attached list to be on hand from two o'clock onwards for police interrogation. The hotel lounge is the place for them until they are wanted. We can do it in the place they call the office, and of course I would like you to be present and I reckon you will have some questions to ask. (Sir Abercrombie could picture Grimm's blue eyes twinkling as he wrote that sentence.) *You are at liberty to add to the list if you wish. The names are in order as I wish to take them. We may as well weed out all red herrings while we are about it. I will do my best to be there at two prompt but am very rushed what with doctor and fingerprinting and other things.*

Yours truly,
George Grimmett

Sir Abercrombie smiled to himself at the mixed metaphor, but regretted that he was to have no conference with Grimmett before the interrogations began. If Inspector Evans was not to be present, however, there was really no reason why he should not indulge his sense of theater and play out the part of Gifted Amateur to the end. He glanced apologetically across the table at Dr. Tom, who seemed to be immersed in his thoughts and his after-lunch pipe, and turned to the 'attached list.'

> *Mr. George Thripp*
> *Mrs. Wiernick*
> *Mr. Frank Hibberd*
> *Major C. Kemp*
> *Mr. J. Jones-Griffith*
> *Mr. Peter Lumley*
> *Mr. Donald Ferguson*

Lewker glanced round the dining room, considering the eleven people who sat at the other tables. Ten of the dinner meet guests had left for their homeward journey before the news of Mark Stonor's death became known; they included all the married couples except Mr. and Mrs. Thripp and none of them appeared to be concerned in the case. The news of what had happened, and that a police investigation was in progress, had spread among the remaining guests as if by magic; it was generally assumed, apparently, that there had been foul play, and the shadow of the word MURDER hung almost visibly over them though Sir Abercrombie had not heard the word uttered. Eve Wiernick was there, appearing for the first time since her husband's death. She looked pale but composed in her dark gray tweed suit, and her conversation with Charles Kemp, who shared a table with her, was desultory. Jones-Griffith and Frank Hibberd, at the next table, had even less to say to each other. Richard Paton was lunching with Donald Ferguson and his niece and seemed to be trying, in somewhat difficult circumstances, to bring a smile to Flora's face. The only audible conversation came from the table where the Thripps and Peter Lumley were listening to Mrs. Hengist's cacophonous voice relating her adventures on a traverse of the Meije in 1909.

"Plainclothes man for a fiver," growled Dr. Paton.

Lewker, whose back was to the door, turned. The broad-shouldered man who stood in the doorway conferring with the waitress must be Sergeant Price, he decided; and was confirmed in that opinion when the broad-shouldered man began to tread with catlike nicety from table to table murmuring some inaudible request at each. He paused beside the actor-manager and bent over him confidentially. His soft Welsh voice had a singsong inflection.

"I was to remind you, sir. Two o'clock in the office."

He passed on, soft-footed. Dr. Tom blew a cloud of smoke.

"Seems I'm out of it," he murmured as Sir Abercrombie got up. "Remember me if you want someone to hold the chap down. Whoever he is."

Lewker nodded and went quickly from the room. It was already a quarter to two and he had yet to locate his ultimate clue. His observation of the other tables had shown him that coffee had only just reached one of them and he counted on five safe minutes for what he had to do. In his pocket was a sheet of brown paper and some string. He went upstairs. Four minutes later he entered his own room with a brown-paper parcel under his arm.

A thin rain whispered on the bedroom window. Through the blurred panes the rocks on the mountainside gleamed palely like the underbellies of stranded fish; a helmeted constable wearing a cape stood on guard outside the corrugated-iron shed. Sir Abercrombie spent some little time in examination of the contents of his parcel before repacking them very carefully in their wrappings, and then took pencil and paper and sat in front of the electric fire which had witnessed their first gropings towards the truth in this odd maze of lies and violence. At the end of ten minutes his sheet of paper was still blank. That cinematograph memory of his, the queer gift by which he was able to project on a mental screen all that his eye had subconsciously observed and hear again all that his ear had heard, had given him the answer to this problem and no notes were needed. He scrawled three short sentences for Grimmett's eye and went downstairs.

It was a little after two o'clock when he came down to the hall, to find Inspector Grimmett just arrived and divesting himself of his raincoat while he talked rapidly in a low voice to Sergeant Price. A police constable, uniformed but helmetless, stood just inside the door and another was standing woodenly beside the door of the hotel office with his large red hands clasped in front of him.

"Good afternoon, sir," said Grimmett; he was very solemn and formal. "You're ready, I take it? Sir Abercrombie Lewker," he added to the sergeant, "will be present by the desire of the assistant commissioner. Sergeant Price, sir, will be taking notes. Shall we go in?"

His eye fell on the brown paper parcel which the actor-manager carried under his arm but he made no comment. As they went into the office he spoke a name to the constable beside the door, who turned and went towards the door of the lounge.

The typewriter, Sir Abercrombie noticed as he entered the little room, had gone from the desk, and the table had been placed with one chair behind it and one at each end. A fourth chair stood opposite the table, leaving barely enough room for the electric fire to stand at a comfortable distance in a corner. Grimmett took the chair behind the table and laid some typewritten papers in front of him, together with three small envelopes and his pocket magnifying glass. Sergeant Price, who had produced a large notebook and a fountain pen from his pockets, sat at the farther end of the table and Sir Abercrombie, after placing his parcel beneath the chair, seated himself at the other end. They were hardly settled before the constable opened the door and George Thripp came in.

"Sit down, please," said Grimmett, his formality gone and his square countenance benevolent. "Mr. George Thripp?"

Sergeant Price made a note of the name. Thripp sat down and blinked at them through his glasses.

"Yes," he said testily. "Yes, of course. I've not the slightest idea why I am required—"

"We shall not keep you long, sir. Can you tell us at what time Mr. Peter Lumley arrived here on Friday evening?"

"It was afternoon rather than evening. He arrived with his aunt, Mrs. Hengist, at just after half past four."

Grimmett shot a significant glance at Lewker. "Thank you. One other question, Mr. Thripp. You heard a shot this morning on your way up to Llyn Llydaw. What time was it then?"

"I didn't go up to Llydaw. I turned back, as I told you, near Llyn Teyrn, and I turned back because I'd looked at my watch and found it was getting near breakfast-time—twenty to nine, to be exact."

"You heard the shot then, sir?"

"About two minutes after I had turned, I should say. Yes. About two minutes later."

"We may say, then, that the shot was fired at eight-forty-two. Did the sound appear to come from near at hand?"

Thripp reflected. "Hard to say, hard to say," he muttered. "There was a light breeze from the southwest, you know, and the shot—I *think*—was fired upwind from me. At a guess, and knowing little about rifle-shots, it might be half a mile or less."

Grimmett glanced sideways at Sir Abercrombie, who shook his head.

"Thank you, Mr. Thripp. That's all we have to ask you."

Thripp got up. At the door he paused and turned to peer fiercely at them.

"I would like to say," he quavered, "that I earnestly, *most* earnestly, hope that you will succeed in bringing the president's murderer to justice."

In his emotion he failed to grasp the fact that the door opened inwards and spent some seconds wrestling with it before the constable outside released him.

"Mrs. Wiernick, please," said the inspector; he turned to Lewker. "I'm dealing with the death of Mark Stonor primarily, sir, but as the other business is bound up with it we're taking that into account. In the first case we've got enough to go on, but short of a confession I don't see my way to prove the Wiernick murder."

"Neither do I, Grimm," nodded Sir Abercrombie. "You are convinced, then, that Wiernick was murdered?"

Grimmett looked surprised. "Why, yes. But there's not enough evidence to convince—"

He broke off quickly as Eve Wiernick entered the room. There was no sign of discomposure on her vividly beautiful face or in the grace with which she went straight to the chair and sat down uninvited, crossing admirable legs.

"I'm very sorry indeed, Mrs. Wiernick," said Grimmett, looking it, "to have to question you at such a time. The very recent death of your—"

"Shall we leave this out?" she broke in, looking steadily at him. "I'm perfectly willing and able to answer questions, especially if I'm allowed to smoke."

There was a moment of awkward bustle as the inspector hastily got out his cigarette case and held the match for her cigarette. Eve inhaled deeply.

"Thanks," she sighed, expelling smoke. "What d'you want to know?"

Grimmett coughed and rustled his papers. He had always some difficulty in maintaining his composure when faced with a pretty woman.

"Just this, Mrs. Wiernick," he said apologetically. "Did your—um— late husband, Professor Julius Wiernick, receive any threatening or anonymous letters recently?"

Eve shook he head. "Not to my knowledge. Probably I wouldn't know if he did. Who'd want to send him anonymous letters, anyway?"

"That's what we have to find out, Mrs. Wiernick. Can you tell us if there's been any sign, any change in his manner, to show that he might have received an anonymous threat to his life?"

"No—nothing. He was always the same, always bitter and—" She stiffened suddenly and her eyes opened wide. "His life! It's Mark Stonor's death you're investigating, isn't it? There wasn't anything—wrong with my—my husband's death, was there?"

Her self-possession was gone. The thought behind her agitation was very obvious. Grimmett made soothing gestures.

"The point of my question," he said quickly, "is simply this—that Mr. Stonor had received threatening letters and we believe the same anonymous writer had sent letters to Professor Wiernick. If you have no knowledge of it—"

"I haven't."

"Then my question is answered. I've one more to ask, Mrs. Wiernick, and I'll ask you to accept my assurance that if—" he paused to choose his words—"if your answer involves another person you won't be doing that person a disservice by telling the truth. On Saturday morning, yesterday, you went for a solitary walk into Cwm Dyli. That's recorded in the exercise book provided for the purpose by Mr. Thripp, and your entry says 'Left ten o'clock, back for lunch.' In fact, you were back here at one o'clock, just after Mr. Stonor arrived with the news of the accident on Slanting Buttress."

"That's quite right," Eve said; she had recovered herself and was watching him steadily through a haze of cigarette-smoke.

"Thank you. Had you any purpose in going to Cwm Dyli? A rendezvous, perhaps?"

Eve's green eyes narrowed and for a moment she looked both frightened and angry.

"What's that got to do with Mr. Stonor's death?" she demanded sharply.

"Very little, maybe. We just want to clear up the details, so to speak. You have nothing to fear from speaking the truth, Mrs. Wiernick."

"All right, then," she said slowly. "I'm trusting you on that. Major Kemp was out supervising the cadet exercise. He said he'd come back through Cwm Dyli and suggested I should walk that way and meet him."

"But you didn't meet him?"

"No, because he heard about the accident on his way down and went to see if he could help. You know all about that."

Grimmett nodded. "Yes. Thank you. Did you by any chance meet anybody at all during your walk, Mrs. Wiernick?"

"Not in Cwm Dyli. I waited—I pottered about by the stream for quite a while before starting back." Eve hesitated; evidently she was weighing all her words before she uttered them. "I started out with Frank Hibberd, you know, but we didn't stick together for long. He's a fast walker and I was holding him back, so I told him to go on."

The inspector consulted his notes. "Mr. Hibberd's plan, according to his entry in the book, was to climb Snowdon and return down the Gribin. He would go up past Llyn Llydaw and Glaslyn, I take it?"

"I suppose so. I wouldn't know."

Grimmett stood up. "That's all, then, Mrs. Wiernick. Thank you."

Eve rose and stubbed out her cigarette in the ashtray on the table.

"I don't know what you're getting at, of course," she said evenly, looking straight at the inspector, "but I can tell you this—Charles Kemp's a soldier. He isn't a murderer. He couldn't be."

She walked gracefully to the door, and her word of thanks to the policeman who opened it for her sounded natural and unforced.

"Cool customer—but it shook her up a bit," commented Grimmett. "You'd say she was in love with Kemp, I reckon."

"And he with her," nodded Sir Abercrombie. "Add that she was not in love with her husband, who was a much older man and a somewhat unpleasant character, and you have one of the commonest motives for murder."

"She saw that plain enough, too. But you're not going on that line, sir?"

Sir Abercrombie folded his fingers over his paunch and looked as inscrutable as the Sphinx.

"Do all men kill the thing they do not love?" he boomed oracularly. "This case, Grimm, is as irrational, in some ways, as life itself. There are motives without consequent result, results without apparent motive, coincidences, plausible lies and deceptive truths. Have you ever, in your long and distinguished professional career, encountered a criminal investigation wherein every discovered fact conduced to the detection of the criminal?"

"No, sir. And it's just the facts that don't conduce that I'm trying to get rid of." The inspector paused and eyed the actor-manager narrowly. "That last speech of yours sounded stagey, so it did. I reckon you're going to put on the revelation act."

"Do not be hard on me, laddie," pleaded Sir Abercrombie, twinkling at him. "You know my foibles, and I promise that the curtain speech shall be yours."

Grimmett rubbed his chin, frowning. "If anybody else offered to hand me his solution on a plate," he muttered, "I'd—oh, well. If you're not on the same track as me, Sir Ab, I'm afraid you've backed the wrong horse this time."

The actor-manager did not respond to this challenge or the sharp glance that accompanied it. Grimmett looked at his papers and called the name of Frank Hibberd to the constable at the door.

"That will be E-R-D, sir?" inquired Sergeant Price, flicking over a page of his notebook.

The inspector nodded. "And it's I-E-R in 'Wiernick'," he added. "You can check with my list afterwards."

Frank Hibberd came in, glancing keenly at the three as he sat down at Grimmett's genial invitation.

"Star Chamber stuff, eh?" he remarked.

"I hope not, sir," returned Grimmett comfortably. "There has to be a jury after this, you know."

Hibberd nodded. "I sit rebuked. You know your history. What can I do for you?"

"Just tell us, briefly, your movements on Saturday, sir, please."

Brevity and clearness characterized Hibberd's account of his activities on the morning of the Slanting Buttress accident. He had started out about ten with Mrs. Wiernick, left her near Llyn Teyrn to go on alone, reached the summit of Snowdon at eleven-fifteen, descended to Bwlch-y-Saethau and thence down the Gribin. He had heard the whistle-blowing as he started down the Gribin and had put on speed to join the others on their way to the rescue.

"A remarkable *tour de grande vitesse*," commented Lewker. "Your time to the summit of Snowdon could well be a record, Hibberd."

"Possibly," said Hibberd indifferently. "I'm in good form. I was trying to make the best time I could. Ran some of the way."

The inspector had taken a section sheet of the Ordnance Survey map from his papers and was studying it.

"Descending to Bwlch-y-Saethau, sir," he said, looking up, "you'd get a view down into the valley on the south and also towards the crest of Lliwedd."

"When I got below the mist. Yes."

"Did you see anyone on the crest or in the valley?"

"Someone was coming up from the valley. Too far off to see whether it was a man or a woman. Didn't see anyone on Lliwedd."

Sir Abercrombie glanced at Grimmett and put a question. "Could you distinguish the color of the anorak this person was wearing?"

"Not at that distance. He or she must have been a good mile away."

Grimmett frowned at the map again. "What time was it when you saw this person, Mr. Hibberd?"

"About eleven-twenty-five, I should say. Not later than eleven-thirty, anyway."

"Thank you," Grimmett said slowly; he looked slightly perturbed. "Sir Abercrombie?"

Lewker nodded and leaned forward.

"You will remember our short conversation of last night about the village of Khamche," he said. "It was there that Professor Wiernick, in 1954, committed what was locally considered a most flagrant form of sacrilege and thereby endangered the safety of your Himalayan expedition."

"That's right," Hibberd said; his piercing blue eyes held a gleam of reminiscent anger. "Did it out of sheer devilry, as far I could see. The man's a damned—was, I mean—" He stopped and shrugged his shoulders. "Oh, well, let it go."

"And Galu Regmi, one of Kemp's cadets, comes from this same village of Khamche," pursued the actor-manager. "Do you not find that a remarkable coincidence?"

"No. The world's not a big place any more. I've met two Rover Scouts from my home town hiking in Kashmir and three years ago there was a Sherpa staying at the Pen-y-Gwryd. I had a word with Galu Regmi this morning. He tells me there's a Gurkha lad at Shorehurst now, comes from a village a day's march from Khamche. Plenty of Nepalese joining the British Army since our Indian Army packed up."

Lewker thanked him and the inspector said that he had nothing more to ask. Hibberd rose and went out with a leopard's casual ease of movement. Grimmett told the constable to bring in Major Charles Kemp.

"We're weeding 'em out, Sir Ab, as well as finding out a thing or two," he observed. "I checked on Regmi with the other cadets before I came in this afternoon. He was with them on the other side of Bwlch Cwm Llan at eleven o'clock yesterday. Hibberd's story isn't so easy to check for Saturday, but this morning one of the girls here took a cup of tea to his room at half past eight and he was sound asleep. Mind you, I'm trying to keep an open mind, in spite of being pretty certain of my man. I don't forget it's just possible the two deaths could have been unconnected."

"I cannot sufficiently admire your attitude, Grimm," said Sir Abercrombie, beaming at him. "And I would very much like to know what you make of the figure seen by Hibberd coming up the valley south of Lliwedd at half past eleven on Saturday."

The arrival of Major Kemp forestalled Grimmett's reply. Kemp responded heartily to the inspector's "Good afternoon, sir," and sat down at his ease, a smile on his thick lips. There were signs of tension (Lewker noticed) in the tautness of muscle and tendon at the angles of his jaw, but this relaxed as soon as Grimmett put his first question.

"For the purpose of your exercise, Major, you had spare rifles and ammunition brought here and stored in the shed on the car park. How many rifles and what ammunition?"

"Six rifles." Kemp was terse and businesslike. "Two boxes of ammo, one of blank and one of live."

"By live ammunition you mean cartridges containing bullets?"

"That's it. For target-practice on dummy figures when the attackin' force reached objective. The locals had been warned to keep clear and I had two chaps over there patrollin' the area. They'll have been waitin' since noon to be picked up by the lorries, incidentally."

Grimmett nodded. "I hope we'll be able to release your men before very long, Major. I'd like you to tell us how these rifles and cartridges were issued, if you will. And how they were returned to your store."

"Righty-ho."

With an occasional question from the inspector, Kemp gave a concise account. The cadets each had their own rifle, the L 1-A-1 twenty-round magazine model as used by parachute troops. They had each been issued with one twenty-round clip of live ammunition for the exercise. The ammunition boxes contained thirty clips, so six clips of live ammunition remained in the box. At seven a.m. this morning the major had gone to the shed with Lumley and Jones-Griffith and issued them with a rifle apiece and twenty rounds of blank.

"The ammunition boxes were not locked?" queried Grimmett here.

"No," admitted Kemp. "But the shed was. There's only one key and it's kept hangin' up in the hall. I considered it safe enough."

"When you issued the clips of cartridges to Lumley and Jones-Griffith did you take them from the box yourself?"

Kemp knitted his brows. "No, I didn't, come to think of it. I was in a hurry. Thought the lads might get to the Bwlch before we did—that's what happened, in fact. I showed 'em the box and said 'Get a clip', and turned away to get the rifles from the case."

"The box with the six clips of live ammunition was near the box of blank, and the lids of both were removed?"

"Far as I remember, yes," replied the major, looking worried. "But if you're thinkin' one of the two helped himself to twenty rounds of live ammo then, you're wrong, Inspector. Both magazines were loaded with blank when I returned them to store this morning."

"Yet," Grimmett said quietly, "there were only five clips of live cartridges in the box when I examined the shed an hour ago, Major. I'll return to that in a minute. Did you lock the shed door after issuing the rifles?"

Yes, Kemp had locked up and returned the key to its place. They had gone very fast up the track in spite of the mist and darkness. The crossing of the flooded causeway had delayed them, but on the other side they had trotted to restore the warmth to their chilled bodies. He had never gone so fast, Kemp said, in his life. They were coming up the path towards Glaslyn when they heard voices on the Gribin ridge in the mist above them. He had been devilish glad to call a halt, and as there was no point in their going on, Lumley and Jones-Griffith had turned back, while Kemp went more slowly up to the foot of the Gribin to meet the cadets and receive the acting corporal's report. He had left them resting and eating the last of their rations while he made his way back to the hotel over the pass below Crib Goch, the route by which (he believed) Jones-Griffith had returned, to avoid the flooded causeway.

"Mr. Lumley took another route back?" Grimmett asked.

"Yes. Said he was goin' back round the other side of Llydaw. Solitary sort of bloke, Lumley."

"What time was it when they turned back?"

"Oh-seven-five-oh," Kemp said. "I looked at my watch when we heard the lads on the Gribin."

"And you yourself reached the hotel at—?"

"Oh-nine-two-oh—and that was fast goin'. I was devilish hungry. Came straight in for breakfast."

"That's all very clear, Major," Grimmett said. "Now, on examining the rifles in the shed, I found four cases containing six rifles each and one open case containing five. I take it your cadets returned their weapons this morning on arrival—Regmi included—and those in the open case would be the rifles you've called spare."

"Right. One spare missing." The major stuck out his underlip ferociously. "Pinched to kill poor old Stonor with. And if I could get my hands on the—"

"Just so, sir. About the cadets' rifles, now. The clips in the magazines were all empty?"

"They were. Accordin' to what I've learned every round was expended on the dummy targets—except one. A bloody young fool named Tillotson kept one back in case he got a chance at a mountain hare, so he says. He loosed it off comin' down from Bwlch Moch, which is the shot we heard at breakfast. And Cadet Tillotson," added Kemp with a scowl, "is for it when we get back to Shorehurst."

"And the rifles returned by Mr. Lumley and Mr. Jones-Griffith had full clips of blank cartridges?"

"Jones-Griffith's had. Peter had fired one."

The inspector stiffened and stared at him. "You're sure of that, Major?"

"Took out the clips myself. Peter told me he'd fired one—just to see if it worked, he said—on his way back."

"Oh. I see."

Grimmett, clearly, was at a temporary loss. He frowned at his papers, coughed, glanced at Sir Abercrombie. The actor-manager raised one eyebrow but otherwise remained Sphinx-like. He guessed that Grimmett was wondering whether to go into the possibilities of Lumley having substituted one bullet containing cartridge for one of the blanks; but if this was so the inspector decided against it, for his next question was related to a different matter.

"On Saturday, Major, your cadets crossed Bwlch-y-Saethau, descended the valley south of it, and crossed Bwlch Cwm-y-Llan. You, with Mr. Lumley and Mr. Jones-Griffith, followed them nearly to Bwlch Cwm-y-Llan to see that all went well. Is that correct?"

"Quite correct."

"You turned back about nine o'clock, Mr. Lumley says, but then you separated. Mr. Jones-Griffith went on down the valley to Nant Gwynant, where he lives. You, I understand, made a long circuit round the southern slopes of Lliwedd and into Cwm Dyli—where you expected to meet Mrs. Wiernick."

Charles Kemp's eyes narrowed and he flushed a little, but his voice was casual enough as he replied.

"Did Eve tell you that?"

"Yes, Major."

"Well, I didn't meet her anyway. I saw Stonor and charged round to the bottom of Slanting Buttress."

Grimmett consulted the map again. "It would be about noon when you encountered Mr. Stonor. You took three hours to cover something like three miles of mountainside, then."

"Well, what about it?" demanded Kemp sharply; he had lost his easy manner. "I took my time and it's devilish rough terrain. It also happens that I'd arranged to meet Eve at noon. All right?"

"All right, sir," returned Grimmett stolidly. "Now as to Mr. Lumley. His plan, as he tells me, was to go up to Bwlch-y-Saethau and then meet Miss Massey when she finished her climb. Did he start back straight away?"

"No. He wouldn't need to." The major was at ease again. "He'd do it in under the hour and Flora wouldn't finish the climb before eleven. I left him squattin' under a rock tryin' to light a fire made of moss and old bilberry roots. There's a touch of the Boy Scout about Peter."

Grimmett nodded dubiously. He picked up a slip of paper on which he had made a note or two.

"Returning to rifles and ammunition, Major," he said, "did you record the serial numbers of the rifles issued?"

"No. It didn't seem worth it and it was devilish dark."

"What sort of lighting did you have?"

"Couple of torches. There's no electric light in the shed."

"So it would have been quite easy, in those circumstances, for Mr. Lumley to take a clip of cartridges from the wrong box?"

"I wouldn't say easy. Possible. But if you want my opinion, he didn't. Jones-Griffith was a foot away and I don't see how he could have failed to notice. And I've told you there was a clip of blank in his magazine."

"Just so, sir," said the inspector blandly. "And—one last point—was the door of the shed locked when you went there this morning to return the rifles?"

"It was." Kemp stood up. "Nothing more I can tell you?"

Sir Abercrombie appeared to come out of his placid meditations.

"During the past forty-eight hours, Kemp," he boomed, "you have been much with Lumley. Has he, to your perceptive eye, appeared to be brooding over some dark secret?"

The major stared and then laughed. "Broodin'? Broody's the word you want. Peter's in love, that's his trouble. I don't want to be rude, but if you're thinkin' Peter went off his rocker and shot Mark Stonor you'd better think again. He couldn't plan a job like that with his head full of Flora." He paused at the door. "Like me to send in another bod for the ordeal?"

"If you will," agreed the inspector. "Mr. Jones-Griffith, please."

When he had gone Lewker looked questioningly at Grimmett who grinned faintly and rubbed his chin.

"I know, sir," he said. "It's like trying to pick up quicksilver, so it is. You think you've got something definite and it rolls away as soon as you touch it. There were prints on the rifle, by the way, but they were Stonor's. It had been handled with gloves as well."

"As was to be expected, Grimm. Did anything new emerge from the police surgeon's examination? You were very quick with that, incidentally."

"Had him ready and waiting, sir. He's one of these bright boys using the latest methods, congelation of different blood-groups and whatnot.

He gave us two things. There was a contusion on the back of Stonor's skull—Dr. Paton missed that—which suggests he was stunned when he was knocked over. The other thing's time of death. This chap's very cocksure about it. Lays it down Stonor had been dead not less than four and a half hours, not more than six, when he examined him at one o'clock."

"Thus establishing the time of death as between seven o'clock and half past eight," murmured Sir Abercrombie. "That does not help you a great deal. You can eliminate Kemp, perhaps, but Peter Lumley and Jones-Griffith were within half-an-hour's fast walk, at ten minutes to eight, of the place where Stonor was killed."

"That's what I meant about quicksilver," nodded Grimmett despondently. "You can't quite get hold of anything. Still, I'm hoping to get something on the rifle and ammunition issue. If Jones-Griffith—"

He stopped short as the man he named came in.

Jones-Griffith's long humorless face showed his nervousness and he sat down slowly on the very edge of the chair as though to be ready for instant flight. Grimmett's Saxon geniality did not put him at his ease. To the inspector's opening questions about his movements on Saturday morning and the day following he answered monosyllabically, confirming the information already received. On the subject of the issue of rifles and ammunition he became more communicative, evidently realizing that the questioning was not designed to incriminate him. Major Kemp, he said, had been in a great hurry. He had pointed out the box of blanks and told them to take a clip each while he got out the rifles.

"You had a torch?" Grimmett asked.

"I had one and Major Kemp had one. Mr. Lumley and I took our clips from the box—"

"Just a moment, sir. Did you see Mr. Lumley take a clip from the box of blank ammunition?"

"In point of fact, Inspector, I gave him one myself. Then Major Kemp showed me how to insert the clip in the magazine."

"At this time," Grimmett said slowly, "the box with the live ammunition was close to the box of blank, and open. Mr. Lumley was still in the shed while you were being shown how to load the rifle by Major Kemp. Is that right?"

"Quaite raight, Inspector," agreed Jones-Griffith. "He remained standing near the boxes. At least, I presume so."

"You were not looking at him?" snapped Grimmett.

"Well, no. I was holding the torch while Major Kemp put in the magazine."

"Thank you," said the inspector with a sigh, and looked towards Sir Abercrombie.

"I have two questions, Mr. Jones-Griffith," Lewker said. "For the first, would you say that the loading and firing of the rifle with which you were issued was a difficult matter, requiring instruction from an expert?"

"Far from it, Sir Abercrombie." The guide was emphatic. "The whole thing is quaite simple, even for a person laike mayself who has little knowledge of any kaind of firearm. There was really no need for Major Kemp to show me how to load it."

"Mr. Lumley loaded his rifle himself?"

"Yes. The method is quaite obvious. The clip of cartridges slides into—"

"Precisely. My second question relates to your return this morning and the surrender of your rifle to Major Kemp. Pray describe your procedure to us."

Jones-Griffith showed a tendency to revert to his original nervousness. He answered slowly and warily, his glance going repeatedly to Grimmett's face to watch the effect of his words. He had come back via the Pig Track—the route over Bwlch Moch—to avoid wading through the water on the causeway, he said, and had reached the hotel at twenty minutes to nine. After breakfast—

"You were not, I think, in the dining room for breakfast?" interpolated Lewker here.

"Er—no." Jones-Griffith appeared embarrassed. "I am acquainted with the good people of the hotel. I breakfasted in the kitchen."

After breakfast, he continued, he had gone out to his motorcycle, which was standing in front of the sheds where the cars were garaged, to make an adjustment to the carburetor. He had seen Peter Lumley walk out of the mist on the car park and enter the hotel.

"What time?" snapped the inspector quickly. "Had Lumley got a rifle?"

Jones-Griffith answered carefully. "The raifles had slings. Mr. Lumley carried his raifle slung on his shoulder. The taime would be about twenty past naine or perhaps a little later."

"Did he go to the shed where the rifles were stored?" Grimmett demanded.

"Oh, no. It was still very misty, of course, but I feel quaite sure Mr. Lumley walked straight past the shed. He took his raifle into the hotel with him. It was after half past naine when Major Kemp came out—the cadets were just arraiving—and a little later Mr. Lumley and I went with him to the shed and returned our raifles."

"Ah. Then, if Sir Abercrombie has no further questions, that will be all, Mr. Jones-Griffith. And thank you."

Jones-Griffith got up with obvious relief and went out.

"From which, Grimm," remarked the actor-manager as the door closed, "I infer that another possible suspect has been weeded out."

"Where's his motive?" countered the inspector. "Not a shadow of one. There's opportunity of a kind in both cases, but I reckon it's not worth bothering about when you consider what we've got on Mr. Peter Lumley."

"Your difficulty, I fancy, will be in establishing Lumley's motive."

"That's right enough, sir. We may have to go a long way after that— get on to the Swiss police to ferret out what he was doing in Zermatt, maybe dig up this Dr. Zukmayer Ferguson mentioned. But I reckon I've got enough to hold him on, even if he doesn't give us some more himself. He'll lie about it, of course."

Sir Abercrombie eyed him thoughtfully. "You pin your faith, for the moment, to Opportunity, it seems. But had not Jones-Griffith opportunity to kill Stonor? In so thick a mist, he could have left Kemp, doubled back on to the Pony Track, crossed the causeway and committed the murder."

"And got back to Pen-y-Pass at eight-forty? That's unconfirmed, I know, but the hotel people can give us a check. No, sir—it's cutting it too fine. And remember, he was quite likely to run into Lumley, who'd reach the end of the lake from the other side. Lumley now, had all the time he wanted."

"But the murder, in that case, was unpremeditated, Grimm. For Lumley could not have known that the cadets would be early on the Gribin or that Kemp would decide that he could turn back at ten minutes to eight."

"Unpremeditated or not," Grimmett said doggedly, "he's the only one who could have done it, ruling out Jones-Griffith on lack of motive and poor opportunity. He was up here in time to put that letter in Ferguson's car, too."

"And how, pray, did he do it, most ingenious inspector?"

"It's Lumley who was ingenious. As I see it, he came round the end of the lake on to the track, spotted Stonor without Stonor spotting him—"

"In a thick mist? And Stonor, Grimm, was found more than a hundred yards away from where Lumley would have joined the track, on a section of it along which Lumley would not go on his way to Pen-y-Pass."

Grimmett nodded. "That's so, sir. But I'll say instead that Lumley saw or heard Stonor on the track and followed him. He knocks him down, gets the idea of rigging a fake suicide, and kills him with the rifle shot. He goes off at once down the track, or more probably keeps just off it in the mist. He's got no rifle with him now. He doesn't have to risk getting the shed key from the hall because he's made a skeleton key from a bit of wire—you gave me that, sir. He goes into the shed and takes another of the spare rifles and a clip of blanks. There's still enough mist to hide him from any chance observer. Then he goes and hides on the hillside some-where for a bit and finally marches down the last bit of the track again with his rifle all complete."

Grimmett's brow had furrowed more than once during this reconstruc-tion, and by the time he reached the end of it he was speaking slowly and thoughtfully. Sir Abercrombie nodded at him sympathetically.

"There be some mysteries still, is it not so?" he boomed. "If this was unpremeditated murder, why does Peter Lumley prepare a skeleton key? Why does he steal a clip of bullet-armed cartridges when he does not know that he will have a chance of using one to kill Stonor? When did he fire that single blank cartridge, and why?"

Grimmett scratched his jaw and frowned. "Call it premeditated, then," he said stubbornly. "He'd planned to turn back anyway, making an ex-cuse—feeling ill, or a wrenched ankle or something. Kemp's decision saved him having to do that." He shifted uneasily on his chair. "This gets us nowhere, anyhow. I'll have Lumley in."

"Wait, Grimm," said Lewker quickly. "There are, I fancy, some rel-evant facts which you are ignoring. Shall I recite them?"

"If you wish, sir."

Sir Abercrombie leaned back with his hands clasped on his stomach and fixed his eyes on the ceiling.

"The letters," he said. "Their wording, the way in which they were brought to our notice, the date on which Donald Ferguson received his first letter according to the statement of Flora Massey. The windows. That of Mark Stonor's room, which is next to ours and invariably open, and that of Donald Ferguson, which is accessible from an outhouse roof at the back. The rifles. Those issued to Lumley and Jones-Griffith were fitted with slings for carrying. The rifle that killed Stonor had no sling. The conversations that you and I have overheard during the past two days, in particular one about the lifesaving propensities of colored an-oraks. The relevance of the fragment of string and the sample of grit may not be so apparent, but I hope you have them in those envelopes?"

"I have, sir." The inspector was staring at him in some bewilderment. "Any more—um—relevant facts?"

"You might also consider the fact that George Thripp heard a rifle-shot at about eight-forty-two, a time that is outside the limits so boldly given by the police surgeon. Also the fact that Mark Stonor started out for his walk at twenty past seven of a chilly morning and had walked rather less than a mile and three-quarters to the place of his death." Lewker brought his gaze down from the ceiling and beamed at Grimmett. "Would he loiter or linger anywhere on such a morning, Grimm? Is it not extremely likely that he walked at a good pace to the spot where we found him and was killed there about—shall we say?—ten minutes to eight, by someone who followed him and lay in wait when he turned?"

"Ah! If it comes to things that are likely, sir—"

"I beg your pardon, Grimm. I undertook to give you facts alone. There are, of course, the circumstances of John Lumley's death on the Matterhorn to be taken into account, and the manner in which we heard of them. Mark Stonor's jealous care for the honor of the Foothold Club is, or was, an undoubted fact. So is the tendency of a guilty conscience to perceive danger before it has really appeared, as I should have remembered earlier. And we observe, I hope, that if Peter Lumley left on Stonor's body the rifle issued to him by Major Kemp, then he either handled it with gloved hands from the moment it was issued or else succeeded in removing every one of his fingerprints from it. But these things are as inscrutable, invisible, as a nose on a man's face, or a weathercock on a steeple. And"—he looked at his watch—"it is half past three. Shall we proceed?"

Grimmett stopped blowing through his mustache and opened his mouth. Then he closed it again and straightened his broad shoulders.

"Sir Ab," he said resolutely, "I'm going ahead according to plan. Sergeant, there's another chair in the corner there. Bring it out, please, and put it by the other one. Constable! I want Mr. Peter Lumley in here."

"Why, pray, the additional chair?" inquired Lewker as the sergeant complied.

"I want Lumley in first, alone. Then I'm going to confront him with Mr. Ferguson. There's a chance we can break him down that way."

The actor-manager's eyes glinted with an indefinable excitement.

"To confront him with Mr. Ferguson," he repeated as though he liked the words. "An excellent plan, Grimm. I hope you will allow me to participate in the confrontation? And forgive me if I indulge my histrionic art? I am in the mood for something in Ercles' vein, a touch of the Bastard's plain cannon-fire, and smoke, and bounce—but I do assure you 'twill be much to the point."

"Well—" began Grimmett doubtfully.

The door opened and Peter Lumley came in.

Chapter XII

Sir Abercrombie Prevaricates

The ominous word *hangdog* came into Sir Abercrombie's mind as he watched Peter Lumley undergoing Grimmett's questioning. This, he admitted to himself, was probably because Lumley slouched in his chair as though he was suspended from a hook at the back of his neck, and resembled, with his shaggy sweater and his hair over his eyes, Monty the hotel dog. Curious that Flora Massey should seem to prefer this large, plain, sullen young man to the equally large but far more prepossessing Richard Paton.

The inspector was dealing gently with his man, though it needed all his patience. Lumley was uncommunicative and almost monosyllabic, and everything had to be dragged out of him as with a pair of forceps. Grimmett had begun by asking him to describe his movements on Saturday morning, and this—though he had not remarked on it—had obviously worried him. Why were these chaps bothering about Saturday morning when Stonor had been killed today? Grimmett said nothing to enlighten him. Sentence by sentence he extracted from Lumley the man's own account of his doings. He had gone over Bwlch-y-Saethau with Jones-Griffith and Kemp round about eight o'clock on Saturday. Then down the valley keeping well behind the cadets. He had no idea what time it was when they separated in the valley bottom. Kemp had pushed off up the south slope of Lliwedd. Jones-Griffith had gone down the valley to Gwynant. He himself had pottered about, had a snack, lit a bit of a fire just for the hell of it. Did a bit of bouldering. Bouldering was practice-climbing on boulders. Started up the valley. Time? Might have been getting on for eleven. Might have been later—hadn't got a watch.

"You were to meet Miss Massey when she had finished her climb, I understand," Grimmett said.

"Yes."

"Wouldn't you have been late for that meeting? I'm told she would have finished the climb about eleven."

"Fixed up to meet her on Bwlch-y-Saethau. She'd wait."

"Did you see anyone when you were alone in the valley?"

"No."

"Or while you were walking up it?"

"No. Or yes. Saw someone coming down off Snowdon on to the Bwlch."

"Could you recognize this person?"

"Too far off. Too tall for Flora, though."

The inspector plodded on gallantly, extracting his account of how he had reached the Bwlch, heard shouting that seemed to indicate that someone was in trouble, and assumed that it was on Slanting Buttress. He had decided it must be near the top of the climb and had hurried up the snow-covered crest and descended the top pitches. He had done the climb himself several times previously.

Grimmett left it there and passed on to the morning of Stonor's death. While he was taking Lumley through the proceedings in the temporary ammunition store, Sir Abercrombie reflected that there was something approaching an alibi for the possible murder of Wiernick in Peter's replies. Hibberd had seen a solitary person coming up the valley, Lumley had seen a solitary person where Hibberd had been. The time must have been about right in spite of Lumley's vagueness.

"You didn't join the path at the end of the lake, then?" Grimmett was saying patiently.

"No."

"What *did* you do, Mr. Lumley?"

"Dropped down into Cwm Dyli. There's a big slab there, Teyrn Slab. Climbed it."

"Carrying your rifle?"

"On my back. It had a sling."

"Did you fire your rifle, Mr. Lumley?"

Lumley looked a trifle sheepish. "Yes."

"Why?"

"Seemed a pity not to. See if it worked."

"What time would that be?"

"Dunno. Before I did the climb. Must've been getting on for nine."

"Did you hear any other shots?"

"No." A spark of intelligence glinted in the dull brown eyes. "If Stonor was shot before eight, I wouldn't hear it. Wind blowing down the cwm. I was up the cwm. Mist blanketing noise."

Grimmett nodded, sighed, and frowned at his notes.

"Now, Mr. Lumley. Last summer you were in Zermatt. Was that as a result of something you had read in the magazine published by the Swiss Alpine Club?"

Lumley's glance shifted quickly from Grimmett to Lewker and back again.

"Partly," he said. "Wanted to traverse the Matterhorn anyway."

"In 1934 your father, John Lumley, was killed on the Matterhorn. Do you agree that the circumstances of his death were—let's say—curious?"

Lumley shifted his massive shoulders. "One year old when it happened. Read the report a long time afterwards. Nothing curious about it, except it's funny he unroped."

"Ah!" The inspector leaned forward, his blue eyes narrowing. "But that was curious enough to make you go to Zermatt to investigate this matter twenty-seven years later. What did you discover, Mr. Lumley?"

"You've got it wrong," Lumley said sullenly. "A body had turned up. Might have been my father's. I wanted to know. Saw the guides who brought it down."

"Yes?"

"It wasn't my father. Body of a little chap. Father was big."

"You also made inquiries about the circumstances of your father's death?" pressed Grimmett.

"No, I didn't."

"You knew the other three men who were with John Lumley on the Matterhorn in 1934?"

"Knew who they were. Wiernick, Ferguson, Stonor. Why?"

Grimmett's gaze bored into him. "Two of those men, Mr. Lumley, have been killed in the past forty-eight hours. Perhaps you can tell us why?"

"No, I can't." Lumley's eyes fell before the inspector's. "Dunno what you're getting at," he mumbled.

Grimmett, still watching him, raised his voice. "Constable! Ask Mr. Ferguson to come in."

Peter Lumley's big frame moved slowly in the chair. His hands, which had been dangling loosely between his knees, came up to rest on his thighs and his body straightened itself. He looked at Sir Abercrombie, who appeared to be taking his after-lunch nap, and then at the intent Grimmett.

"What's this about?" he demanded, quietly enough. "A link between my father's death and Stonor's? Wiernick, too?"

"I think you know what that link is, Mr. Lumley."

"I don't. Looks as if you think I shot Stonor. I didn't. Couldn't if I'd wanted to. Blank cartridges in my rifle—easy to check that."

The inspector sighed and turned as the door opened. Donald Ferguson came in, followed by the constable. As the latter closed the door, to remain standing inside the little room, Lewker caught a glimpse of the other policeman crossing the hall to take his place.

Ferguson nodded to Lumley and looked questioningly at Grimmett, who pointed to the vacant chair.

"I want your help, sir," he said as Ferguson, looking slightly puzzled, sat down. "We had from you, in confidence, an account of the circumstances in which Mr. John Lumley met his death in 1934. Sir Abercrombie here assured you then that your confidence would be respected unless the cause of justice required us to use your information. Well, the cause of justice does now require that."

"Oh, aye?" said Ferguson slowly.

"I have reason to believe," Grimmett went on, "that Mr. Lumley is aware of those circumstances. He denies this—"

"I never denied it!" Lumley said impatiently. "I saw the report. I had the details from Thripp."

"But the true details, Mr. Lumley, you discovered only six months ago, I think. At Zermatt."

Ferguson cocked a grizzled eyebrow at Lewker. "What's this?" he demanded uneasily. "You're no' putting the thing on Peter?"

"That's what they're trying to do, sir," Peter said between his teeth. "Beats me why."

"Heavens, Inspector!" Ferguson was genuinely astonished and indignant. "What's Peter to do with it? If you ask me, Mark Stonor shot himself—and I'm thinking you'll know why, after what I told you."

"There's very good reason to think otherwise, Mr. Ferguson," said Grimmett. "Mark Stonor was murdered."

"I'll no' believe it," Ferguson said loudly.

Sir Abercrombie stayed the inspector's reply with a gesture.

"I fear this will be a heavy blow for you to bear, Ferguson," he said gravely. "You are, I think, very fond of your niece?"

Ferguson nodded. His eyes were troubled.

"And Miss Massey is greatly attached to Peter Lumley?"

"Aye. She is."

"Then she will need help and sympathy, for one who is dear to her is to be—"

"For God's sake!" Lumley almost shouted the words; his sullen taciturnity had broken at the mention of Flora. "Come into the open, can't you? Where's your proof?"

Grimmett sat up very stiffly. "Now, Mr. Lumley," he began.

"Pray allow me, Inspector," interrupted the actor-manager in a voice that suggested distant thunder.

He rose slowly to his feet, his pouchy face transformed to the grimness of a judge pronouncing a death sentence, and leveled an accusing finger at Peter Lumley.

"Wretched youth!" he boomed, and there was nothing comic about that apostrophe. "Has it not occurred to you that there is a telephone in this hotel? That the Swiss police, the hospital in Zermatt, and a certain clinic in Munich, can all be reached by means of that telephone? We know, Lumley, that you discovered that the body brought down by the glacier was that of your father. You identified it by the shirt and trousers which were its only clothing. Your further investigations revealed the name of a doctor who assisted in the rescue. You went to Munich, you saw that doctor and won from him the full and true story of how your father met his end. The doctor's name was Zukmayer."

"Zukmayer!" Ferguson repeated in a whisper as he paused.

Peter Lumley's eyes stared incredulously from a face suddenly suffused with crimson. "Lies!" he said hoarsely. "Damned lies!"

"Peace, sirrah!" thundered Sir Abercrombie, his form dilating until he seemed to tower above the table. "Will you deny that you learned how your father had been left to die—that the disgraceful business had been hushed up by the three men who had been his comrades?" He dropped his magnificent voice to a sort of prophetic rumble. "I feel the knowledge rankling and seething in your mind through the long months of autumn, Lumley. I feel the dull heat of anger smoldering until it bursts into flame, the flame of desire for vengeance. Those three men should pay for their misdeed. And first they should know that the secret was out. The anonymous letters were the preliminary—"

"Letters!" Lumley lurched to his feet, his eyes glittering dangerously. "What letters? What the hell are you playing at?"

"Constable!" snapped Grimmett, and the policeman was beside Lumley's chair in two strides.

"Sit down, Mr. Lumley," said Lewker sharply, and was sullenly obeyed.

Ferguson had put both hands to his head like one whose mind is in turmoil. Between the white bandages his face looked gray and old. At the actor-manager's side a very worried Grimmett was tugging urgently at his sleeve. Sir Abercrombie ignored the appeal.

"You asked, Lumley, where is our proof," he boomed on. "That you shall have. Inspector Grimmett has in his possession all but conclusive evidence in the matter of Mark Stonor's murder. I am being frank with you. One last item of evidence is needed—proof that you were in fact the author of the anonymous letters. Were that proof in our hands—"

"Hold on," Ferguson said suddenly, taking his hands from his head; he looked at Grimmett. "I wasn't going to tell you this. I see now I'll have to. Flora told you she went to my car and found one of these letters there on Friday evening. She didn't tell you—because she didn't know—that I'd seen that letter put there."

"What's that?" Grimmett snapped. "Did you see who put it there?"

"Aye." The word was like a groan. "I saw him, plain as I see you."

"The time?" questioned Sir Abercrombie gently.

Ferguson thought for a moment. "It would be just half past six. I saw the clock in the hall as I went out. I'd got my suitcase from the car earlier but I'd left some other things. It was dark and the car was in a barn. When I got to the door of the barn I saw a torchlight flash and someone opened the door of my car and put an envelope on the front seat. The light showed me his face."

"You didn't grab him?" demanded Grimmett. "Why was that?"

"He didn't see me and I went away. You see, Inspector, I thought the note might be a what-d'ye-call-'em—a *billet doux*—for Flora."

"Then this man was—?"

Ferguson covered his face with his bandaged hands.

"Peter Lumley," he said.

"You bloody liar!" said Lumley in a low voice.

The color had drained from his face and he was staring at Ferguson as though the man was a ghost. Sir Abercrombie, who had remained standing, sat down with a sigh of satisfaction.

"I take it, Ferguson," he said slowly, "that you would swear to the time at which you saw Lumley placing the envelope in your car?"

"Aye, I would," said Ferguson without looking up.

"Thank you. For truth is truth, in Shakespeare's words, to th' end of the reckoning, and but for your timely revelation the end of the reckoning might have been different. I, myself, had toyed with the theory, a fanciful one perhaps, that Mark Stonor was the anonymous letter-writer."

Ferguson jerked up his head. "Stonor?"

"Yes. It seemed to follow, once it was established that it was you, not Stonor, who had been John Lumley's partner on the Matterhorn traverse and who had left him for dead."

"I? But I told you—"

He checked himself quickly. Sir Abercrombie regarded him curiously.

"You would not contest Dr. Zukmayer's statement?" he inquired mildly. "Or the information acquired by Peter Lumley at the Zermatt hospital?"

Ferguson hesitated. His glance went swiftly from Lumley's sullen perplexity to Inspector Grimmett's worried frown and returned to the actor-manager.

"No," he said slowly. "No."

"You told us the truth about John Lumley's death, with the trifling exception that you—very naturally—substituted Stonor's name for your own, not wishing to incur possible and unmerited odium. That is correct?"

Again Ferguson hesitated.

"Yes," he said at last, reluctantly. "You'll no' blame me, I hope? It was a pure mistake, but—"

"Just so." Sir Abercrombie, who had heard Grimmett's breath whistle sharply through his mustache, dropped a hand on the inspector's. "Pray allow me, Grimm. You see, Mr. Ferguson, Mark Stonor had a favourite child—the Foothold Club. He had created that child and cared very greatly for its reputation. When the committee nominated you as president elect, at the special meeting held as usual towards the end of November, he had no say in the matter. But he would be most strongly opposed—or so it seemed to me—to a man with a secret but very large blot upon his mountaineering record becoming president of the Foothold Club. A man of his nature, unworldly, simple, most meticulous in matters of personal integrity, might well consider that the oath of silence he and Julius Wiernick had taken debarred him from mentioning his opposition, even to you yourself. Casting about in his mind for some method of making you decline the honor of the presidency, he hit upon the idea of the anonymous letters—thus ran my theory. He would adopt this idea with reluctance, for it was foreign to his nature, and knowing that his threat to divulge your secret was a hollow one, since he would never break his word, he added a veiled threat to your life. It was not well done. The attempt at disguising the style—"

"Aye, aye," broke in Ferguson impatiently. "No need to go on, Lewker. It was no' Stonor—we know that now—and in any case he received one anonymous letter himself."

Lewker raised his eyebrows. "Did he, Ferguson? Do you remember approaching me with a request to make the speech of welcome on Friday night? We were outside this hotel, beside my car, and my car was standing directly beneath the window of Stonor's room, which was open. The time was about ten minutes past seven."

"I do. Well?"

"You showed me a slip of paper, about the size of these anonymous notes we have seen. You talked in a low voice because there were two persons within earshot. It is not impossible that Stonor looked out to see who was below, that he saw, in the light from the lower windows, the handing over of the paper, and that he assumed—being unable to hear what was said—that you had found the anonymous letter in your car and had decided to ask me to detect the sender. My—ah—gifts of investigation," added Sir Abercrombie, looking modestly down his nose, "are known to some senior members of the Foothold Club."

"By gum!" said the inspector, clapping a palm on the table.

"Yes, Grimm. Still theorizing, Ferguson, I thought it not unlikely that the president, to disarm possible suspicion, had decided to present me with an anonymous letter purporting to have been received by himself. As emerged later, it had been typed on the hotel typewriter, which he had been using for the preparation of his speech that evening. It was plain from the wording of the letters that they were addressed to one person only."

Ferguson shook his head sagely. "It won't do, Lewker," he said evenly. "Wiernick had a letter too."

"So he did," nodded Sir Abercrombie, shaking his head sadly in apparently unconscious mimicry. "And Wiernick is dead, is he not? He cannot tell us whether that letter was in his pocket when he died, or whether it was put there afterwards—when, for example, his body was being carried into the car-park shed with your assistance. Stonor is dead, and cannot tell us—"

"This rigmarole gets us nowhere," Ferguson interrupted impatiently, getting up. "If you've got nothing more to ask me, Inspector, I'll ask to be excused from this—this recitation of whigmaleeries."

"Sit down!" There was no 'sir' from Grimmett this time. "Answer me this. What made you tell us Stonor was the man who left John Lumley to die, when Stonor would have denied it as soon as it was put to him?"

Ferguson looked at the door, at the impassive constable, at Peter Lumley sitting bolt upright with his fists clenched, at Sir Abercrombie Lewker who had passed a slip of paper to the inspector and was now removing the string from an untidy brown-paper parcel. He sat down very slowly and wetted his lips with his tongue; but he did not speak.

"There's only one explanation that I can see," Grimmett answered for him. "You knew Stonor could not deny it. You knew Stonor was dead, before the body had been found."

The constable, obedient to his jerked finger, moved behind Ferguson's chair. The man found his voice, though it was a mere croak.

"You're no' saying I killed Stonor! It's a bluidy lie!"

"I think not." Lewker set his half-opened parcel on the table before Grimmett. "That description, however, applies to your tale of Peter Lumley placing the letter in your car. At half past six on Friday evening— you were prepared to swear to the time—I was in the Pen-y-Gwryd Hotel and Peter Lumley was a few feet away from me."

"You—you damned mountebank!"

"I fear your comment, if rude, is just. I do admit to a trifle of lying also, for lies invite more lies. Your story of Lumley was invited, though ill-considered. I confess that, in fact, I do not know whether Dr. Zukmayer of Munich is alive or dead, and that no telephone calls have gone from here to Zermatt. Lies, you see, may deceive a liar into admitting a truth— as you, deceived by my indictment of Lumley here, admitted that you were the man who left his father to die."

Ferguson made an obvious effort and pulled himself together.

"You're making a great mistake, Inspector," he said in a steady voice. "I didn't kill Mark Stonor. I couldn't have killed him. I was in my bed and asleep when he was killed—that's guessing," he added hastily, "that it was done before breakfast."

"A good guess," commented Sir Abercrombie; he glanced at Grimmett, who was studying the slip of paper he had passed to him. "Will you conclude, Inspector?"

Grimmett nodded. His tone when he began to speak was formal and courteous.

"There's been some deception, Mr. Ferguson, but that's at an end. I've some facts for you." He held up the pair of ancient rope-soled shoes, the soles much tattered and frayed, which he had taken from Lewker's parcel. "Do these belong to you?"

After a long moment Ferguson nodded.

"Your initials, a bit faded, are on the canvas at the back of the heels, I see," Grimmett went on; he took up his magnifying-glass and scrutinised the toe end of the sole of the left shoe. "The shoe is still wet, I notice, and there are particles of grit among the worn strands of hemp. These may correspond, on a closer examination, with a sample of grit"— he held up an envelope—"taken from a footprint found near Mark Stonor's body. The hemp of the sole is badly frayed and starting to rot. Here"—he opened a second envelope and carefully removed from it a fragment of what looked like string—"is a wisp of hemp which was found in the footprint. Looking at it through my glass, I would say that it is the same material as forms the sole of this shoe. That's only an opinion, and it'll be confirmed or disproved by scientific examination."

He looked inquiringly at Ferguson who had closed his eyes and allowed his chin to sink on his chest. Peter Lumley shifted uneasily in his chair.

"Look," he said in a low voice. "Do I have to stay now?"

"I think we owe you the full explanation, Mr. Lumley, and Mr. Ferguson also. That's why I'm dealing with you—and him—like this."

An almost unrecognizable voice came from Donald Ferguson's lips.

"You've no proof. Let's hear what I'm supposed to have done."

"Very well." Grimmett spoke more briskly. "You won't contest that you were in the hall last night when Mark Stonor announced where he was going this morning and at what time. You got up well before that time. Your bedroom, as we know, is accessible from an outhouse roof below the window, and your old rope-soled shoes made the descent safer as well as ensuring silence. You went to the shed on the car park and opened the door with this." He took the piece of bent wire from the third envelope and held it up. "You were a locksmith in Glasgow and opening a simple lock by such means was child's play to you. You took a rifle and a clip of ammunition and locked the door again, throwing the key away. You went up the track to Llyn Llydaw. It was dark and a thick mist, but you'd been that way a good many times and the track's plain enough. At the lake you waited. Stonor came, and you killed him. May we look at the knuckles of your right hand, Mr. Ferguson? I see the bandage has been extended to cover them."

Ferguson said nothing. Nor did he move, except that his head sank lower.

"Very well," said the inspector quietly. "They are, of course, bruised or abraded due to the blow that knocked Stonor down. You shot him and contrived an arrangement you hoped would look like suicide. The shot, if it was heard, would be put down to Major Kemp's Army exercise. You returned to the hotel, either by the track or keeping on the hillside to avoid the slight risk of being seen, and climbed back into your room."

He stopped. Ferguson had thrown back his head and squared his shoulders. His lips were trembling but there was a faint smile playing about them as he nodded to Sir Abercrombie.

"I'd no' a hope, had I?" he said.

And then, suddenly and shockingly, he dropped his head on his bandaged hands and burst into a dreadful dry sobbing.

Peter Lumley got up quickly. Grimmett muttered something to Lewker, who rose also and went out of the room with his hand on the shoulder of the younger man.

"You are wanted in there, Constable," he said to the man on duty at the door; and to Peter, "You are wanted elsewhere. She will bear the news the better if it comes from you."

Peter looked at the door which had just closed behind the policeman.

"Isn't there anything I can do for—him?" he asked dully.

Sir Abercrombie shook his head.

"Where the offense is, let the great axe fall," he boomed. "What you can do for Flora is a thousand times more important."

Epilogue

"We find that he was wilfully murdered and with malice aforethought," said the foreman of the coroner's jury.

"Yes. And"—the coroner was carefully formal—"do you find anyone guilty of the murder of Mark Stonor?"

"We do, sir."

"Will you say this person's name?"

"We—we find," said the foreman shakily, "that Donald Gillespie Ferguson did wilfully murder Mark Stonor."

Half an hour later Sir Abercrombie Lewker's Wolseley bore Inspector Grimmett away from the courtroom at Llanberis where the inquest had been held. It was late in the afternoon of Tuesday, and the wintry sunshine that all day had touched slope and summit with gold was deepening its hue to a rich strawberry pink. The aged car plodded up the windings of the pass and panted to a halt on the Pen-y-Pass car park. Lewker and Grimmett got out and walked slowly up the hillside to a spot whence they could see the sky colors changing and darkening over the sea to westward, and there seated themselves on two convenient rocks. Grimmett removed his tweed hat and Sir Abercrombie lit his pipe.

"And that's that, until the trial," said the inspector; he rubbed his forehead with the back of his hand. "It's a bit tricky, so it is, arresting a man on the verdict of a coroner's jury. It's not a legal arrest, you know, until the coroner's signed the warrant."

Sir Abercrombie nodded, drawing meditatively at his pipe.

"I wonder, Grimm," he said after a moment, "whether he will confess to the murder of Julius Wiernick."

Grimmett looked at him sharply. "He did kill Wiernick, then?"

"Of course, Grimm. I was reasonably certain of that as soon as Flora Massey told us her uncle had been receiving the anonymous letters, though indeed the possibility had been in my mind from the first."

"You reckon Ferguson thought Wiernick had been sending him the letters, Sir Ab?"

"I do. Consider, Grimm. Here is a man with wide prospects opening

186

before him. He has a knighthood in view, he will conceivably become a great public figure. He learns, from the first anonymous letter, that someone is prepared to divulge the secret he thought hidden forever, and to him that someone can only be one of the other two men who had sworn to keep the secret. It does not occur to him—as it did to me—that the first letter was sent shortly after the meeting at which he was nominated as president-elect of the Foothold Club. He sees a wider threat, something which may well mean publicity for that secret and a shocking blow to the foundations he has laid for his grand entry into public life. The guilty conscience, you see, will always magnify the danger of guilt revealed."

"But why pick on Wiernick, Sir Ab?"

Lewker took his pipe from his mouth and considered the bowl reflectively. The rich light flooding the opposite mountainsides lent a touch of the Demon King's spotlight to his pouchy face.

"Because," he said, "of the two possibles, Julius Wiernick was by far the more likely. Wiernick was the *enfant terrible* who liked to hurt with his tongue. Wiernick had recently been disappointed in his hopes of a knighthood. Wiernick might be implying that he would reveal the secret in his forthcoming book unless Ferguson relinquished his anticipated directorship of youth centers and perhaps his knighthood also. I think something that Wiernick said at breakfast on Saturday would confirm his opinion." The actor-manager's voice became the professor's nasal tone. " 'A red windproof could quite conceivably save a man's life in certain circumstances. Don't you agree, Ferguson?' "

"Ah!" Grimmett exclaimed. "I get you. John Lumley's windproof."

"Precisely. And so Wiernick's fate was sealed. It was carefully done. Ferguson, you remember, took down the book which was to suggest Wiernick's attempt at varying the chimney pitch of Slanting Buttress. The place was ideal for his simple plan. With Flora out of sight on the traverse, he had only to wait until Wiernick was far enough up the rock-wall above and then jerk the rope as hard as he could. Wiernick was certain to be pulled off, and almost certain to be killed in that fall of a hundred and forty feet before the rope checked him."

"Why put the letter in Wiernick's pocket, though?" frowned the inspector.

"The guilty conscience again, Grimm. Ferguson knew it would seem just a little odd to his fellow-climbers that Wiernick should fall off. When he heard that I proposed to go up and look at the rock-face above the chimney he was afraid. The letter he had received the previous evening was in his own pocket and he made an opportunity of transferring it to

Wiernick's, thinking—as Mark Stonor thought by a similar process—to disarm any possible suspicion of himself." Sir Abercrombie relit his pipe, frowning between puffs. "I scarcely like to imagine Ferguson's state of mind that evening when he discovered that the letter-writer was still alive and active. You recall Flora's description? 'Uncle Donald stood absolutely rigid when he saw the envelope, and then he grabbed it and ripped it open.' "

"And then he knew he'd killed the wrong man," Grimmett nodded. "He knew it was Stonor who'd sent him the letters. But he'd see, wouldn't he, that Stonor only wanted him to back out of being president? Why kill Stonor?"

"That," replied Sir Abercrombie gravely, "was the very mistake I made, Grimm. I had the framework of the matter in my hand before Stonor started out for his last walk, and I assumed that because I saw no cause for the ending of his life Ferguson would see as I saw. I reckoned without the other factors that would drive Ferguson on—his fear that Stonor would give away that secret and so reveal a motive for his killing of Wiernick, his realization that all danger would end if Stonor were to die, the very fact that he had killed once and got away with it. Even so, I fancy he would not have risked a second murder had not opportunity presented itself so temptingly."

He stood up and massaged the seat of his trousers. The rock held the winter cold and would hold it for many weeks yet. With the passing of the last sunlight the phantasm of coming spring fled from the darkening hillsides and the flood of cold shadow rose, engulfing the pass and seeping into the far folds of the mountains. Against the glow of the western sky the enormous pyramid of Crib Goch stood black and forbidding. A car, humming up the road from Llanberis, added its temporal note to the eternal and changeless harmony of distant mountain streams.

"One thing I haven't got, Sir Ab," said Grimmett, rising to stand beside him. "Flora Massey's statement that Wiernick, as he fell, screeched something that sounded like '*Jack!*' "

"If Flora had been a more experienced climber, Grimm, I fancy she would have known what it was that Wiernick really shouted." Sir Abercrombie tapped out his pipe against the rock and put it in his pocket. "She said, you remember, that he seemed to be yelling a furious command. When a leader on a rock-climb feels the rope dragging at his waist he shouts urgently for it to be slackened. What Julius Wiernick actually shouted in the instant of his fall was '*Slack!*' "

He threw a last glance round him at the purple summits and the darkening slopes, and began to walk slowly down to the Pen-y-Pass Hotel with Grimmett. The car had stopped before the door of the inn. Peter Lumley and Flora Massey got out. Peter's arm went round her and they passed into the inn together.

THE END

About the Rue Morgue Press

"Rue Morgue Press is the old-mystery lover's best friend, reprinting high quality books from the 1930s and '40s."
—*Ellery Queen's Mystery Magazine*

Since 1997, the Rue Morgue Press has reprinted scores of traditional mysteries, the kind of books that were the hallmark of the Golden Age of detective fiction. Authors reprinted or to be reprinted by the Rue Morgue include Catherine Aird, Delano Ames, H. C. Bailey, Morris Bishop, Nicholas Blake, Dorothy Bowers, Pamela Branch, Joanna Cannan, John Dickson Carr, Glyn Carr, Torrey Chanslor, Clyde B. Clason, Joan Coggin, Manning Coles, Lucy Cores, Frances Crane, Norbert Davis, Elizabeth Dean, Carter Dickson, Michael Gilbert, Constance & Gwenyth Little, Marlys Millhiser, Gladys Mitchell, James Norman, Stuart Palmer, Craig Rice, Kelley Roos, Charlotte Murray Russell, Maureen Sarsfield, Margaret Scherf, Juanita Sheridan and Colin Watson..

To suggest titles or to receive a catalog of Rue Morgue Press books write P.O. Box 4119, Boulder, CO 80306, telephone 800-699-6214, or check out our website, www.ruemorguepress.com, which lists complete descriptions of all of our titles, along with lengthy biographies of our writers.